Beowulf

*A New Translation for
Oral Delivery*

BEOWULF

*A New Translation for
Oral Delivery*

By Dick Ringler

Hackett Publishing Company, Inc.
Indianapolis/Cambridge

Copyright © 2007 by Hackett Publishing Company, Inc.

10 09 08 07   1 2 3 4 5 6 7

For further information, please address
        Hackett Publishing Company, Inc.
        P.O. Box 44937
        Indianapolis, Indiana 46244-0937

        www.hackettpublishing.com

Cover design by Brian Rak and Abigail Coyle
Interior design by Elizabeth L. Wilson
Composition by Agnew's, Inc.
Printed at Edwards Brothers, Inc.

Library of Congress Cataloging-in-Publication Data

Beowulf. English.
  Beowulf : a new translation for oral delivery / by Dick Ringler.
    p. cm.
  Includes bibliographical references.
  ISBN 978-0-87220-893-3 (pbk.)—ISBN 978-0-87220-894-0 (cloth)
  1. Epic poetry, English (Old) I. Ringler, Dick. II. Title.
  PR1583.R56 2007
  829′.3—dc22   2007009152

Contents

About the Cover Art   vi
Prefatory Note   vii
Map   viii
Introduction   ix
  The Story   ix
  Oral and Written *Beowulf*s   xvi
  Legend and Lore   xxv
  Narrative Strategies and Structures   xxx
  The Hero   lii
  Christianity and the Problem of Violence   lxxxii
  The Poet   xcvi
  The Meter of the Translation   c
Appendix   cx

Beowulf   1

People and Places in *Beowulf*   167
Three Shorter Old English Poems   174
  "The Fight at Finnsburg"   174
  "A Meditation"   177
  "Deor"   184
Suggestions for Further Reading   187

About the Cover Art

This image of the Devil from an early eleventh-century manuscript in the British Library (MS Cotton Tiberius B.v) suggests how an Anglo-Saxon audience might have imagined Grendel:

> The fingertips
> of the heathen foe's
> horrible claw
> were like nails,
> like enormous spikes
> of iron or steel (1968–73)

and

> in the eerie dark
> his eyes darted
> rays of raging
> red hellfire (1451–54)

Prefatory Note

For the most part, the present translation of *Beowulf* is based on the text and notes in Fr. Klaeber's third edition of the poem (see Suggestions for Further Reading, p. 187), though I have consulted a wide range of other editions and commentaries, and not infrequently abandoned Klaeber's readings and explanations in favor of others.

References to passages in the translation are by verse number. References to the Old English original are by line number in Klaeber's edition (with notation of a-verse or b-verse always provided).

With regard to its verse form, this translation is designed to provide an imitation—rigorously self-consistent within certain fixed limits—of the meter of the Old English original and thus to mimic (to the extent that this is possible) its acoustic qualities, phrasing, and general momentum. (See further pp. c–cxiii.)

As regards its content, the translation is naturally shaped and informed by the translator's understanding of the original, and the present Introduction tries to make some of the elements of that understanding explicit. But *Beowulf* is a remarkably complex work—multivalent, mysterious, sometimes baffling—and a number of other quite different understandings are possible (and can be found in the extensive literature on the poem). It was felt, however, that for readers approaching the work possibly for the first time, a single coherent interpretation would be more helpful than a smorgasbord of alternative and warring theories. For brave souls who are eager to press ahead into the *selva oscura* of interpretive controversy, Andy Orchard's *Critical Companion to "Beowulf"* (D. S. Brewer, 2003) will serve as a satisfactory point of entry.

As the translator, I gratefully acknowledge the many different kinds of help I have received over the years from Frederic G. Cassidy, Alger N. Doane, Kenneth L. Frazier, Norman P. Gilliland, Peter C. Gorman, John D. Niles, Frederick Rebsamen, Karin Ringler, and Jane A. Schulenburg. For any deficiencies in the present work—and no doubt they are legion!—I make the same apology that King Alfred the Great made when offering the world his translation of Boethius' *Consolation of Philosophy:* "Everyone must say what he says and do what he does according to the capacity of his intellect and the amount of time available to him."

The Geography of *Beowulf*

Introduction

The Story

This synopsis is provided in order to ease the reader's approach to what sometimes seems a bewilderingly complex text. It summarizes the content of the poem and provides clarifying and explanatory comment.

[Prologue] **Scyld Scefing**
Scyld Scefing, founder of a famous dynasty of Danish kings, arrives mysteriously in Denmark as a small child at a time when the Danes are without a ruler. (It seems likely that this situation arose because Heremod, the last king of the previous dynasty, was cast out by the Danes on account of his tyrannical and unkingly behavior.) Scyld's glorious reign is described, as are his death and funeral.

I **Hrothgar and the Danes. Grendel**
Scyld Scefing's descendants are tallied as far as his great-grandson Hrothgar, a famous war leader who expanded Danish power and prestige and built the great meadhall Heorot. Here he and his followers live joyously until they are attacked by Grendel, a giant man-eating demon descended from Cain.

II **Grendel's Persecution of the Danes**
The monster's nightly raids go on for twelve years, bringing such confusion and despair to Hrothgar and his people that some of the Danes take up devil-worship in an effort to avert their fate.

III **Beowulf Sails to Denmark**
Beowulf, a youthful nephew and companion of Hygelac, king of the Geats (a people living north of the Danes in what is now southern Sweden), sets out with fourteen followers to help Hrothgar. When the Geats arrive in Denmark,

Hrothgar's coastguard challenges them and demands to know who they are.

IV   **Beowulf and the Coastguard**
Without giving his name, Beowulf explains why he has come. The coastguard, impressed by the visitor's speech and bearing, allows him to enter Denmark and shows him the way to Heorot.

V   **Beowulf and Hrothgar's Sentry**
At the door of the hall, Beowulf and his followers are challenged by a sentry and again asked to identify themselves. Beowulf now reveals his name, and the sentry obtains Hrothgar's permission for the visitors to enter Heorot.

VI   **Beowulf and Hrothgar**
Beowulf greets Hrothgar, presents his monster-slaying credentials, and pleads to be allowed to defend the Danes' great hall against Grendel.

VII   **Beowulf and Hrothgar (Continued)**
Hrothgar reminds Beowulf that he once helped Beowulf's father Ecgtheow when the latter was in desperate trouble. He invites the visitors to join the Danes' feast and seats Beowulf (we later discover) in a place of honor between his own young sons, Hrethric and Hrothmund.

VIII   **Unferth's Version of Beowulf's Swimming Feat**
Unferth the court spokesperson, motivated by personal envy (and perhaps embodying the Danes' collective resentment about their need to be rescued by a foreigner), launches a public attack on Beowulf, claiming that he has misrepresented his credentials. As Unferth tells it, Beowulf once engaged in—and lost—a swimming race against a warrior named Breca. Beowulf replies that it was not a race at all but a joint heroic exploit, and that even so he emerged from it with more credit than Breca did.

IX   **Beowulf's Version of the Feat and Hrothgar's Reaction**
After concluding his own account of the swim, during which he slew numerous sea monsters, Beowulf delivers a counterattack, charging Unferth with the murder of his own brothers, and the Danes—as a people—with cowardice. Beowulf's boldness and resolve awaken hope in Hrothgar and his queen Wealhtheow, and Hrothgar puts Beowulf in charge of the meadhall for the coming night.

X   **Beowulf and His Men Wait for Grendel in the Hall**
           The Geatish warriors get ready for bed as Grendel ap-
           proaches the hall.

XI   **Beowulf and Grendel Fight**
           Grendel seizes and eats one of Beowulf's followers, then at-
           tacks the hero himself. As soon as Beowulf meets the attack
           by grabbing Grendel's arm, the monster realizes he has met
           his match and tries to flee.

XII   **Beowulf's Victory**
           Beowulf wrenches off Grendel's arm. Mortally wounded,
           the monster escapes to his lair in the fens. Beowulf nails the
           arm to the gable of Heorot as a trophy.

XIII   **The Danes Celebrate Grendel's Defeat**
           The next morning the Danes track Grendel's bloody foot-
           prints to the deep pool where he lives. Afterward, while they
           are riding back to Heorot, a poet composes a song in praise
           of Beowulf, first comparing him to the great hero Sigemund
           the dragon-slayer, then contrasting Sigemund with the
           wicked Danish king Heremod, and finally contrasting
           Heremod (whom the Danes had good reason to hate) with
           Beowulf (whom they now have good reason to love).

XIV   **Hrothgar Thanks Beowulf**
           Hrothgar expresses his gratitude to Beowulf and adopts
           him as a son (by military adoption). Beowulf apologizes for
           his failure to hold onto Grendel and prevent him from get-
           ting away.

XV   **Hrothgar Rewards Beowulf**
           Heorot is readied for a victory feast, which is presided over
           by Hrothgar and his silent nephew Hrothulf (who sits next
           to Hrothgar as if he were co-ruler or heir apparent). Hroth-
           gar presents Beowulf with a number of gifts, among them
           his own richly decorated war saddle.

XVI   **Entertainment at the Victory Feast: The Tale of Finn and
           Hnæf (Beginning)**
           A court poet tells the tragic story of a famous Danish tri-
           umph of the past: how King Hnæf, on a visit to his sister
           Hildeburh and her husband Finn, king of the Frisians, is
           treacherously attacked and slain by Finn. The son of Hilde-
           burh and Finn is also killed in the fighting, and his body is
           burnt alongside his uncle Hnæf. (A fragmentary Old English

poem, "The Fight at Finnsburg" [see pp. 174–77], contains material that supplements this account.)

XVII   The Tale of Finn and Hnæf (Conclusion)
The next spring, after a bitter winter during which weather conditions force him to remain at Finn's court in Frisia under the protection of a treaty, Hnæf's lieutenant Hengest avenges Hnæf's death by killing Finn. Hildeburh is taken back to her people. When the poet concludes his tale of Hildeburh's sorrows, Hrothgar's queen Wealhtheow is shown to be worried about the future prospects of her own young sons in the light of Hrothulf's ominous preeminence at court and her husband's recent adoption of Beowulf.

XVIII   Wealhtheow's Gifts to Beowulf
Wealhtheow thanks Beowulf and gives him a robe and a marvelous neck-ring, then pleads with him to look after her sons and their interests. (We are told that Beowulf's king and uncle Hygelac subsequently lost this neck-ring when he was slain during a reckless and unprovoked attack on the Frisians in the Rhineland.) When darkness falls the Danes once again take possession of their meadhall.

XIX   The Attack by Grendel's Mother
Seeking vengeance for her son's death, Grendel's mother raids the hall. She kills Æschere, Hrothgar's closest friend and confidant, and recovers her son's arm.

XX   Hrothgar's Despair
Hrothgar, stricken, mourns the death of his old friend and describes the eerie and sinister place where the monsters have their lair.

XXI   The Journey to the Monsters' Lair
After rallying the demoralized king, Beowulf travels to the monsters' pool, where he dons his armor and prepares to swim down to their underwater hall, taking with him a sword lent to him by Unferth.

XXII   Beowulf Fights Grendel's Mother
Beowulf says goodbye to Hrothgar and swims down to the monsters' lair, his descent taking a good part of the day. When he reaches the bottom, Grendel's mother seizes him and carries him inside her underwater hall, where a battle ensues that Beowulf would have lost (we are told) had he not been helped by God.

XXIII   **The Return to Heorot**
Beowulf kills Grendel's mother with a giant sword that he finds in the monsters' lair, then looks for Grendel's body and cuts off its head. Taking the head and the hilt of the sword with him, he swims up to rejoin his followers, and they return to Heorot.

XXIV   **Hrothgar and Beowulf Talk**
After studying the images and inscription on the hilt of the giant sword, Hrothgar praises Beowulf, asserting that he is very unlike the miserly tyrant Heremod (the earlier king of the Danes with whom he had already been contrasted in Section XIII). Hrothgar warns Beowulf against pride and avarice.

XXV   **Hrothgar Counsels Beowulf**
Pride, he says, along with greed for temporal riches, leads to disaster. Since death is the inevitable lot of all of us, we should pursue eternal values. Hrothgar cites his own career and his long humiliation by Grendel as an example of pride and the fate that awaits it. The next morning, their mission accomplished, Beowulf and his men are eager to set out for home.

XXVI   **Beowulf and Hrothgar Part**
Beowulf thanks Hrothgar for his hospitality, promising to return to Denmark if his help is ever needed again. Hrothgar prophesies that Beowulf will one day be an outstanding king and thanks him for establishing a relationship of peace and friendship between the Danes and Geats, who were once enemies.

XXVII   **Beowulf Goes Home**
Beowulf and his men return to the land of the Geats and set out immediately to report to their king Hygelac. (Hygelac's queen Hygd is contrasted with Modthrytho, a princess who was infamous for wicked behavior until tamed by her husband Offa.)

XXVIII   **Beowulf Reports to His King**
Beowulf greets Hygelac and tells him what happened in Denmark, describing his reception by Hrothgar and Wealhtheow and outlining Hrothgar's plan to patch up a quarrel with his enemies the Heathobards by marrying his daughter Freawaru to their king Ingeld.

[XXIX–XXX]   **Beowulf's Report Concluded**
Beowulf foresees the failure of Hrothgar's plan. He describes his fights with Grendel and Grendel's mother.

XXXI   **Beowulf's Reward. His Long Reign as King. The Coming of the Dragon**
Beowulf is lavishly rewarded by his king Hygelac and confirmed in the possession of his ancestral estates. Much later, after Hygelac has died and his son Heardred has been killed by the Swedes, Beowulf succeeds to the throne and rules prosperously for fifty years until a flying, fire-breathing dragon is roused to wrath by an intruder who sneaks into the burial mound where it lives and rifles its treasure.

XXXII   **The Dragon's Vengeance**
After a review of the earlier history of the treasure, the poem describes how the angry dragon starts to ravage the land of the Geats.

XXXIII   **Beowulf Prepares to Fight the Dragon**
When he learns of the dragon's depredations, Beowulf decides to fight it single-handedly and has an iron shield made for himself. (Background information is provided about past hostilities between the Geats and their neighbors and traditional enemies the Swedes.)

XXXIV   **Beowulf Arrives at the Dragon's Mound**
The hero, accompanied by eleven chosen companions, approaches the dragon's mound. Uneasy about the coming encounter, he says goodbye to his followers and reviews his life, emphasizing his relations with the Geatish royal house.

XXXV   **Beowulf Fights the Dragon**
After reviewing the bitter history of warfare between Swedes and Geats, and also Hygelac's rash and fatal raid against the Franks and Frisians in the Rhineland, Beowulf challenges the dragon and the two foes engage. During the dragon's first onslaught, Beowulf is deserted by all but one of his followers, his faithful young kinsman Wiglaf.

XXXVI   **Beowulf is Mortally Wounded**
Wiglaf reproaches Beowulf's cowardly companions and vows to stand by him. When the dragon attacks for the second time, Beowulf's sword Nægling fails him. In the third attack he receives a fatal wound.

XXXVII   Beowulf and Wiglaf Kill the Dragon
              Between them, Wiglaf and the mortally wounded Beowulf
              kill the dragon. Beowulf, dying, says that he is confident of
              the righteousness of his life and reign but regrets having no
              son and heir. He sends Wiglaf into the mound to bring out
              a sample of the treasure so he can derive comfort and con-
              solation from the sight of it.

XXVIII   Beowulf's Death
              After gazing at the treasure and expressing his gratitude to
              God for letting him win such a prize for his people, Beowulf
              designates Wiglaf his successor. (Earlier, in Section XXXVI,
              attention had been drawn to the ominous fact that Wiglaf's
              father Weohstan once killed the brother of Eadgils, the pres-
              ent king of Sweden.) Beowulf asks to be buried in a mound
              near the sea. His soul departs from his body.

[XXXIX]   Wiglaf Rebukes Beowulf's Cowardly Retainers
              Beowulf's ten cowardly companions, skulking back from
              the woods, are rebuked by Wiglaf and punished with dis-
              grace and the loss of all their privileges.

XL   Prophecy of Future Warfare between the Geats and Their
              Enemies
              A messenger, sent to tell the rest of Beowulf's army about
              his death, foresees assaults on the Geats from the Franks
              and Frisians (who are still concerned to avenge Hygelac's
              raid on the Rhineland) and the Swedes.

XLI   The Background of Swedish Hostility
              The Swedes want vengeance for the death of their great king
              Ongentheow, slain by Hygelac's forces during an earlier
              clash between the two peoples.

XLII   The Dragon's Hoard Is Plundered
              (An account is given of the curse on the treasure.) Wiglaf
              and his companions plunder the hoard, then transport it,
              along with Beowulf's body, to Whale Headland.

XLIII   Beowulf's Funeral
              Amid gloomy hints of a national disaster awaiting the
              Geats, Beowulf's followers burn his body and inter its ashes,
              along with the treasure plundered from the dragon's hoard,
              in a great burial mound.

Oral and Written *Beowulf*s

The Oral *Beowulf*

In his important book on the early Germanic tribes, written about 100 A.D., the Roman historian Tacitus mentions some of the subjects treated "in their ancient songs, which are the only kind of historical tradition among them."[1] Tacitus thinks it strange that a people's vernacular oral poetry ("their ancient songs") could be the sole means whereby their "historical tradition" (i.e., their memory of the past) was transmitted from one generation to the next. This was certainly not the way things were done in Rome, not at least in the days of the historian—the highly *literate* historian—Tacitus. But it was standard practice among the early Germanic peoples, who were, by and large, illiterate until the time of their conversion to Christianity.

Today the oral poetry of these peoples has disappeared and is as unrecoverable as the breath of those who sang it, except for fragments and snatches, reflections and refractions, that survive embodied in the much later *written* texts of the Old Icelandic Poetic Edda, the Middle High German *Nibelungenlied,* and—most magnificent of all—the Old English narrative poem *Beowulf.*

Beowulf is obviously not an "oral poem" in the primary sense of the phrase, since none of us is ever going to listen to it in a live performance by a tenth-century Anglo-Saxon *scop* ("poet," literally, "shaper, creator"), or at least not until time machines come into common use. Nor is it likely to be an "oral poem" in the sense that it is a written text resulting from someone— a "scribe" of some sort—taking down *verbatim* the words of a performance by an oral singer. It is much more probable that it was, at least in a form verging on that in which we have it today, a written production from the outset, the work of a literate—and perhaps even fairly learned—individual who was intimately familiar with the oral poetry of his people and modeled his own poem closely upon it.[2] This oral poetry was not only very much alive

---

1. *Carminibus antiquis, quod unum apud illos memoriae et annalium genus est. Cornelii Taciti de Origine et Situ Germanorum,* ed. J. G. C. Anderson (Oxford: Clarendon Press, 1938), sec. 3.

2. We do not know who this individual was, so we call him "the *Beowulf*-poet." While it is possible that the individual in question was a woman, the interests and attitudes that are on view in the poem, as well as what we know about the circumstances of literary production in Anglo-Saxon England, strongly suggest that its author was male.

in his day but was popular among all classes of society, from kings to peasants.[3] Moreover, it was (and this is of decisive importance) the only form in which poetry was known to exist in Old English, the vernacular language of the Anglo-Saxons.[4]

The rootedness of *Beowulf* in Anglo-Saxon oral poetry is shown by its reliance on many of the devices and techniques employed by traditional poets to facilitate oral production and improvisation (e.g., set formulaic phrases) and to mark the boundaries of scenes and sections (e.g., deliberate repetition of thematically significant words, or "echo-words"). It is shown, too, by the fact that, whatever may have been the immediate form in which his materials reached him, the *Beowulf*-poet insists that they have behind them the authority of oral tradition: "We have heard tell . . ." (1), "I have never heard . . ." (75), "I have heard it said . . ." (1553), and so on.

In fact, the *Beowulf*-poet's interest in oral poetry verges on the professional, and his intimate knowledge of how it is produced, and for what purposes, is made clear in a number of places. After Beowulf's fight with Grendel, for example, some of Hrothgar's Danes track the dying monster's bloody footprints to the pool where he lives with his mother. Afterward, as they ride back to Heorot, racing their horses out of sheer "high spirits" (1730),

> sometimes a thane
> of the king's would perform,
> a consummate poet
> who knew and could sing
> numberless tales,
> could relate them in linked

---

3. The Venerable Bede's account of Caedmon, an illiterate cowherd who began producing oral poetry as the result of a vision in a dream, attests to its popularity at the lower end of the social spectrum. The lyre found in the royal ship burial at Sutton Hoo, as well as what we are told about King Hrothgar in *Beowulf* (4213–15), attests to its popularity at the higher end.

4. The *Beowulf*-poet knows that poetry, in an oral culture, serves a wide range of communicative purposes, including some that are today the province of other media (television, magazines, newspapers). For example, Grendel's dozen years harassing the Danes were of such universal interest

> that news of his raids
> was known everywhere,
> leaping from land
> to land in songs. (299–302)

> language, in words
> arrayed properly,
> and who was already at work
> blazoning Beowulf's
> brilliant achievement,
> composing a poem
> of praise, skillfully
> weaving its web. (1734–47)

We see here that the young hero has no sooner performed his first great heroic deed than it is being transformed into poetry, poetry that—passed orally from singer to singer and generation to generation—was intended to keep the memory of his achievement green far into the future. What the author of *Beowulf* wants us to believe—and perhaps believes himself—is that we are witnessing here the birth, the moment of creation, of a panegyric song about one of the deeds of his great hero.

The passage is also interesting as a sort of *ars poetica* in miniature: it contains references to both the alliterative *style* of Old English verse (its "linked / language") and its *content* ("numberless tales" drawn in large part from the world of heroic legend). We learn more about this content from a remarkable passage enumerating the repertory of the Danish king Hrothgar, who was himself a composer and singer of oral poems. We are told that the king

> knows legends and songs
> from long-gone times:
> sometimes he would play
> sweet melodies
> on his sounding harp,
> sometimes sing songs
> sorrowful but true;
> sometimes he would tell
> astonishing stories,
> strange but moving;
> and sometimes the old
> sad-hearted king,
> mastered by age,
> would lament his youth
> and broken strength,
> his breast surging
> with immense sorrow
> as he remembered the past. (4211–28)

Among "songs / sorrowful but true" will have been oral poems about "historical" subjects, that is, poems like those retold, alluded to, or summarized in the "digressions" in *Beowulf* (and in the short lyric "Deor," printed on pp. 184–86). Among "astonishing stories, / strange but moving" will have been poems dealing with folklore material like monsters and dragons. Among personal statements about a singer's past, containing reflections on lost youth, old age, and bitter memories of days that are gone, will have been elegiac lyrics like "A Meditation" (see pp. 177–83).

We catch sight, too, of what must have been another typical subject of Anglo-Saxon oral poetry in the lament sung by Beowulf's followers at his funeral:

> Slowly, then, twelve
> sons of princes
> rode on horseback
> around the barrow,
> lamenting their leader
> in mournful lays;
> they complained of their plight
> but praised the king,
> applauded his virtue
> and prowess in war,
> were generous in judgment,
> just as retainers
> should always be,
> honoring their lord
> with worthy love
> and words of praise
> when fate leads him
> forth from the body. (6337–54)

Once again, here, we are present in the *Beowulf*-poet's imagination and our own at the birth of a piece of oral heroic poetry, but this time a dirge— "Beowulf's Funeral Song," we might even call it.[5]

---

5. It is quite remarkable how closely this whole scene parallels the eyewitness account by the Byzantine historian Priscus of Panium of the funeral of Attila the Hun conducted by his Germanized followers (453 A.D.): "In the middle of a plain in a silk tent his body was laid out and solemnly displayed to inspire awe. The most select horsemen of the whole Hunnish race rode around him where he had been placed, in the fashion of the circus races, uttering his funeral song as follows: 'Chief of the Huns,

The *Beowulf*-poet and the tradition he represents would have regarded oral songs of this kind, transmitted down through the centuries by a succession of singers, as containing authentic historical information about the ancestral heroes of their people, as well as about their gods, their laws, their belief and value systems, and anything else that was felt to be important enough to be delivered intact from the present to the future.

But it is not information that would be regarded as accurate or reliable by modern "scientific" historians. Anyone who has played the game of "telephone" will appreciate how quickly and easily data that is transmitted orally deteriorates in the process of transmission. Words and messages become garbled, and the expectations and imaginations of the players quickly step in to "straighten things out" and "restore coherence," so they suppose, but actually to create ever more confusion. Singers of oral poetry may also, in the course of time, spice their narrative up by importing into it all sorts of nonhistorical matter (e.g., man-eating monsters and dragons). And they may reshape personalities and events in order to express a moral or teach a lesson. This may lead to great works of imaginative literature; it does not lead to accurate history.

The Written *Beowulf*

Once the skills of writing and book production were introduced to the Anglo-Saxons by Christian missionaries in the 600s, it became possible for vernacular poetry to be created and transmitted in writing as well as orally, and there followed a long period of time—extending up to and even beyond the end of the Anglo-Saxon age—when oral and written cultures coexisted and overlapped, constantly cross-fertilizing one another. It is at some point during this period that we must imagine the initial creation of a written version of *Beowulf*, composed in a manner indistinguishable from that of oral poetry (remember that it was the only manner in which poetry in the vernacu-

---

King Attila, born of Mundiuch his father, lord of the mightiest races, who alone, with power unknown before his time, held the Scythian and German realms and even terrified both empires of the Roman world, captured their cities, and, placated by their prayers, took yearly tribute from them to save the rest from being plundered. When he had done all these things through the kindness of fortune, neither by an enemy's wound nor a friend's treachery but with his nation secure, amid his pleasures, and in happiness and without sense of pain he fell'" (C. D. Gordon, *The Age of Attila: Fifth-Century Byzantium and the Barbarians* [Ann Arbor: University of Michigan Press, 1960], 110–11). The differences in emphasis between what is sung by Attila's followers and what is sung by Beowulf's are as interesting and enlightening as the ritual formalities are similar.

lar was possible or imaginable) and containing historical memories and folk-lore material that had been handed down for centuries in oral tradition.

It is not possible to gauge, today, the extent to which the various elements that are brought together in the written text of *Beowulf* had already been combined in oral tradition, and the extent to which their present combination is the result of a unique act of amalgamation and consolidation on the part of a literate poet (or literate poets).[6] Whatever may have been the case, we have now reached the point, almost certainly sometime in the mid- or late Anglo-Saxon period, when a long, coherent, written narrative in verse, with Beowulf as its principal subject, has coalesced out of oral antecedents.[7]

What happened next is that manuscripts of this written narrative were copied, one from another. Evidence of this process remains today in the unique surviving manuscript in the presence of certain types of scribal error that imply a history of recopying. There may at one time have existed a number of manuscript copies of the poem, but we will never know how many. *Beowulf* is hardly unique in this respect: most Old English poems survive to-day in single copies. What it means, however, is that most of the Old English poetry that once existed and was lucky enough (or in some cases privileged enough) to be written down, perished either during the Anglo-Saxon period itself or the centuries that followed. Such works had to run the gauntlet of the Norman Conquest of 1066 (the linguistic impact of which was ultimately of such effect that within three centuries it would have been hard for anyone in the country to read Old English prose and well-nigh impossible to read Old English verse) and the wholesale destruction of manuscripts that followed Henry VIII's dissolution of the monasteries and the dispersal of their libraries in the early sixteenth century.

Beowulf is one of the lucky survivors of this process of random culling. As a long secular narrative work on a heroic subject, it is unique among surviving Old English poems, and this uniqueness has important consequences. While it is true that other surviving Old English poems—such as the three that are published in this book—shed a good deal of light on *Beowulf* and its cultural and intellectual background, they do not tell us much about what

---

6. That is why often, in the pages that follow, when readers come across the phrase "the *Beowulf*-poet," they ought to substitute for it the more accurate (if somewhat un-wieldy) formula "the *Beowulf*-poet, or the tradition upon which he bases his work."

Students of the poem have sometimes claimed to detect signs of multiple author-ship in the surviving text. But it contains nothing to contradict—and much to support—the view that it is the work of a single creative intelligence.

7. It is not possible to assign a precise (or even an imprecise) date to this. Linguistic criteria, which were once all the rage, are no longer regarded as furnishing a sound basis for dating the text.

Anglo-Saxons would have regarded as its *genre,* that is, what *kind* of poem Anglo-Saxon readers would have considered it to be, nor whether they would have regarded it as a good or bad example of that kind. Furthermore, comparative material is lacking that might enable us to explain many of the puzzling features of the text and make certain kinds of critical judgments about it.

To take a contrasting and highly revealing example: almost all the Icelandic family sagas that were ever written have survived, often in multiple manuscript copies, and the richness of this legacy allows us to discuss them as a group, to identify the typical and characteristic features that identify them as a class or genre, to date them vis-à-vis one another (and thus to say something about the rise, development, and decline of the entire genre), and even—by counting and comparing the number of surviving manuscript copies of individual sagas—to determine their relative popularity in their own day and thus to make judgments about whether modern criteria for literary excellence jibe with those of the society that originally produced them.

None of this is possible in the case of *Beowulf.* The only strictly comparable work in Old English of which anything is known is the poem "Waldere," about the hero Walter of Aquitaine; it survives in two short fragments, neither of which shows any of the features of *Beowulf* that strike us today as most interesting or puzzling, though the mere fact of its existence *does* suggest that *Beowulf* represents a kind of poetry that was familiar to the Anglo-Saxons.

We would understand many of the features of *Beowulf* better if we had a few other texts that were like it (or even a single text that was like it). Sympathetic readers today feel that it is a masterpiece, a work of original and startling genius. Would an Anglo-Saxon reader have agreed?

It is possible, of course, that no genre of similar and comparable poems existed in Anglo-Saxon England and that *Beowulf* was, even in its own day, *sui generis,* a unique work whose author may have been inspired by nonnative models (like Virgil's *Æneid*) to create an extended narrative poem. This hypothesis has struck some readers as very attractive, since it would explain a number of features in the work that make it an oddity among early Germanic narrative poems. But it cannot be proven.

The Surviving Manuscript and Modern Editions of the Poem

The unique surviving text of the Old English *Beowulf* is preserved today in the British Library in London, where it forms part of a manuscript volume bearing the traditional designation MS Cotton Vitellius A.xv. This volume consists of two originally separate manuscripts that are now bound together. The second of these (folios 91–209 in the composite manuscript) contains

The first page of the text of *Beowulf*. © British Library Board. All Rights Reserved. MS. Cotton Vitellius A.xv, f. 132. By permission of the British Library.

three pieces of Old English prose, *Beowulf,* and the Old English poem *Judith.* It has been thought by some that the reason these five texts were brought together in Anglo-Saxon times and included in a single manuscript is that all of them deal in one way or another with giants and monsters.

The text of *Beowulf* occupies 70 folios (140 pages) of the composite manuscript (folios 132–201ᵛ). It was copied out, mainly in the West Saxon dialect, by two scribes writing sometime in the late 900s or early 1000s. The poem itself bears no title in the manuscript, where its text is divided into forty-four sections, most of which are preceded by Roman numerals.[8] Sometimes the section divisions correlate so neatly with what seem to be units or blocks of the narrative that one is tempted to regard them as going back to the poet;[9] at other times they appear to be perfectly arbitrary.

The manuscript is likely to have been produced in one of the many monasteries of late Anglo-Saxon England (we do not know which one) and to have remained in the library of that monastery, increasingly unintelligible as the years went by,[10] until it was "liberated" in the time of King Henry VIII, when the monasteries of England were dissolved (1535). In 1563 it was in the hands of the antiquary Lawrence Nowell. It ended up in the library of the great Elizabethan collector Sir Robert Cotton (1571–1631), which became one of the founding collections of the British Museum Library (now the British Library) in 1753.[11]

---

8. There is an unnumbered "prologue" and Roman numerals are lacking for Sections XXIX, XXX, and XXXIX. These sections were probably known as *fitte* ("fitts") to contemporary Anglo-Saxons. They are of very unequal length, the shortest containing 86 verses and the longest 284.

9. Section I, for example, begins with a genealogy of the Scylding kings of Denmark (105–26) and concludes with a genealogy of their enemies, the Grendel clan (221–27). These genealogies, so clearly balanced and contrasted, seem to mark the outer boundaries of a narrative unit. Section XIII has a complex, intricate, and demonstrable internal structure that seems to identify it as another narrative unit (see pp. xlviii–li).

10. E. G. Stanley provides evidence that Old English verse may have ceased to be fully understood as early as the twelfth century (Eric Gerald Stanley, ed., *Continuations and Beginnings: Studies in Old English Literature* [London: Nelson, 1966], 105, n.). This is especially likely to have been true in the case of *Beowulf,* which is a difficult text.

11. In 1731 the Cotton collection was ravaged by a terrible fire that destroyed many famous manuscripts. The edges of the parchment pages containing the text of *Beowulf* were scorched in the fire, and this set in motion a process of flaking that ultimately led to the loss of many letters standing at the beginning and end of lines.

Modern interest in the poem was first kindled in the late eighteenth century, not because of its literary merit but because of the light it was thought to shed on the history of Iron Age Scandinavia. The first edition of the Old English text was published in 1815, and the first Modern English translation in 1837. Thus, although it is perfectly correct to regard *Beowulf* as the earliest important piece of poetry in the English language, it is necessary to remember that it remained completely unknown—and unable to exert any influence on literary developments—until the nineteenth century.

The standard scholarly edition of the Old English text is *Beowulf and the Fight at Finnsburg,* edited by Fr. Klaeber, 3rd ed. (Boston: D. C. Heath and Company, 1950). Its introduction and notes, though now somewhat dated, still cover most of the relevant bases.[12] They are covered in more up-to-date fashion in Andy Orchard's invaluable *Critical Companion to Beowulf* (Cambridge: D. S. Brewer, 2003). For a handy edition of the Old English text with a Modern English translation on facing pages and plenty of helpful notes, see Howell D. Chickering, Jr., *Beowulf: A Dual-Language Edition* (New York: Doubleday Anchor Books, 1977). See also the Suggestions for Further Reading (pp. 187–88).

Legend and Lore

It is customary to approach *Beowulf* as a mixture or synthesis of legend ("fabulous elements") and lore ("historical elements"). The poet, or the tradition he represents, has fused these elements so seamlessly together that neither can be disengaged from the other without producing a very different —and essentially crippled—work. Not that people do not *try* to disengage them: we often see in comic-book or motion-picture redactions of the poem the elimination of as many of its "historical elements" as possible, and in hard-nosed rationalistic criticism there is sometimes an inclination to discount the "fabulous elements" as not worthy of the attention of serious people. W. P. Ker, writing in 1904, can be taken as representative of this stern but ultimately unhelpful approach to the poem: "In construction it is curiously weak, in a sense preposterous; for while the main story [i.e., the story

---

12. A new edition of this foundational work is in preparation: R. D. Fulk, Robert E. Bjork, and John D. Niles, eds., *Klaeber's "Beowulf"* (Boston: Houghton Mifflin Press, forthcoming).

of a monster-slaying hero] is simplicity itself, the merest commonplace of heroic legend, all about it, in the historic allusions, are revelations of a whole world of tragedy, plots different in import from that of *Beowulf,* more like the tragic themes of Iceland." This, according to Ker, "is a radical defect, a disproportion that puts the irrelevances in the centre and the serious things on the outer edges."[13] No doubt some readers of the poem today will feel that Ker's points are well taken; others will see them as the product of too much respect and admiration for more "mature" and "classical" models, too little regard for the child in all of us who would sometimes prefer watching *King Kong* to *King Lear.*

It is not necessary to say much here about the "fabulous elements" in the poem: Grendel, his mother, and the dragon. It is important to point out, however, that these monsters are of two distinctly different kinds: Grendel and his mother, though they are human in origin, represent grotesque distortions of humanity. Grendel, for example, can be interpreted as a projection (and symbol) of humanity's proclivity to violence, as is clearly implied by his descent from Cain. The dragon is more elemental, a nonhuman, antihuman force of nature, as his weapon of choice—fire—immediately suggests. Dragons are awesome creatures, too, and signs of things to come: in 793, to herald the approaching Viking raid on the monastery of Lindisfarne, "terrible portents appeared over Northumbria, and miserably frightened the inhabitants: these were exceptional flashes of lightning, and fiery dragons were seen flying in the air."[14]

The "historical" portions of *Beowulf* offer more difficulty to a modern reader than the "fabulous" portions, since they introduce us to a large number of unfamiliar events and a large cast of unfamiliar characters (or it might be better to say "a large cast of characters with unfamiliar names," since the human types represented by these characters are familiar and instantly recognizable).

Most of the human characters in *Beowulf* have the same names as real historical persons who lived in or near Scandinavia in the late 400s and early 500s, and the events actually took place at that time (to the extent that they ever took place at all). Subsequently, memories of these persons and events were transmitted for many centuries in the form of oral poetry, and during this period they were subject to all the types of distortion and contamination that characterize oral transmission, including in this case the infusion of

---

13. W. P. Ker, *The Dark Ages* (London: Thomas Nelson and Sons, 1955), 54.

14. G. N. Garmonsway, tr., *The Anglo-Saxon Chronicle,* revised edition (London: Everyman's Library, 1954), 253.

"fabulous" elements. Some of the oral traditions originating in Scandinavia made their way to England, and it was there that the written text of *Beowulf,* more or less as we have it today, took shape in the mid– or late Anglo-Saxon period, during the time when oral and literary cultures overlapped.

The realization that actual historical persons and events underlie *Beowulf* is the fruit of modern scholarship, and it was (not surprisingly) historians in Scandinavia who first understood that the poem could shed light on a very dark period in the history of their part of the world, a period for which reliable documentary sources were few and often unreliable.

We owe the most striking discovery of this scholarship—it has been called the most important discovery ever made in the study of *Beowulf*—to the Danish scholar N. F. S. Grundtvig, writing in 1815 and 1817. Grundtvig noticed that Beowulf's uncle and liege lord Hygelac, who is represented in the poem as dying in a seaborne raid against a tribe called the Hetware,[15] can be identified with an historical Scandinavian king named Chochilaicus who died in a raid against the Attuarii, a people who lived near the mouth of the River Rhine and were allied to the Franks. The clash is recorded in the *Historia Francorum* (*History of the Franks*) of Gregory, Bishop of Tours,[16] and its mention there allows it to be dated around 520 A.D. Grundtvig's discovery is thus not only the foundation of our belief today that real personalities and events underlie the account of early Scandinavia in *Beowulf,* but it enables modern historians to assign rough (and admittedly extremely hypothetical) dates to the reigns of all the Scandinavian kings and queens mentioned in the poem.

By analyzing the pieces of information about these figures that are scattered throughout *Beowulf,* combining it with information from later Scandinavian sources (where many of them were also remembered, generally much more dimly), and reassembling it in schematic format, it is possible to produce genealogical tables of the kings of the Danes, the Geats, and the Swedes that can be of great help to modern readers in their struggle to follow the complex dynastic relations and politics that are the subject of so much of the poem.

---

15. Beowulf is said to have accompanied his uncle on this expedition and to have been its only survivor. The raid is alluded to several times in the poem, and it is clear that Beowulf regarded Hygelac's death as the greatest tragedy of his own life.

16. Chochilaicus (misspelled Chlochilaicus) is Gregory's Latinization of the name of a chieftain who probably called himself—in his own tongue—something like Hugilaikaz. This name later became Hygelac in Old English by normal processes of phonetic development.

Genealogies of Scandinavian Kings

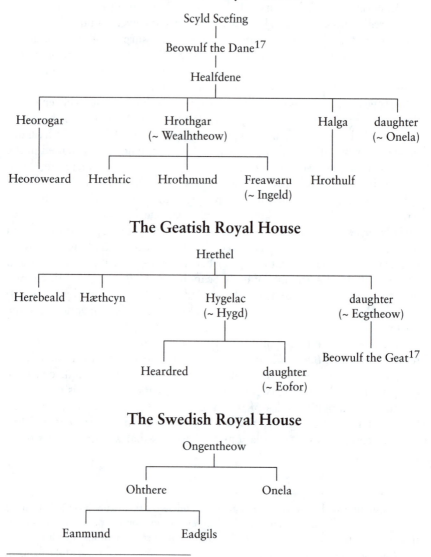

The Danish Royal House

Scyld Scefing

Beowulf the Dane[17]

Healfdene

Heorogar — Hrothgar (~ Wealhtheow) — Halga — daughter (~ Onela)

Heoroweard   Hrethric   Hrothmund   Freawaru (~ Ingeld)   Hrothulf

The Geatish Royal House

Hrethel

Herebeald   Hæthcyn   Hygelac (~ Hygd)   daughter (~ Ecgtheow)

Heardred   daughter (~ Eofor)   Beowulf the Geat[17]

The Swedish Royal House

Ongentheow

Ohthere   Onela

Eanmund   Eadgils

17. It is important not to confuse these two Beowulfs. The poet himself is careful to keep them distinct, referring to the Danish king as *Beowulf Scyldinga* (53b), "Beowulf of the Scyldings," and the hero of the poem as *Beowulf Geata* (676a, 1191a), "Beowulf of the Geats."

Reconstructing in detail the political and familial relationships of these kings, as well as their motivations for acting in the way they do, has been one of the enduring preoccupations of *Beowulf* scholarship. The poet seems to take it for granted that his original audience was not only very interested in material of this sort but closely familiar with it, so he does not always feel a need to dot the i's and cross the t's: he assumes that a few quick allusions or summary statements will conjure up for the mind's eye of that audience a whole pageant of events and personalities. This means, unfortunately, that his audience today is often left in the dark about backgrounds and details that the poet takes very seriously and feels passionately about, and the poem —especially its second half concerned with the Geats and their powerful neighbors the Swedes—tends to flit past as a confusing and boring rigmarole of kings' names and military campaigns. It is only when one reads this part of the poem in slow motion (as it were) that it begins to make sense and yield up its riches.

The poet realizes that the Scandinavian dynasties that are his "historical" subject lived in the past, a past he idealizes as a time when people—people like Beowulf's Geats, at least—

> treated friend and foe
> with firmness, constancy,
> and all honor
> in the ancient way. (3727–30)

The poet also realizes that back beyond this time of "the ancient way"— however long ago that may have been!—stretches a much deeper past. The dragon, for example, had been guarding its treasure for three hundred years when a thief robbed it, starting the chain of events that led to Beowulf's death. "Three hundred years" is a "poetic" number, of course, not to be taken literally—except as suggesting the poet's awareness of the very large tracts of time that make up the past.

Even farther back than the dragon's discovery of the treasure is the period of the "heathen lords" who originally mined the gold from the ground and later placed a curse on it and whose last living representative consigned it back to the earth (4462–4539), where it lay for a thousand years (6098–6100).[18]

---

18. This is on the assumption that a single group of "heathen lords" owned the treasure before it was buried, not two different groups at two different times. This anonymous race of "heathen lords" is probably intended to recall the Romans, whose long occupation of Britain was surely a fact familiar to the poet, as it was to his contemporaries, and whose caches of buried treasure probably came to light even more

We plunge even deeper in time—and into the Biblical history that the poet and his contemporaries regarded as prologue to their own—with the poet's references to Cain and Abel (214–15 and 2523), to "those bold giants / who rebelled against God" (225–26), and to "the story / of earth's creation / ages ago" (180–82)—beyond which of course it is not possible to go.

Narrative Strategies and Structures

The way in which the *Beowulf*-poet marshals his materials and organizes his narrative sometimes strikes modern readers as the oddest thing about his poem, and the hardest to understand and sympathize with. Some of his narrative techniques—the ones that seem obvious and familiar to an audience today—require no comment here; it is the more unfamiliar and apparently idiosyncratic tactics and strategies that need explanation. When it is properly understood, the structure of *Beowulf* is seen to be masterful and to mirror in the most startling and expressive way the moral and philosophical concerns of its author. It is fair to say that the way the poem is constructed, both as a whole and in part, is an integral part of its meaning and message.

As we embark on an analysis of the architecture of *Beowulf*, both the grand sweep of its overall design and the intricacies of some of its details, it is well to bear in mind that it is not really possible to say how many of its structural features are the work of our (hypothetical) literate poet and how many of them reached him ready-made in the materials and traditions upon which he drew. Whatever their source, the text as we have it today shows an intense interest in formal structures of all kinds, many of them based on juxtapositions, cycles, balances, and symmetries; these are among the most characteristic features of the poem, and studying them provides valuable insight into the workings of the poet's mind and craft.

The central, organizing narrative of *Beowulf* is obviously the story of the hero's life, achievements, and death. For the most part, this narrative unfolds

---

regularly in his day than they do in ours—when they turn up with quite surprising frequency. It is interesting, too, that the dragon's mound in the poem seems to combine features of a Stone Age or Bronze Age tumulus (burial mound) with those of a Roman building. Both types of structure were fairly thick on the ground in the poet's day, when they distinguished themselves so much from the mainly timber construction of the Anglo-Saxons that they were thought of in the poetic tradition as "the work of giants" (*enta geweorc*), an idea the *Beowulf*-poet refers to twice in his original (2717b, 2774a). See also "A Meditation" (pp. 177–83), where the ruins discussed by the poet are clearly Roman in origin.

in a straightforward chronological way. The details of the historical background, on the other hand, are presented in more fragmentary nonlinear form —but not haphazardly!—and the narrative darts forward and backward in time as it weaves its elaborate tapestry of the kings and queens and wars and weddings of pre–Viking Age Scandinavia. The past, the present, and the future are all on view in the poem, but they are not bound by the usual laws of sequentiality, and thus of cause and effect: the actual order in which they are presented allows for many striking effects of juxtaposition and contrast, irony and pathos.

The main narrative falls into two parts that are concerned with two defining moments in its protagonist's life: his first great heroic achievement as a young man, which won him wealth and fame and a high position in the aristocratic society of his day, and his death as an old man fifty years later. There is no transition between these two parts of the poem: they are deliberately juxtaposed and sharply contrasted. The join between them occurs unexpectedly in the middle of one of the poem's numbered sections, just after Beowulf has been given enormous rewards by his uncle Hygelac, the king, in recognition of his achievements:

> Both of them, the king
> and Beowulf, had land
>   in that country,
> the king much more,
> the whole kingdom,
> since he was higher in rank.
> It would come to pass
> in the cruel wars
> of the harsh future,
> when Hygelac was dead
> and his son Heardred
> had been slain in combat. . . . (4393–4404)

After this we are in altogether new territory. We never see Beowulf aging; one moment he is young, vigorous, confident, crowned with success, and looking forward to a promising future; the next moment—fifty years later!— he is ancient, doubt-ridden, and doomed. This sudden juxtaposition gives us a jolt that is nicely calculated to make us realize that no matter how much time may elapse between our own youth and old age, it is really only the blink of an eye, which is certainly how it feels in retrospect. This abrupt but studied contrast of the hero's youth and old age is thus part of the poet's ongoing insistence on the inevitability of reversal (*edwenden*) in human affairs. A philosophical position—an interpretation of life—is being articulated here through the use of structure.

But it is not only the hero who is suddenly old and doomed in the second part of the poem; so, it seems, is almost everyone else. Unlike the first part, with its cast of hopeful young warriors and its evocation of an optimistic world in which evil can be thumpingly defeated and virtue brilliantly rewarded, the second part is filled with old, depressed, doomed individuals: the last survivor of an unidentified tribe (who buries his treasure so that no one else will ever be able to enjoy it), an aged father (who must see his own son hanged on the gallows), old King Hrethel of the Geats (who dies of depression after one of his sons murders another), and the grim old Swedish king Ongentheow (slaughtered in the poem's bloodiest and most uncompromising scene of human beings fighting and killing each other). If the first part of the poem suggests that long-standing international conflicts can be peacefully resolved by the outstanding virtue of a single heroic individual, the second part shows a whole culture breaking down in wars and foresees a bleak future of doom and disaster. And if the first part of the poem is concerned with beginnings (the creation of the world, the building of Heorot, the launching of Beowulf's heroic career), the second part is about endings (Beowulf's death and the end of both his family, the Wægmundings, and his people, the Geats, as well as the end of the world).[19] The second part of the poem is thus much gloomier than the first, and its darkening trajectory is an accurate image of the trajectory of most human lives and all human societies.[20]

The emphasis on the contrast between youth and age is fundamental to *Beowulf* and is reinforced by a number of balances and symmetries: the youthful Beowulf of the first part of the poem has his counterweight in ancient King Hrothgar, and this pairing is balanced in the second part by its inversion, the contrast between ancient King Beowulf and youthful Wiglaf.

The contrast between the two parts of the poem, established in the first place by their abrupt juxtaposition, was first noted and emphasized by J. R. R. Tolkien in 1936.[21] It is paralleled—on a much smaller scale—by a number of other stark juxtapositions. Often the intended effect of these is to show that nothing in the secular world lasts for very long, neither good fortune

---

19. The last of these is not described, but the mere use of the word *woruldende* (3083b) at the very close of the poem is suggestive.

20. The portrayal in the second part of the poem of a hero grown old who dies in a last great battle, as well as the curious "aging" of everyone else, may reflect a common theme of pre-Christian Germanic poetry: like Beowulf, the great northern hero Hrólfur kraki and all his comrades grow old and then perish—fighting as old men— in a last great battle.

21. "*Beowulf*: The Monsters and the Critics," Sir Israel Gollancz Memorial Lecture, British Academy, 1936 (*Proceedings of the British Academy*, XXII [1936]), 245–95.

nor bad, happiness nor sorrow, and that one of the things individuals must always be prepared for is a reversal of their present situation. German university students used to place a skull on the table around which they sat drinking; this served as a *memento mori*, a reminder—at moments of intensest pleasure and joy—of what life ultimately had in store for them. The *Beowulf*-poet's preferred way of driving this message home is to show us human beings and the things they have created in their fullest glory and grandeur, and then instantly to dart into the future and show them dead or in ruins—with juxtaposition again being used to make a philosophical or moral point. For example, the poet describes the building of the great hall that Hrothgar intends to symbolize his power and glory:

> He named it Heorot,
> he whose word and will
> had wide dominion.
> He stood by his vow,
> distributing gold
> from the hoard, while high
> overhead the great
> wooden rafters
> waited for floods
> of fire to enfold them,
> for the fated day
> when the tragic hate
> of two in-laws
> would flash into flame,
> into fierce warfare. (156–70)

We may or may not know, when we hear or read this, the identity of the "two in-laws" or the details of the burning of Heorot, but that hardly matters: what the poet wants us to understand is that the moment Heorot has been built and stands before us in its fresh and highly symbolic glory, it is already as good as destroyed.

Another chillingly successful example of juxtaposition, once again used to emphasize people's ignorance of what the future holds in store for them, achieves its effect by creating a sort of collision between present and future. This occurs in the account of the banquet served in Heorot to celebrate Beowulf's victory over Grendel. Here Queen Wealhtheow gives Beowulf a great neck-ring (or torque), "one of the worthiest / ever worn on earth" (2391–92), and the poet—in his associative, digressive way—turns momentarily from the banquet to follow this neck-ring into the future. Beowulf takes it back to Geatland and gives it to Queen Hygd, who lends it to her husband Hygelac, who wears it on his reckless raid against the Franks and Frisians in the Rhineland. "He died there," the poet tells us,

> swinging
> his desperate shield,
> and his grey mailcoat
> and that great neck-ring
> fell afterwards
> into Frankish hands,
> when warriors of less
> worth plundered
> the field where corpses
> of defeated Geats
> held lifeless sway. (2417–27)

Our jaunt into the future concludes with a bitter and ironic oxymoron—how can anyone "hold lifeless sway"?[22] When the poet tells us this, our imagination has us standing in the Rhineland, observers of the greatest disaster of Beowulf's life (as he sees it): the death of his beloved uncle Hygelac. And now comes the shock of juxtaposition, as we are wrenched abruptly back to the present and the banquet in Heorot:

> There was loud applause
> and Wealhtheow spoke
> before the waiting court. (2428–30)

No one is applauding the fact that Geatish corpses are strewn over a lost battlefield. They are applauding Wealhtheow's gift to Beowulf of a great neckring. But then (and this is the whole point) when you are men living in ignorance of the future and applauding something, "Ye know not what ye applaud."

Another, somewhat different use of juxtaposition is found toward the very end of the poem, when the Geats at Beowulf's funeral watch their king's body being consumed by flames. Their grief at losing him and anxiety about what is going to happen to them next in this dangerous world without their great protector are summed up in the moving portrayal of one of the mourners:

---

22. The Old English original takes a phrase that occurs many times in the Anglo-Saxon Chronicle to signal the identity of the victor in a battle (e.g., *þa Deniscan ahton wælstowe gewald*, "the Danes owned possession of the slaughter-place") and treats it to a grim ironic inversion: *Geata leode / hreawic heoldon* (1213b–14a), "the people of the Geats held the corpse-place."

with hair bound tight
and heaving breast
a woman of the Geats
wailed her heart out,
crazed with terror,
crying bitterly
that she dreaded days
of doom and disaster,
invading armies,
violence of troops,
slaughter, exile,
slavery. (6299–6310)

This mounting crescendo of fear and anxiety is followed by—and juxtaposed with—the brief, clipped, and somewhat opaque statement: "Heaven / swallowed the smoke" (6310–11; *Heofon rece swealg* [3155b]). As a climactic utterance coming hard upon the heels of the desolate wail that precedes it, this bald objective statement offers no sympathy and no hope.

Ironic or poignant juxtapositions like these are found at many points in the poem. Another characteristic feature of the structure of *Beowulf* is the emphasis in the text on cycles and cyclicity. It has often been pointed out that the poem begins and ends with a funeral and that this provides a sort of cyclical framework for the whole narrative: the beginning foreshadows the end and the end harks back to the beginning. But there is a crucial difference between the two funerals: whereas the death of Scyld Scefing opens the way to glory and triumph for his heirs and their race, Beowulf has no heirs, and it is abundantly clear that his death will be followed by the destruction of his people. Contrast as well as cyclicity is involved here.

There are many small-scale cycles in the poem and these can often be identified by the presence of "echo-words." These are words or phrases that occur two or more times within such a short hailing-distance of each other that their repetition is unlikely to be merely accidental. Echo-word cycles often mark the beginning and end of scenes and actions and thus help identify separate building blocks of the narrative. As a sort of "punctuation for the ear" the device would have been very useful in a living oral tradition (to which it may well owe its origin). As a rule, the present translation does not try to reproduce the effect of echo-words, but an excerpt from the original will suggest how they work. The particular scene (or action) here is a self-contained passage (1224–82) in which Hrothgar's queen Wealhtheow goes round the hall Heorot distributing mead before returning to her seat. The beginning and end of the passage are given here in both Old and Modern English, with the echo-words in the former printed in boldface type:

Eode Wealhþeow forð,	Wealhtheow, Hrothgar's
cwen Hroðgares	queen, adept
cynna gemyndig,	at court etiquette,
grette **goldhroden**	went round the room,
guman on healle,	<u>radiant in gold,</u>
	greeting the thanes.

[51 verses omitted]

	Hrothgar's consort,
eode goldhroden	<u>radiant with gold,</u>
freolicu folccwen	solemnly returned
to hire frean sittan. (612b–41b)	to sit by her lord. (1224–82)

Echo-words are also frequently used to build suspense and underpin climaxes. In the original of the account of Grendel's approach to Heorot (702b–21a), the verb *com* ("he came") is repeated three times, each time in a context that shows the monster drawing progressively closer to the door of the hall. This sequence is imitated in the translation (1404–41). It creates—and was almost certainly intended to create—a buildup of terrified apprehension (and we may even imagine the poem's original hearers glancing nervously toward the door of the room in which they were sitting).

Echo-words in combination with repeated (and parallel) phrases can be used to create climaxes of great power that emphasize the symbolic significance of certain pivotal actions, for example Beowulf's delivery to Hrothgar of the giant sword-hilt he has brought back from the monsters' lair:

Ða wæs gylden hilt	the giant hilt
gamelum rince,	passed from the peerless
harum hildfruman	prince of warriors
on hand gyfen,	to Hrothgar, the best
enta **ærgeweorc;**	of rulers; it passed
hit **on æht gehwearf**	into the keeping
æfter deofla hryre	of the king of the Danes
Denigea frean,	after demons had died,
wundorsmiþa **geweorc,**	that dread monster
ond þa þas worold ofgeaf	Grendel, the foe
gromheort guma,	of God himself,
Godes andsaca,	and <u>his murderous</u>
morðres scyldig,	<u>mother; it passed</u>

ond his modor eac;   into the possession
on geweald gehwearf of the most exalted lord
woroldcyninga   of the present world,
ðæm selestan   the prince of kings,
be sæm tweonum known everywhere
ðara þe on Scedenigge in Scandinavia. (3354–72)
sceattas dælde. (1677a–86b)

This is a truly impressive and resonant climax.

Or take the outstanding and quite terrifying moment when Beowulf and the Danes reach the monsters' pool and come to the end of their search for Hrothgar's comrade and friend Æschere, who was last seen being borne away from Heorot in the clutches of Grendel's mother:

Denum eallum wæs, And **what did they find**
winum Scyldinga   on the brink of that pool,
weorce on mode   bringing them grief,
to geþolianne,   bringing them great
ðegne monegum,   bitterness of mind,
oncyð eorla gehwæm, **what did they find** there
syðþan Æscheres   with woe and fear
on þam holmclife   and anguish, **what**
hafelan metton. (1417b–21b) but Æschere's head? (2834–42)[23]

When discussing how the poet manipulates his climaxes, it is appropriate to mention one of the most important and large-scale climax sequences in the poem: the series of three challenges that are issued to Beowulf after his arrival in Denmark. (Readers familiar with folktale structures will recall that such impediments to a hero's progress generally tend to appear in groups of three.) These challenges come from a Danish coastguard, a sentinel at the door of Heorot, and Unferth, Hrothgar's *þyle* ("official spokesperson or orator," presumably some sort of chief minister). The challenges are increasingly serious and increasingly public, and together with the hero's responses they occupy over 750 verses, a huge proportion—roughly one-sixth—of the

---

23. Here the translation makes use of echo-words, embedded in a series of rhetorical questions, to simulate a climax that is achieved in the original by means of syntactic suspension: the poet employs an elaborate sequence of repetitions to iterate and reiterate the Danes' dismay and terror but defers mentioning the cause of it—the direct object *hafelan* ("head")—until the climactic position at almost the end of the sentence.

entire poem. Modern readers sometimes feel that these exchanges take up much too much space, delaying the really interesting part of the story—Grendel's assault on the hall and his battle with the hero—for an unnecessarily long time. But the more one studies these three challenges, the more clearly one perceives that they not only ratchet up suspense (by deferring the battle we are looking forward to so eagerly) but also answer a number of important questions about Beowulf himself: does he, when we see him in action, if only verbally, display the qualities of mind and character that we expect in a great hero and that will enable him to triumph over Grendel? What is important here, and what justifies the leisurely pace of the narrative, is that Beowulf's responses to the three increasingly difficult challenges give us increasing respect for his character and ability; the poem would be much poorer, and assertions about the hero's caliber much less persuasive, without this long sequence of challenge and response.

The poem contains at least one climax sequence that is in effect covert (or "buried") in the text as we have it today. It is not possible to know whether this is a deliberate and subtle tactic on the part of the poet or results from his failure to understand a climax sequence expressed more straightforwardly in his source materials. It concretizes the theme of "reciprocal violence," which plays a large role in the poem, as it did in the society that the poem depicts, where it was endemic at both the personal or family level (feud) and the international level (war). The poet, after Grendel's mother has avenged her son's death in Heorot by killing Hrothgar's counselor Æschere, is distressed by the reciprocal casualties of feud, saying:

> What grim barter
> that gold-hall had witnessed,
> lives of loved ones
> lost in a deadly
> game of swapping! (2607–11)

It was typical of feuds in early Germanic society that as their tit-for-tat violence continued it tended to move up the social scale, claiming ever more prestigious victims.[24] This escalation of a typical feud seems to be represented in *Beowulf*, in symbolic fashion, by the "buried" climax sequence under discussion here, and which may be represented as follows:

---

24. Various Scandinavian sources—Icelandic sagas and Norwegian laws—show that this feature of feuds alarmed thoughtful people in those cultures who valued order and stability in society.

— the Danes lose a *mitten* or *glove* (the name of Beowulf's companion who was killed by Grendel is Hondscioh [cf. German *Handschuh*], which literally means "hand-shoe") [4152].[25]

— the Grendel clan loses a *hand* (Grendel's) [1940].

— the Danes lose first a *hand* (Hrothgar's confidant Æschere, who is called a "hand" [2686] by synecdoche, because he hands out treasure to his followers), then a *head* (Æschere's [2842]).

— the monsters lose a *head* (Grendel's [3180]), which brings the vengeance cycle to a close (and does so at almost the exact halfway point of the text—a striking fact).

It is hard to believe that the symmetry of these references, and the increasing value of the objects referred to, is coincidental.

Another remarkable structural feature of *Beowulf,* and one that has sometimes struck readers as ill-conceived, is the hero's lengthy recapitulation of his adventure in Denmark when he returns home to the land of the Geats (3999–4294). Dissatisfaction here stems, as it often does in similar cases, from a failure to recognize differences between what is deemed "important" and "unimportant" in our own society and the heroic society depicted by the poet. Readers today are troubled by the fact that Beowulf's report, which goes on for almost three hundred verses, covers narrative ground with which they are already thoroughly familiar (even though the account is sometimes differently inflected). It is not so important—though it is certainly interesting—that the poet spices up the repetition by revealing certain pieces of information that had been omitted earlier at points where it would have seemed natural to mention them, such as the name (Hondscioh) of the Geatish warrior murdered by Grendel at Heorot. More important is the fact that this account of events by the hero in his own voice allows us to admire his modesty at a critical moment of self-presentation. Moreover it enables us, thanks to Beowulf's description of Hrothgar's plan to marry his daughter Freawaru to the Heathobard leader Ingeld and his projection of what is likely to happen afterward, to marvel at what a canny grasp this young warrior has of the forces that govern men's behavior in his society. Even this, however, is perhaps insufficient to explain why the recounting of earlier material goes on for as long as it does. Indeed, the poet himself, using the hero

---

25. The poet's desire, as part of a competing structural tactic, to defer mentioning Hondscioh's name until after the Geats' return to their own country (see pp. xli–xlii), means that his name does not occur at the point in the narrative where its relevance as the first item in a climax sequence would have been most obvious.

as his mouthpiece, openly admits that the narrative needs speeding up: "It would take too long / to tell you, my king," Beowulf acknowledges at one point (4185–86). And the recapitulation ends with Beowulf's extremely head-over-heels summary of his adventure with Grendel's mother, a summary in which the account's merciless abbreviation is deliberately emphasized by a masterful and climactic echo-word sequence:

> It is well known, now,
> how I went to fight
> the ghastly guardian
> of the great deep;
> how we grappled together
> in grim combat;
> how at last my blade
> lopped off the head
> of Grendel's mother
> in her gloomy hall;
> how the sea turned red;
> how I swam upward
> after a narrow escape
> (I was not yet doomed);
> and how once again
> wise Hrothgar,
> Healfdene's son,
> gave me handsome gifts. (4269–86)

Why, then, does the poet subject us to this long recapitulation of familiar events, when he himself realizes that it is neither more nor less than that? The reason is undoubtedly that both hero and poet feel the need, especially in the light of Beowulf's unpromising boyhood (4366–75) and Hygelac's skepticism about his ability (3984–93), to show him giving a full and substantive account of his great triumph in the very presence of those who had earlier doubted him and whose opinion of him will be sharply revised as a result of hearing his words. The length and weight of Beowulf's report are thus essential to "justify" the tremendous rewards that follow, rewards that mark his coming of age and entrance into his inheritance, and that reduce to insignificance, in their value for Beowulf's self-esteem and future career among his people, the trinkets given him by Hrothgar, glorious though these are.

Although the central narrative of *Beowulf* unfolds in chronological and linear fashion, the poet often eschews linearity, providing us with certain kinds of information not when it would be most relevant or useful to have it (from our point of view) but when it serves other and more important purposes (from his point of view). An elementary but important example is provided by the way in which he defers his first mention of the hero's name—while unambiguously letting us know he is deferring it—until the moment when it can be introduced into the poem with the greatest possible éclat. This postponement goes on for almost three hundred verses (387–685), with the poet bending over backward in his effort to come up with ways of referring to the hero that will *not* involve using his name: he is "Hygelac's thane" (389), "the prince" (405), "a seasoned sailor" (415), the "bold captain / of the band of comrades" (515–16), the "man of the Geats, / the mariners' chief" (679–80). Finally, when our suspense about how and when the name will actually be introduced has been wrought to a considerable pitch, the hero himself proclaims resonantly, in his own voice and at a moment when suppression of his identity is no longer possible—and revealing it will be most effective—*"Beowulf is min nama"* (343b), "My name is Beowulf." The effect is thrilling.[26]

A more complex example of the deferral of "relevant" information is provided by Grendel's murder of Beowulf's follower Hondscioh. Two things are striking here: first, that the follower is nameless when he is first mentioned (1480), which adds to the horror of his sudden death and dismemberment; and second, that Beowulf, whose role as a leader is to protect his men, does nothing to avert Hondscioh's fate, but is represented as coolly taking advantage of an opportunity to study Grendel's modus operandi:

> for there lay Hygelac's
> kinsman, alert
> and carefully watching
>   how the murderer
> meant to proceed. (1472–76)

Why does Beowulf do this? The whole incident comes into clearer focus when Beowulf returns to his own people and gives his king Hygelac a report about the adventure in Denmark. Here, back home where friends and family knew the dead warrior and will mourn him, Beowulf's words reflect his own respect, affection, and sorrow. He not only tells us the man's name,

---

26. The audience's interest in Beowulf's name and identity that this arouses is later turned to account in ways that could be meant to be humorous. When Hrothgar is told the name of this visitor who (we have every reason to believe) is a complete stranger to him, he announces that he not only knows who he is but has actually met him in the past (743–48). And Unferth begins a speech that is designed to diminish Beowulf by inquiring insolently, "Are you / the Beowulf . . . / whom Breca defeated . . . ?" (1010–12)—as if the world is full of Beowulfs!

personalizing him, but explains why he could not have been saved: he lay nearest the entrance and thus naturally became the first victim when the monster burst suddenly into the hall:

> Quickly he killed
> my comrade Hondscioh,
> quietly asleep
> closest to the door,
> a girded hero;
> Grendel devoured
> my faithful friend
> with foaming jaws,
> swallowed him whole
> at a single gulp. (4151–60)

Hondscioh is no longer a nameless, hapless victim but in his own way a hero, and one who is remembered as such.

This is a relatively unimportant example of the poet's tactic of deferring relevant information. But extremely important and indeed revelatory pieces of information can also be deferred. For example, we might imagine that we should be told, at the point when Beowulf first resolves to visit Denmark or when his ship first approaches the Danish coast, that there has long existed a state of war between the Geats and the Danes. Had we been told this, the knowledge would have increased our appreciation of the hero's boldness, resolution, and generosity in embarking on this venture, and it would also have explained his ambiguous reception—formally polite but wary and suspicious—by the Danish coastguard. It is not, however, until Hrothgar's very last speech to Beowulf, spoken just as the hero is about to leave Denmark forever, that this particular piece of information is divulged. The king says to Beowulf:

> Thanks to your valor
> the thanes of our two
> nations, my Danes
> and your noble Geats,
> will live in friendship,
> and the long terror
> of warfare cease
> that they once suffered.
> While my power endures,
> peace shall prevail
> and gifts be exchanged

as a gage of the love
and trust uniting
our two nations. (3709–22)

Clearly Beowulf is being presented here as an international peacemaker engaged in what we would now call "conflict resolution" on a grand scale, and the poet has chosen to let us know this at a moment when the achievement will redound most gloriously to his credit and will also take on its full meaning as one of the most significant—and personally disinterested—outcomes of his visit to Denmark.

Even more striking, perhaps, is the way the poet keeps his counsel about Beowulf's unpromising youth until after the hero has returned to his own country:

Once, in his boyhood,
the thanes of his people
had thought him useless
and King Hrethel
had declined to give him
approval or praise
through presents at mead;
they all looked on him
as an idle youth,
a lazy princeling. (4366–75)

Beowulf himself, for very good and obvious reasons, makes no mention of this when presenting his credentials to Hrothgar and the Danes: to advertise the fact that his own people had once held such a low opinion of him would have been very counterproductive. Later, however, after he has so effectively proved himself, his unpromising youth can be remembered by the poet simply as an incident from the past that is not only shorn of any predictive force but stands in brilliant opposition to the hero's recent triumph, emphasizing it by contrast. The "objective correlative" of the complete rehabilitation of Beowulf's reputation is Hygelac's presentation to him of his father Hrethel's sword (4379–86), since it is likely to have been at Hrethel's court that the boy Beowulf was so humiliatingly misprized.[27] The gift of the sword symbolically cancels the misprision.

---

27. The poet does not tell us this explicitly, saying only that the lord of the Geats (*drihten Wedera* 2186a) would not give him much in the way of gifts on the mead-bench. It is hard to imagine what "lord of the Geats" can be meant, if not Hrethel.

The trick of divulging important information only at the point at which it will be most dramatically or thematically effective occasionally results in two statements, at different points in the poem, that seem to contradict each other—and were sometimes regarded by early scholars as evidence of the poet's poor control of his material.

In listening to an oral poem, the hearer cannot of course flip back a hundred pages to check something in the text, nor can he consult an index. This is likely to encourage, on the part of poets, what might be called "contextual opportunism": a striving for immediate effects in immediate contexts at the expense of narrative consistency over the long haul. Who is going to notice? Furthermore, audiences will have been conditioned to expect not unique, coherent, self-contained works, but multiple versions with conflicting details, and consequently there is no reason why they should have felt rigid inner consistency—especially in matters of detail or ornament—to be a particular virtue. This easy tolerance of such harmless discrepancies in an oral tradition might easily be continued in a written tradition based upon it.

For example, toward the beginning of *Beowulf,* when the poet's emphasis is on the widespread support and encouragement that the hero receives in his homeland when he decides to visit Denmark, we are told:

> Much as they loved him,
> men did not try
> to dissuade the prince
> from his set purpose
> but urged him on. (403–7)

The hero himself claims much the same thing in his first speech to Hrothgar:

> I was urged, therefore,
> by my own people,

Beowulf himself claims to remember things differently, telling us that after he was admitted to the Geatish royal household at the age of seven

> Good king Hrethel
> guided and loved me,
> gave me handsome gifts
> and upheld our kinship. (4859–62)

Is the apparent discrepancy to be explained as a lapse of the poet's, or is it simply an example of the hero's tact and diplomacy?

by the worthiest
and wisest among them,
to come to the court
of King Hrothgar. (829–34)

It would hardly do to tell us at this point in the story that Beowulf's people tried to *dis*courage him from going to Denmark because they lacked confidence in him. Yet after his success there, and his return to the land of the Geats, that is how his lord Hygelac remembered things:

I was racked with fears,
alarmed and anxious;
I lacked confidence
in your ability;
I begged you constantly
not to encounter
that pernicious fiend,
but to leave the Danes
alone to settle
their grudge against Grendel. (3984–93)

There is obviously no point in arguing about which of these versions is "accurate." They both are. In the first instance, Beowulf wants to persuade Hrothgar that he is the right man to fight Grendel, and thus he wants to suggest that his venture is endorsed wholeheartedly by his own people; in the second, in the new context provided by his recent success, what can be safely and appropriately emphasized is Hygelac's love for his nephew and anxiety about his fate. In many similar cases of apparent discrepancy in *Beowulf,* each of the discrepant items is entirely appropriate in its own immediate context.

The total lack of accord between Unferth's account of Beowulf's swimming feat and Beowulf's own account of it, on the other hand, should obviously not be regarded as an inadvertent contradiction on the *Beowulf*-poet's part but rather as a deliberate and intentional discrepancy. It is clear that Unferth's version is malicious and that Beowulf's is ostensibly motivated by a desire to set the record straight and to present himself in the best possible light; it is clear, too, that the different purposes of the two speakers explain much of what differs in their accounts. However, it is also important to recognize that the presence side by side of two such variant versions undoubtedly reflects the experience of audiences of Anglo-Saxon oral poetry, who from time to time would have heard different versions of traditional stories, varying in large or small details and in emphasis.[28] The two accounts of the swim are thus in a sense like oral doublets, and the fact that such doublets existed in the oral tradition is being exploited here by the *Beowulf*-poet for purposes of characterization and dramatic conflict.

Another interesting aspect of the work's narrative technique is the author's approach to developing suspense. Any anxiety we might be inclined to feel about Beowulf's impending clash with Grendel is repeatedly undercut by assurances that the hero is going to triumph. What is important to the poet here is not ratcheting up suspense but highlighting Grendel's overconfidence and foolish faith, on the brink of his impending discomfiture, that things will go tonight as they have gone in the past. Similarly, any suspense we might feel about the outcome of Beowulf's fight with the dragon is repeatedly undercut by forecasts that the hero is going to be killed; but this is clearly done to increase the irony—and pathos—in the poet's picture of a man who has always been successful now embarking on something that we know will be his undoing.

On the other hand, the poet cannot be charged with *always* revealing everything in advance; sometimes he holds his cards very close to his chest. For example, the very existence of Grendel's mother remains a well-guarded secret until the moment when she suddenly bursts onto the scene. These completely different strategies suggest that since the poet knows that many members of his audience are likely to be familiar with his story in advance, he decides that playing in various ways with their expectations will be a useful way of holding their attention and showing his mastery.

The last—but certainly not the least important—features of structure to be discussed here are the poem's so-called "digressions." "Digressions" is not a very satisfactory term for them, perhaps, since it suggests that these passages "wander away" from the central narrative and are excrescences unconnected with it and irrelevant to it—which is far from being the case. But in spite of the unsatisfactoriness of the term, we will continue to use it here.

The "digressions" vary enormously in length, ranging from the briefest, which is only ten verses (the Hama digression [2393–2402]), to the longest, which is almost two hundred verses (the Finnsburg digression [2131–2317]). They consist sometimes of summary allusions to, and other times leisurely retellings of, well-known heroic stories or portions of those stories. The short poem "Deor" (see pp. 184–86) consists almost entirely of the sort of material we find in the "digressions" in *Beowulf*, but in "Deor" it remains in the form

---

28. Compare the two extant versions of what happened at Finnsburg: the Finnsburg digression in *Beowulf* (2131–2317) and "The Fight at Finnsburg" (pp. 174–77).

of discrete chunks and is not embedded in (or integrated into) any sort of large master narrative.[29] Since both the digressions in *Beowulf* and the "chunks" in "Deor" rely on their original audience's prior familiarity with the stories they allude to, they are often stenographic and elliptical, which makes them difficult for modern readers to understand unless they are accompanied by extensive commentaries. But they are very important in the *Beowulf*-poet's scheme of things and have a number of critical functions vis-à-vis his central narrative, serving to throw light on the contexts in which they occur and also to confirm that the story told of Beowulf and his associates has its place in a vast network of interlocking historical and semihistorical memories. The digressions provide important information about the cultural and political contexts in which the characters live, move, and have their being, and they also show what motivates men and women in the heroic society depicted in the poem. Sometimes they offer a critique of the society's values, especially its generally futile violence-control mechanisms and institutions (e.g., the swearing of formal oaths, political marriages, etc.). Sometimes the "digressions" fill in parts of the hero's life that were elided in the fifty-year-long eyeblink between his youth and old age. And sometimes they expand the time frame by dipping into the past as far as the creation of the world and into the future as far as the destruction and dispersal of the Geats. The poem would be a poor thing indeed without its "digressions." The fact that they are usually the first thing to be jettisoned when the text is reconfigured as a comic book or a book for children is a sure indication of their weight and importance.

The poet's reference to Wayland the smith (907), though hardly a "digression" at all but rather a simple "allusion," shows very clearly how a reference to extrinsic story materials can enrich and focus the text of *Beowulf*. All members of the poet's original audience will have been familiar with Wayland (*Weland* in Old English), the semidivine artificer whose story is told in surviving Old Norse sources, both poetry and prose.[30] Wayland's popularity in Anglo-Saxon England is shown by the fact that he appears in the first stanza of "Deor" (see p. 184), features impressively on a whalebone jewelbox in the British Museum (the Franks Casket), and is recalled in a remarkable passage in King Alfred the Great's Old English translation of Boethius'

---

29. Which is not to deny that the "chunks" in "Deor" are purposefully and meaningfully arranged in a narrative framework of their own.

30. The story is told brilliantly (but allusively and elliptically) in the Icelandic "Völundarkviða" (one of the poems in the Poetic Edda) and in full detail (but of course in a divergent version) in *Þíðriks saga af Bern* ("The Saga of Theodric of Verona"), a work produced for the Norwegian court at Bergen but based on poems carried there by merchants from the Low German area.

Consolation of Philosophy.[31] In the Old English poetic tradition, jewelry and weaponry made by Wayland represented the ne plus ultra in beauty and efficacy, and anyone owning an object with this provenience would treasure it accordingly and make sure it was passed on to his descendants. Since kings often gave warriors outstanding weapons—which were at the same time treasures—in recognition of heroic achievement (see 4379–88), items like this could signal one's ancestors' (or one's own) accomplishments and status. "Those good weapons / were an honor to their owners" (660–61), the poet says of the Geatish warriors when they first arrive at Heorot.

The glory and prestige of Wayland's workmanship, attested in these references, will have been present in the minds of all Anglo-Saxon hearers or readers of the poem when Beowulf tells Hrothgar that if Grendel should kill him, Hrothgar should

> send Hygelac
> the grey mailcoat
> that guards my breast,
> the work of Wayland;
> it was once King Hrethel's. (904–8)

The effect is that of a tremendous spotlight being turned on Beowulf as he concludes his first speech to Hrothgar. In the speech itself he had persuasively presented his credentials to the king and the Danish court; but his mailcoat, in its shining symbolism, is a credential more persuasive than any that could be expressed in mere words.

It would take a long time to analyze all the "digressions" in *Beowulf* and show the many ways in which they are tethered to their contexts,[32] but one particularly instructive example must be examined in detail. It is a sort of "double digression" and forms the centerpiece of the section of the poem labeled XIII in the manuscript, a section whose internal structure is unusually clear. The section describes events in Denmark on the morning after Beowulf's fight with Grendel. It will save time to summarize its content in schematic form; the structure is cyclical and consists of cycles within cycles, their cyclical character being marked by repetitions and echo-words. It is a masterpiece of symmetrical construction:

---

31. Alfred asks, "Where now are the bones of the wise Wayland, the goldsmith who was once so famous?" (*The Anglo-Saxon Poetic Records: A Collective Edition* [hereafter referred to as *ASPR*] V, 166.)

32. A valiant (and for the most part convincing) effort to analyze them and justify their presence on contextual grounds is Adrien Bonjour's *The Digressions in "Beowulf"* (Oxford: Basil Blackwell, 1950).

[1673–1704] The Danes gather at Heorot from far and near to stare at Grendel's arm, nailed to the gable as a trophy. Then they follow the monster's bloody footprints to the pool into which he has plunged to die.

[1705–33] Mounting their horses, they ride back to Heorot, excitedly discussing Beowulf's triumph. **Sometimes** they race their horses

[1734–47] and **sometimes** one of the king's thanes, "a consummate poet / who knew and could sing / numberless tales" (1736–38), composes and sings a poem to celebrate Beowulf's victory.

[1748–1801] The only part of this "poem within the poem" that we ever get to hear are two of its "digressions" (which by itself suggests the importance of the role of digressions in the mind of the *Beowulf*-poet). In the first of these, Beowulf is implicitly compared to Sigemund, one of the greatest and best-known Germanic heroes. Various events of Sigemund's career are recalled, including the dragon-slaying that brought him his greatest fame:

> Sigemund's courage
>   was so absolute
> that in after years
> he was remembered by men
> as the most exalted
> of princely exiles. (1796–1801)

This praise of Sigemund is intended, of course, to magnify Beowulf, who is being compared to him.

[1802–26] At this point the poet recalls another princely exile, "the Danish / despot Heremod" (1803–4), who is introduced in a second digression to stand in contrast to Sigemund,[33] since Heremod was a king who went haywire, turning his back on two of the most conspicuous kingly virtues, the duty to protect his men and to reward them with gifts, and thus betraying the hopes of his people:

---

33. It is possible, indeed probable, that Heremod was the last member of the dynasty of Danish kings who preceded Scyld Scefing and his descendants and that his exile and death were the direct cause of the Danes' "time of trial / and terrible grief / lacking a leader" (29–31).

He lost the hearts
of loyal followers
who looked to him for help,
who thought that their prince
would thrive in virtue,
inherit the great
high-seat of his father
and lead Denmark.[34] (1816–23)

[1827–30] Finally the poet contrasts Heremod and Beowulf, thus bringing the double digression full circle and taking us to the end of the "poem within the poem" (i.e., Hrothgar's court poet's praise of Beowulf).

[1831–33] The next passage ("**Sometimes** the horsemen / measured sandy paths," etc.) returns us to the central narrative by picking up the series of anaphora initiated earlier (1727) and thus bringing us back to the horsemen racing their horses.

[1834–48] The Danes gather at Heorot to stare at Grendel's arm, just as they did at the beginning of the section, and there—climactically—they are joined by Hrothgar and Wealhtheow and their retinues.

The 176 verses of Section XIII, which display this elaborate structure, show the complexity and intricacy of which the *Beowulf* poet is capable when he really puts his mind to it.[35] And of course the elaboration of *form* here serves in the end to focus attention on and thus emphasize important *content*: the presentation of two patterns or models of behavior—the glorious positive one (Sigemund) that Beowulf must strive to emulate, and the ugly negative one (Heremod) that he must try to avoid.[36] Thus the two digressions send a very

---

34. On the collocation of the two figures of Sigemund and Heremod in this digression, see pp. lxxi–lxxii, n. 54.

35. Furthermore, the synopsis of Section XIII provided here tells only part of the story. The beginning and end of the passage are crowded with echo-words and echo-synonyms, identifying it as a narrative unit:

morgen 837a	morgenleoht 917b
guðrinc monig 838b	scealc monig 918b
gifhealle 838a	sele 919b
wundor sceawian 840b	searowundor seon 920a

36. The way in which a positive example is followed by a contrasting negative one

clear message about how Hrothgar's court poet sees Beowulf measure up to criteria for heroic and kingly behavior; in doing so, they show how digressions like this are capable of shedding great light not only on the immediate contexts in which they occur but also on the value system and meaning of the poem as a whole. Many of the digressions in *Beowulf* have multiple resonances with their contexts, and whole volumes could be written—and have been written!—about the complex relationships involved.

It is worth mentioning that the *Beowulf*-poet seems quite aware of the complexity of the story he is telling and of the need to reassure his hearers and readers about the coherence of his central narrative. He does this by recapitulating the Grendel clan's descent from Cain when he introduces Grendel's mother (2516–25); by recalling the events of Grendel's initial raid on Heorot (signaling the beginning of his feud with the Danes) just before Beowulf cuts off the monster's head (signaling its end) (3157–67); and—most significant of all—by tethering the second part of the poem (Beowulf's old age) tightly to the first part (Beowulf's youth) by means of a careful back-reference at the point where the hero is about to go up against the dragon, overconfident because of his past success: had he not

> survived many
> violent clashes
> and fierce encounters
> since those far-off days
> when his grip had crushed
> Grendel in combat
> and his quick courage
> had cleansed the hall
> of noble Hrothgar? (4699–4707)

The *Beowulf*-poet's ordering of everything in his poem, both narrative content and ethical reflection, is highly "artificial." His determination that much of the work's "meaning" should manifest itself through abrupt juxtapositions, contrasts, cycles, and other such structural devices, and his consequent preference of disjunct to conjunct narrative order, results in the poem being a remarkably complex web of narrative and ethical strands.

---

is paralleled by the poet's fondness for balancing negative (litotistic) and positive statements of the same theme (see, for example, 154b–61a and 1025b–29b).

This, incidentally, is Sigemund's only appearance in the poem. But Heremod appears again as an antitype of Beowulf in a substantial digression in Hrothgar's speech of advice to his newly adopted son (3417–43).

The Hero

Beowulf is deeply concerned with values: both the nature and quality of the traditional values of the heroic society it depicts, and the success and failure of individuals in attempting to live up to those values. Most of the major characters in the poem, and some of the minor ones, are intended to be—at least in part—models or "exemplars" or representatives of virtuous or vicious behavior, and the purpose of their "exemplary" presentation is moral and didactic. In this they are like the gallery of figures who populate the Venerable Bede's *Ecclesiastical History of the English People,* written in the early eighth century: "For if history relates good things of good men, the thoughtful listener is spurred on to imitate the good; or if it records evil things of evil men, the devout and earnest listener or reader is encouraged to avoid everything harmful and perverse and follow what he knows to be good and pleasing to God."[37] *Beowulf* is full of teachings and lessons, both explicit and implicit, of the kind discussed by Bede, and it would be a serious mistake to think that these are without relevance to a modern audience.

The poem contains an array of memorable and finely drawn characters: the hero himself, whom we see both as a young man full of energy and heroic ardor, and as an old man, still heroic as he goes out to a battle in which he suspects he will die and reflecting on the meaning and achievement of his life; the Danish king Hrothgar, old and feeble but immensely wise, who learns to love Beowulf and adopts him as a son; Hrothgar's queen Wealhtheow, a gentle and attractive figure, apparently a good deal younger than her husband, who lives in a state of perpetual anxiety about what will happen to her two young sons when old Hrothgar dies; Unferth the official court spokesperson, bitter and filled with envy of Beowulf; Beowulf's uncle Hygelac, king of the Geats, a rash and headlong fellow; the nameless "last survivor" of a long-extinct people, melancholy and elegiac; Beowulf's kinsman and successor Wiglaf, who is young, energetic, and concerned to do his duty as a warrior and thane; and the messenger at the very end of the poem who loves purveying bad news at great length, a man (*secg* 3028a) who talks too much and who simply cannot stop talking (*secggende* 3028b),[38] but whose words alert us to future disaster for Beowulf's people.

---

37. Bede, Preface. Sigemund and Heremod, the heroic antitypes who are contrasted so forcefully in Section XIII of *Beowulf* (see pp. xlix–li), might almost have been devised as an illustration of Bede's statement.

38. The poet is "punning" here and suggesting a (nonexistent) etymological relationship between the two words, influenced perhaps by the vastly popular *Etymologies* of Isidore of Seville (ca. 570–636). Anglo-Saxons were fully aware that what

In *Beowulf* the character and quality of the various dramatis personae are often revealed to us directly in their own words. There are many speeches in the poem, and they are usually constructed with great subtlety and show a highly developed sense of drama. The speeches occasionally strike modern readers as too formal and artificial, and it is only when we read them with full understanding of the contexts in which they are uttered and the audiences to which they are delivered that we begin to appreciate the poet's sensitivity and masterful command of his materials.

Unlike the Scandinavian kings and queens who play so large a role in the poem, its hero Beowulf is thought to be a fictional figure who has been soldered onto the historical memories at some point in the process of their transmission. It is impossible to say when or where this happened, since he has been thoroughly integrated into the Scandinavian dynastic materials. Because of the poem's unusual structure, information about the hero tends to reach us scattershot, that is, dispersed here and there throughout the text. It may be useful, then, to summarize the major events of Beowulf's life in conventional chronological order, attaching to them some completely supposititious dates.[39]

- The hero was born ca. 495.
- His father was Ecgtheow, a member of the Swedish/Geatish clan (or family) of the Wægmundings, and his mother a daughter of the Geatish king Hrethel [see p. xxviii].
- At the age of seven (ca. 502) he was taken to the court of his grandfather Hrethel and brought up there in the company of Hrethel's own three sons.
- A few years later he showed his true worth by fighting giants and sea-monsters and engaging in a famous feat of swimming with a foreign prince named Breca.

---

distinguishes men from other animals is their use of language; in another Old English poem, "The Dream of the Rood," the word *reordberend* ("voice-bearing ones") is used as a synonym for human beings (*ASPR* II, 61).

39. These are based on Klaeber's reconstruction (xlv), which like all reconstructions of Beowulfian chronology takes as its starting point the putative date of Hygelac's raid on Frankish territory, ca. 520 A.D. (see p. xxvii). For purposes of general chronological orientation, it is worth noting that—if he had ever really existed—Beowulf (ca. 495–583) would have been a somewhat younger contemporary of the philosopher Boethius (ca. 480–524) and the monastic codifier St. Benedict of Nursia (ca. 480–543).

- Later still (ca. 515) he sailed to Denmark[40] and delivered the Danes and their king Hrothgar from the depredations of Grendel and his mother.
- Returning home to the land of the Geats, he accompanied his uncle Hygelac on a reckless and ill-starred raid against the Franks (ca. 520), swimming back to the land of the Geats after Hygelac's defeat and death, turning down the offer of the Geatish throne made to him by Hygd (Hygelac's widow), and acting as regent for her son Heardred until Heardred came of age.
- After Heardred's death fighting against the Swedes (ca. 533), Beowulf himself became king of the Geats.
- He supported the Swedish pretender Eadgils in Eadgils' successful campaign against his uncle Onela (ca. 535).
- After a fifty-year reign Beowulf died fighting a dragon (ca. 583).

Beowulf is very far from being the sort of hero who is all brawn and no brain. In fact he is presented as an almost ideal combination of physical strength and courage on the one hand, and agility and subtlety of mind on the other, or of *fortitudo* ("strength") and *sapientia* ("wisdom"),[41] to give these two qualities their Latin names. The poet shows us how highly he values the combination of these qualities in several ways, first by outright assertion on a number of occasions. Hrothgar, for example, expresses his total confidence in Beowulf in one of the poem's very rare sequences of long (hypermetric) lines, which stand out metrically from their context and thus emphasize the content of the lines in question:

> Because you have both might and wisdom,
> fierceness in fighting and judgment,
> I am not afraid to support you
> fully with my friendly counsels. (3410–13)

And a few lines later, impressed by a particularly subtle speech of Beowulf's, the king says:

---

40. Klaeber reckons that this happened when Beowulf was about twenty. But people matured much faster in early medieval times than they do today, and it is well to bear in mind that when Beowulf set out for Denmark he may have been considerably younger than Klaeber supposes.

41. This important observation was first made by R. E. Kaske in "*Sapientia et Fortitudo* as the Controlling Theme of *Beowulf*," *Studies in Philology* 55 (July 1958), 423–57.

> God in his wisdom
> gave you, my son,
> these knowing words.
> I have never heard
> such masterful speech
> from a man so young.
> Your might is matchless,
> your mind agile,
> your talk full of wisdom. (3681–89)

Another way in which the poet shows how much he values Beowulf's combination of *fortitudo* and *sapientia* is by bringing onstage several figures who lack one quality or the other and thus fail to meet the poet's criteria for true heroic stature. Beowulf's uncle Hygelac, for instance, though bold and adventurous, seems to lack good judgment (2411–16), and the Danish king Hrothgar, though he is—in his old age—a model of wisdom, is physically enfeebled and thus unable to play an active role in delivering his people.[42]

Not much need be said about Beowulf's physical strength. The very first thing we are told about him is eloquent on this point:

> In that day
> of this life
> no earthly man
> had equal strength
> or equal courage. (391–95)

In the original, this formula (196a–97b) is repeated almost verbatim—an otherwise unexampled procedure on the part of the poet—at the end of Section XI (789a–90b), where the context makes it sound like a song of triumph.

Beowulf's *fortitudo* is shown to full advantage in his fights as a young man against various monsters, including Grendel and his mother, and again as an old man in his last great fight against the dragon, where his sheer physical strength may be less than it once was, but his courage and resolution are undiminished.

One aspect of Beowulf's *fortitudo* needs to be specially emphasized: his prowess as a swimmer. Like the Icelandic saga hero Grettir the Strong, with

---

42. As they are about to leave Denmark, Beowulf and his men express the opinion that Hrothgar "was a king who was blameless (*orleahtre* 1886a) in every respect until old age robbed him of the joys of strength." It is probably the irresolution and helplessness brought about by old age, rather than old age itself or any defect of character in Hrothgar, that is judged to be "blameworthy."

whom Beowulf is thought to have other things in common, one of Beowulf's strongest suits is his strength, ability, and endurance in the water. As a young man he slays monsters in the sea at night (843–44) and engages in a remarkable long-distance swim with a fellow-prince named Breca (1010–1160), during which he slays additional shoals of monsters. In Denmark he swims (in full armor) down to the Grendel-kin's underwater lair, a swim that takes him a good part of the day (2983–90), and later he swims back up again carrying Grendel's enormous head and a giant sword-hilt (3223–50). (The head is so huge that it takes four ordinary men to carry it once Beowulf gets it to dry land [3268–78].) After Hygelac's death Beowulf swims from the mouth of the River Rhine to the west coast of Sweden carrying thirty suits of mail (!) on his arm (4714–36). Indeed, so great is the emphasis placed on his ability as a swimmer that one sometimes wonders whether he was not thought of in the tradition as preeminently a "swimming hero," that is, a hero who excelled in that particular "specialty" (swimming not being a skill that figures prominently in the stories of other leading Germanic heroes).

With regard to Beowulf's *sapientia* we may ask: In what, precisely, does this wisdom consist? The answer is many-sided, since "wisdom" is not so straightforward a quality as "strength"; it includes all sorts of intellectual, social, and interpersonal skills.

An interesting example of the interplay of strength and wisdom, and of how they are mutually reinforcing for Beowulf, is provided by the clash between the hero and Unferth[43] and the way in which this clash is ultimately resolved. Both Beowulf and the poet attribute Unferth's sudden attack on the hero's credentials to drunkenness (1060 and 2934), the poet adding that it was also the result of envy:

> Beowulf's unbidden
> bold arrival

---

43. *Beowulf* criticism has devoted a lot of attention to Unferth and his role at the Danish court and has evolved a number of competing interpretations of this complex and ambiguous figure. The poet seems to think his name is allegorical and means "bad mind" or "evil mind": this is suggested by the way in which he puns on the name in lines 1165b–66b of the original, where he says that both Hrothgar and Hrothulf had faith in the mind (*ferhþ*) of Bad Mind (*Un-ferþ*)—obviously not a very smart thing to do. Punning, incidentally, was very popular among the Anglo-Saxons. Bede's account of Pope Gregory the Great and the English slave boys in Rome is deservedly famous (*Ecclesiastical History,* Book II, Chapter 1), and already by the end of the period the incompetent and hapless King Æðelræd ("Noble Counsel") had acquired the nickname *Unræd* ("Bad Counsel")—whence the name Ethelred the Unready, by which he is known today.

> annoyed him enormously,
> since he was never pleased
>   when anyone
> was honored more
> or more highly esteemed
> than he was. (1003–10)

It is not unlikely that Unferth's attack is simply a traditional part of the story, since it forms the third and most important challenge in a climax sequence and must occur where it occurs for that reason, regardless of whatever motivations may be attributed to him. It is possible, too, since Unferth holds an official position at Hrothgar's court—he is its spokesperson (*þyle* 1165b, 1456b)—that he is a sort of proxy who expresses the corporate resentment of *all* the Danes about their need to be rescued by a foreigner. This at least is strongly suggested by certain features of Beowulf's reply.

Beowulf's problem is that the whole exchange is taking place in public at the Danish court, observed by all the Danes, so everything he says must be very carefully weighed. He must show that he is perfectly in control of the situation; Unferth's charges must be countered politely but firmly and definitively. If Beowulf were an ordinary person listening to Unferth's speech, he might be sorely tempted to fly off the handle and start shouting. But the beginning of his reply lacks any suggestion of real anger and is quietly ironic:

> Friend Unferth,
> fuddled with beer
> you've been babbling away
> about Breca's deeds. (1059–62)

Beowulf proceeds to give his own version of the swim, which provides him with plenty of opportunity to highlight his physical strength and endurance, his *fortitudo*. Only then does he turn his attention to Unferth and the Danes, first saying something that is bound to rub Unferth the wrong way, and then asserting that Unferth's most glorious heroic deed to date is murdering his brothers—an unredeemably evil act, from the Germanic point of view—an act that puts him in the company of both Cain and Grendel and will ultimately (Beowulf assures him) land him in hell:

> I cannot ever
> recall hearing
> such a tale of triumph
> told about you—
> your big battles!
> Breca has never,

> and neither have you,
> known such success
> in battle (I scorn
>   to boast of it!)
> though it is quite clear
> that you killed your brothers,
> your own kinsmen:
> an evil deed
> for which, friend Unferth,
> you will one day roast
> shamefully in hell,
> shrewd though you are. (1161–78)

We have come a long way here from the restraint and relaxed irony with which Beowulf's speech had begun. And when he continues, his focus shifts gradually from Unferth to the Danes whose mouthpiece Unferth is (at least *ex hypothesi*), and he stresses their impotence and humiliation. He even turns one of their honorific titles, "Victory Danes" (*Sige-Scyldingas* 597b), against them in a masterstroke of sarcasm (1194). And he concludes by saying that although Grendel knows he has nothing to fear from the Danes, Beowulf now intends to show him

> the full fierceness
> and fury of the Geats,
> how *they* clear accounts.
> And then, tomorrow,
> when the sun rises
> in the south, clothed
> in morning radiance,
> men will again
> laugh in this meadhall,
> delivered from fear. (1203–12; emphasis added)

Talk about *fortitudo!* It takes tremendous boldness, courage, and resolution for a warrior of the Geats to say these things in a hall full of Danes, especially when we take into account that there is a history of warfare between the two peoples (3714–16). The hero has shown himself to be neither a hothead nor a wimp—not a man who is easily provoked or easily cowed—but one who can be as firmly confrontational as you please if circumstances and context justify such behavior. One might think that after Beowulf's speech the Danes in Heorot, brutally insulted by their guest, would leap to their feet shouting, "Get him!" But nothing of the sort happens. Instead,

> Hrothgar, the white-haired
> ruler of Denmark,
> was filled with relief
> and fresh hope
> that succor was near:
> he had seen the hero's
> quick resolve
> and courage in action. (1213–20)

Quick resolve and courage in action, of course, are precisely the things that will be needed in a contest with Grendel. It is well to remember at this point that just before Unferth launched his unprovoked verbal assault on Beowulf, Hrothgar had said to his guest:

> Now sit at the banquet
> and say what you think;
> tell us how you hope
> to triumph over Grendel. (977–80)

In his crushing response to Unferth's sudden attack, Beowulf has done much more than merely "told us" how he intends to triumph over Grendel—that master of sudden attacks—but has demonstrated how he will do it. No wonder Hrothgar is pleased and decides to give Beowulf charge of the Danes' national monument and shrine for the coming night.

It is interesting that the note of Danish/Geatish rivalry and antagonism that has been sounding in the poem at this point is not allowed to die away before the poet has told us that everything ends in harmony and equally apportioned praise. Yes, Grendel killed a lot of Danes, and yes, God

> would give the Geats
> the glory, thanks
> to one man's strength,
> of worsting their foe,[44] (1393–96)

---

44. The referent of "their" in verse 1396 (Geats? Danes? both peoples?) is deliberately ambiguous:

> Ac him Dryhten forgeaf
> wigspeda gewiofu, Wedera leodum,
> frofor ond fultum, þæt hie feond heora
> ðurh anes cræft ealle ofercomon. (696b–99b)

but this was done

> so that all might share
> the honor, Geats
> together with Danes. (1397–99)

With similar harmoniousness, the clash between Beowulf and Unferth leaves no bitter residue. The next thing that happens in their relationship is that Unferth lends Beowulf his splendid and famous heirloom, the sword Hrunting, to use against Grendel's mother. In doing this, the poet tells us,

> he chose to forget
> his challenge while drunk
> of the night before. (2933–35)

Did he also choose to forget—or at least suppress—his envy of Beowulf? Or has Beowulf's behavior and performance impressed him so much that he has been won over to the hero (as some readers have thought)? Beowulf, in any event, by accepting the loan of the sword, shows that he is perfectly willing to let bygones be bygones.

In the event, ironically, the sword fails Beowulf in his fight against Grendel's mother. But the hero is careful to return it to Unferth

> with appropriate thanks
> for the loan of that old
> reliable weapon,
> that friend in combat;
> he refrained, out of tact
> and wisdom, from faulting
> the weapon's performance. (3618–24)

His whole interaction with Unferth shows Beowulf's firmness in sticking up for his right and reputation (this is surely *fortitudo*, if only verbal), combined with a reluctance to provoke or even to protract hostile engagements with others and a desire to seek instead reconciliation and friendship (surely *sapientia!*). This episode thus nicely exemplifies two of the aspects of Beowulf's virtuous conduct that he feels proudest of as he lies dying at the end of the poem: "I held what was mine / but sought no quarrels" (5474–75).

Beowulf's insistence with these words that he always fought defensively and never offensively illuminates his behavior during his three great monster-fights. The fights themselves—with Grendel, Grendel's mother, and the dragon—are all defensive in nature, his response to a direct physical attack by his adversary. True, on all three occasions he has deliberately put himself in a position where the monster can launch an attack if it wants to, but the initiative always lies with the monster, and the battle is always—on Beowulf's side—a defensive one. This is quite a remarkable thing, and it inevitably raises the question of whether what we have here is the poet's attempt to answer the vexing question—vexing in his day as well as ours—"Is it possible to be a Christian and a warrior at the same time?"[45] Or is there some sense in which the two categories are mutually exclusive? (See p. lxxxi.)

The hero's wisdom is shown also by his extraordinary understanding—extraordinary in a man so young—of the values of the society in which he lives, along with its internal tensions and dynamics. This is clearest, perhaps, in the digression about the Heathobard king Ingeld and his tragic marriage to Hrothgar's daughter Freawaru (4039–4137). The digression, almost a hundred verses long, occurs as part of Beowulf's report, after returning home, to his king Hygelac. It is evident that during his stay at the Danish court he kept his eyes and ears open, observing people and their words and actions, learning all that he could about them, and then putting this information together with his understanding of how things normally worked in his society to make informed guesses about what is likely to happen in the future. At the banquets in Heorot he had watched "Hrothgar's / slender daughter" (4039–40) serving mead to the older warriors and had learned that her name was Freawaru, as he reports to Hygelac:

> This girl is pledged
> to Ingeld, the son
> and heir of Froda,
> the Heathobard king
> so unhappily slain
> in a clash with the Danes,
> and canny Hrothgar
> means for that marriage
> to mark the end
> of old enmities. (4048–57)

Hrothgar intends to use his daughter as a "peace-weaver" (*freoðuwebbe* 1942a),[46] hoping by means of the marital alliance between her and Ingeld

---

45. It also leads one to wonder whether the poet was familiar with early patristic attempts to formulate a doctrine of "just war."

46. Since women performed the domestic task of weaving in Anglo-Saxon society, the word *freoðuwebbe* represents a metaphoric extension of this occupation into the political and international sphere.

to stave off any further warfare between the Danes and the Heathobards, their neighbors to the south.

> But even when a bride
> is beautiful and young,
> the bloody spear
> is rarely idle
> once a ruler is killed. (4058–62)

The poet is as skeptical about the efficacy of this method of controlling violence as he is about the efficacy of oaths and vows and treaties and wergild payments (see the Finnsburg episode, 2131–2317). He is only too aware that women exploited as "peace-weavers" (and their children, too, if the marriage is fruitful) are likely to be ground up by the vengeance machinery if and when it starts up again. In the case of Ingeld and Freawaru, violence is apparently rekindled—with terrible irony—at the wedding itself or shortly afterward, when Ingeld has returned to the land of the Heathobards with his new wife and her complement of Danish retainers. Every time Ingeld walks

> through that ancient hall
> with his happy bride,
> he and every
> Heathobard there
> will hate and resent
> her attendants: Danes,
> entertained like friends,
> but wearing familiar
> weapons and jewels,
> well-known heirlooms
> that had once belonged,
> while hands could still hold them,
> to the Heathobards' sires, (4064–76)

who had been killed in a great battle against the Danes and whose plundered trappings, worn now by the sons of their slayers, are a constant incitement to revenge. One can imagine the tensions at Ingeld's court, which continue until a bitter old warrior, a survivor of the battle in question, eggs a young Heathobard on to exact the long-delayed vengeance.[47] The upshot is that both Danes and Heathobards

---

47. Old warriors are often, in Germanic heroic tradition, assigned the role of re-

> break their agreement,
> the oaths of earls;
> Ingeld's fury
>   is unleashed
> and his love for his wife
> grows cooler, chilled
> by curdling sorrow. (4126–32)

When Beowulf is making his report to his uncle Hygelac, of course, all this is in the future, a tragic birth still hidden in the womb of time.[48] But Beowulf speaks as if it is inevitably going to happen: he knows that this is the way people must and will behave in his society, given their situation and the nature of the forces acting upon them. So Beowulf's statement is not prophecy—he has no preternatural ability to peer into the future—but a "hunch" that is virtually certain to prove correct,[49] and this is why he can say to his lord Hygelac with such absolute certainty:

---

minding lazy or cowardly or merely pragmatic younger warriors of their vengeance obligations.

48. It was probably as a result of the rekindling of this feud between father-in-law Hrothgar and son-in-law Ingeld that the Heathobards invaded Denmark and burned down the hall Heorot. This tragic story in its entirety will have been present in the minds of both poet and audience, and the audience is asked to recall it at the very beginning of *Beowulf,* when the building of Heorot is described and Hrothgar distributes gold in the hall

> while high
> overhead the great
> wooden rafters
> waited for floods
> of fire to enfold them,
> for the fated day
> when the tragic hate
> of two in-laws
> would flash into flame,
> into fierce warfare. (161–70)

The sudden plunge into the future here is (as noted earlier, p. xxxiii) a splendid example of the poet's use of juxtaposition to suggest the instability of earthly glory.

49. There is an interesting parallel in Chapters 21–24 of the Icelandic *Brennu-Njáls saga* ("The Saga of Burnt Njáll"), where the wise chieftain Njáll foresees in remarkable detail the future behavior of some of the other characters.

> I conclude, therefore,
> that this compact between
> Heathobards and Danes
> is highly unstable
> and not to be trusted. (4133–37)

Among the many reasons the poet may have had for glancing at the tragic story of Ingeld and Freawaru in his poem, certainly one of the most important was to give his audience a particularly impressive example of young Beowulf's *sapientia*—his uncannily mature understanding of the way things work in his society.

A further example of Beowulf's wisdom is provided by his interaction with Hrothgar's queen. Wealhtheow has the most substantial female role in the poem (aside from Grendel's mother, who is only partly human and apparently without language). Her name means "foreign bondwoman," and it is possible that she is a "trophy wife" in the most literal sense—booty from one of Hrothgar's earlier military campaigns and perhaps a captive princess. She is represented as a grave and serious woman, at ease in her queenly role, "adept / at court etiquette" (1225–26) and fully aware of the dangerous currents and cross-currents swirling in the waters of the Danish court. She gives the impression of being younger than her ancient husband, by whom she has had two sons named Hrethric and Hrothmund. They are probably in their teens, as suggested by the fact that in Heorot they sit among the youthful warriors (*geogoð*), presumably in the most prestigious place among them.

Wealhtheow is given two speeches in the poem, one addressed to her husband the king and the other, which follows soon afterward, to Beowulf. It is important to remember, when reading these speeches, that they are *public* speeches, and as in all such cases the speaker needs constantly to bear in mind that she or he is being heard not only by the particular person who is ostensibly being addressed, but by a larger audience (some of whose members may not be in sympathy with what is being said). This means, of course, that speakers are constrained in what they can declare openly and may need to indulge in indirection of various kinds, even sending covert messages to other characters. This situation presents a particular problem and opportunity for Wealhtheow. Her two brief speeches show to admiration the subtlety and emotional perceptiveness of the poet, and their reception by Beowulf once again shows his sensitivity to the words and thoughts of others and his quickness of mind.

As her words make clear, Wealhtheow is tormented by anxiety and mastered by one particular fear: in the light of Hrothgar's extreme age and decrepitude, it is likely that he does not have a great deal longer to live, and that when he dies—given what frequently happened in early Germanic society—the throne will be grabbed by his nephew Hrothulf and his own two young sons will be dispossessed (and no doubt "disappeared," so that no counterclaim can ever be made). This anxiety, which has probably been festering in Wealhtheow for a long time, is stirred into active expression by several things that occur just before she makes her speeches. In the immediately preceding scene, the court poet has sung a long tale about bloody doings between Danes and Frisians, centering on the tragedy of the Danish princess Hildeburh, who loses a son in the course of the conflict.[50] This is bound to make Wealhtheow reflect on her own parallel situation. Even more ominous, perhaps, the first of her two speeches comes hard on the heels of the poet's statement that the silent (and sinister?) Hrothulf and the ambiguous Unferth—both of whom she probably has good reason to fear and mistrust—are sitting right next to the king. Since they will hear everything she says, it behooves her to be extremely circumspect. And finally, to add to her troubles, she has recently received the very disquieting news that Hrothgar intends to adopt Beowulf as his son (2349–51).[51] As if the dynastic situation were not already problematical enough! How will she deal with this new threat to her own sons' future? She seems to feel that she can speak about Beowulf's adoption quite openly and straightforwardly to Hrothgar, knowing she will find ready sympathy from everyone at the Danish court:

---

50. The anticipation in this digression of Wealhtheow's plight is a good example of how the story told in a "digression" can stand in ironic or pathetic relationship to something in the central narrative. (Note, too, that both Hildeburh's tragedy and Wealhtheow's worries are relevant to the situation of Grendel's mother, who has just lost her son.)

51. Hrothgar's words to Beowulf in 1892–94 ("Henceforth / I aim to love you / as my own son!" ["*me for sunu wylle / freogan on ferhþe*" 947b–48a]) are probably meant to be taken literally. In the early medieval period, kings (and others) would sometimes adopt promising individuals either by ordinary adoption or by so-called "military adoption," the latter involving a gift of arms. Theodric the Great's letter to the king of the Heruli, offering to adopt him, is relevant to *Beowulf* in a number of ways: "The peoples account it a high honour for a man to be made a son by military adoption, since only he who has shown himself to be worthy is fit to be numbered among the strongest of [the] strong. Our natural children often disappoint us. But the children we choose for ourselves cannot be unworthy. For they achieve their position not by birth but by their merits. . . . Wherefore it is our will that you, who are already declared a hero according to the custom and ceremonial of the folk, should also be made our son in proper fashion through our gift of weapons to you. We bestow upon you horses, swords, shields and other weapons of war" (Eric Graf Oxenstierna, *The World of the Norsemen*, trans. by Janet Sondheimer [London: Weidenfeld and Nicolson, 1957], 91–92.

> Heorot has been cleansed,
> our jubilant hall,
> so enjoy good fortune
> as long as you can;
> but leave the kingdom
> to your *own* children,
> your heirs, when death
> finally comes. (2352–59; emphasis added)

But Beowulf is obviously not the only—or the major—threat to her children's future, and in approaching the danger represented by the taciturn Hrothulf and his probably ruthless ambition, she has to be very careful indeed. She begins by stating her "faith" (it is hard to believe she has much of this!) that Hrothulf can be depended on to show loyalty to the king and his children:

> I have faith that Hrothulf,
> your loyal nephew,
> will look on our two
> youngsters with love
> if you, most gracious
> and dread sovereign,
> should die before he does. (2360–66)

Then she changes tack, reminding everyone—including Hrothulf—of his own helplessness and vulnerability as a child. Surely, she thinks, this will induce in him some fellow-feeling for her young sons. She also reminds him of Hrothgar's generosity toward him, which implies a reciprocal obligation on his part:

> I trust he will treat
> our two children
> with mildness and mercy,
>   remembering
> the warmth and kindness
> with which *we* treated *him*
> when he was himself
> a helpless child. (2367–74; emphasis added)

Wealhtheow seems to be taking advantage of the situation to "co-opt" Hrothulf, as it were, to pressure him into what she regards as desirable behavior by telling him—in this very public context—how he *will* behave. It is a tactic of desperation, of course, and a little pathetic, since she is powerless to exert any real control over his future actions.

What is Beowulf to make of Wealhtheow's words as he listens to them? We know that he is paying close attention to developments at the Danish court, picking up all the information he can and entrusting it to memory (the Ingeld digression shows this clearly enough). As we will see in a moment, he correctly interprets Wealhtheow's speech as a covert cry for help. And as she completes her speech and continues on her rounds of the hall, we are told something we had not been told earlier about the seating arrangements in Heorot:

> She approached the place
> where her princelings sat,
> Hrethric and Hrothmund,
> around them a throng
> of Danish youths
> and, drinking between them
>   on the bench,
> Beowulf the Geat.[52] (2375–82)

These lines end Section XVII of the poem and are treated as a kind of climax.

Wealhtheow's second speech is addressed to Beowulf himself. She praises the fame he has earned, wishes him a prosperous life, begs him to help her sons with his advice ("give these boys / your wise counsel" [2438–39]) and—a moment later—begs him to help them with something *more* than mere advice ("Be good to my boys / and act in their interest" [2452–53]). She concludes the speech with the brave but almost certainly hollow claim that everyone at the Danish court loves and honors everyone else, while

> the nation is united
> and its noble thanes
> drink merrily
> and do as I bid them. (2459–62)

We suspect that this cannot be true, given the ominous hint of a future rupture between Hrothgar and Hrothulf and the emphasis placed on Unferth's unreliability (2327–35); it must be another attempt to put a good face on things and pretend that nothing is rotten in the state of Denmark.

Beowulf does not forget this scene, nor Wealhtheow's desperate (if oblique) plea on behalf of her sons, as becomes clear when he makes his farewell speech

---

52. This tells us something about Beowulf's age and about Hrothgar's and Wealhtheow's interest in promoting a friendship—and a potential future alliance—between Beowulf and their two sons.

before leaving Denmark. Here he thanks Hrothgar for his hospitality and says he will come back eagerly if his help is ever needed again. He concludes:

> And if your son Hrethric
> should someday resolve
> to visit my country,
> he can avail himself there
> of a wealth of friends;
> worthy travelers
> win the worthiest
> welcome abroad. (3671–78)

The likeliest reason that Hrothgar's eldest son might want to visit the Geats is that he is fleeing Denmark and seeking refuge. What Beowulf seems to be doing here, then, is making him a promise of asylum, should he ever need it in the future. This promise must obviously be delivered in such an indirect way that it does not openly and publicly acknowledge the tensions at the Danish court and offend or alarm Hrothulf.[53] It is quite likely to be the intelligence, tact, and subtlety displayed by Beowulf here—to say nothing of his loyalty and gratitude—that prompts Hrothgar to reply in terms that seem, if we fail to take the whole context into account, strangely "over the top," that is, strangely in excess of what would seem appropriate.

> God in his wisdom
> gave you, my son,
> these knowing words.
> I have never heard
> such masterful speech
> from a man so young.
> Your might is matchless,
> your mind agile,
> your talk full of wisdom. (3681–89)

---

53. The manuscript reading here (1836a–37a) is *gif him þonne hreþrinc to hofum geata geþinged [=geþingeð] þeodnes bearn* ("if, then, a glorious warrior, a king's son, decides to visit the courts of the Geats"). The manuscript *hreþrinc* ("glorious warrior") is usually emended by editors to *Hreþric,* the name of Wealhtheow's elder son (and this interpretion is followed in the present translation). It is just possible, however, that the manuscript means what it says and that a kind of wordplay is intended: the actual name of the boy must not be mentioned in the tricky circumstances suggested above, so Beowulf substitutes for it a near-homonym, trusting that Wealhtheow will be able to decipher his meaning.

Beowulf is always capable of learning from everything that happens to him, including, of course, his experiences at the Danish court, and he shapes his own behavior accordingly in the maelstrom of dynastic politics. After Hygelac's death he refuses to accept the offer of the Geatish throne and thereby to supplant his young cousin Heardred, even though the offer is made by the boy's own mother (4737–44) and even though many contemporaries of the poet would no doubt have seen it as a wise and even responsible thing to do ("Woe to the land that is governed by a child!" was a common sentiment in medieval times). Partly he acts this way out of loyalty to Hygelac—this being the deepest loyalty of Beowulf's life—but also no doubt because he appreciates the havoc that dispossessions of this sort have caused (or are bound to cause) at both the Danish and Swedish courts, bringing murders and rebellions and further dispossessions in their train. It is for reasons like this that Beowulf refused

> to usurp his youthful
> cousin's kingdom
> or covet its throne
> or allow the Geats
> to elect him king;
> but he guided the boy
> in governing the land
> until he reached manhood
> and could reign on his own. (4748–56)

In addition to straightforward authorial descriptions of the hero in action, self-presentation in his own speeches, and evaluative comments made about him by others, the poet has another important method of revealing his character: through presentation of his antitype. We saw earlier (pp. xlix–l) that in the "double digression" in Section XIII of the poem, Beowulf was brought into relationship with two very different "princely exiles" (1801) of Germanic tradition: first he was compared to the great hero Sigemund, and then he was contrasted with the failed Danish king Heremod. Heremod is the antitype of both Sigemund and Beowulf, and he haunts the poem, making two explicit appearances in the text.

As a young man Heremod was a person of exceptional promise who was popular with his people and had many loyal followers

> who looked to him for help,
> who thought that their prince
> would thrive in virtue,
> inherit the great

> high-seat of his father
> and lead Denmark. (1818–23)

So far, so good.

> But he lost their hearts
> when sin and sorrow
> usurped his mind; (1824–26)

and in consequence his people deposed him and shipped him off to be murdered by the Jutes. What had gone wrong?

> Mental anguish
> had crippled Heremod:
> he became, in the end,
> an evil burden
> to his own people,
> who were enraged by his wrathful
> and erratic deeds,
> his lawless ways. (1808–15)

   We are given specific information about all this in the "second Heremod digression," which occurs at the beginning of Hrothgar's long speech of moral advice to Beowulf after his triumph over Grendel and Grendel's mother. Here the king praises Beowulf's impressive combination of *fortitudo* and *sapientia;* in the future, he prophesies,

> you will be your land's
> blessing and hope,
> unlike our late
> lord Heremod,
> who brought no blessing
> but bloodshed, grief,
> danger, and death
> to the Danish race. (3415–22)

And now Hrothgar gives us a list of the charges against Heremod:

> In his angry fits
> he killed his comrades
> and close associates
> until forced to flee
>   his fatherland

and the delights of men,
a forlorn exile.
Although God the giver
had granted him strength
above all other
earthly champions,
a baneful crop
of bloodthirsty thoughts
took root in his soul;
morose, close-fisted,
he grudged gift-giving
to gain men's praise,
and both king and country
came to disaster
and long-lasting grief. (3424–43)

Physical strength without wisdom and good judgment is very dangerous. Heremod perverts two of his most important obligations in the lord-follower relationship that was so central to early Germanic military and social organization: instead of protecting his men and promoting their well-being, he murders them; instead of distributing treasure, he hoards it. He has gone psychotic, as we might say today, and the results are disastrous for him and his people.

It is obvious that Heremod with his "wrathful / and erratic deeds, / his lawless ways" (1813–15) stands at the opposite pole of acceptable behavior from Beowulf. Moreover (and this is an important aspect of the contrast between them), the trajectory of Heremod's career is the exact opposite of Beowulf's: Heremod began in popularity and promise but ended being hated, whereas Beowulf began in scorn and contempt but ended in glory. The arc of Heremod's life story is thus the inverse of Beowulf's, and it is this that makes him a perfect foil for (and antitype of) the hero.

If we want to probe beyond the mere fact of their radical unlikeness and the facile psychological labels that we might adduce to explain it, if we want to ask what was the ultimate reason for their different behaviors and destinies, the poet would undoubtedly tell us that God gives men different gifts and different fates.[54] That is the way things are. Hrothgar says to

---

54. This was a popular theme in Old English poetry (see especially "The Gifts of Men," *ASPR* III, 137–40, and "The Fortunes of Men," *ASPR* III, 154–56).

It is interesting to note that the eddaic poem "Hyndluljóð" tells us not only that the high god Óðinn (Woden) gives different gifts to different men, but singles out

Beowulf that he has told him about Heremod "for [his] own dear sake," immediately adding:

> It is truly strange
> in what unlike portions
> the Lord of heaven,
> the absolute Owner
> of everything,
> parcels out property,
> power, and wisdom. (3448–54)

And the poet of "Deor" (see pp. 184–86), whose views on this matter jibe perfectly with those of the *Beowulf*-poet, tells us we must understand

> that in this world
> God is always
> going about,
> granting some men
> glory and honor,
> allotting others
> lives of misery. (62–68)

It is likely that Beowulf's antitype Heremod is on the poet's mind once again—though not explicitly this time—in the great climax that ends the first part of the poem, where the poet is summing up Beowulf's early career:

> And so, with unceasing
> sapience and strength,
> the son of Ecgtheow
> sought after fame
> and pursued glory.
> His soul was untroubled;
> he hewed down none

Heremod and Sigemund as examples of this ("gaf hann Hermóði / hiálm oc brynio, / enn Sigmundi / sverð at þiggja" ["He gave Heremod a helmet and mailcoat, but Sigemund a sword."]). The appearance of these two figures together in this Scandinavian poem as notable recipients of divine gift-giving, and their reappearance in much the same role in *Beowulf*, suggests that contrasting them is a very ancient poetic *topos* in Germanic oral tradition. We may well have here (in *Beowulf*) an example of the survival of a pre-Christian theme into Christian poetry.

> of his hearth companions,
> but guarded the gifts
> God bestowed on him
> with skill and greater
> discretion than any
> warrior on earth. (4353–65)

The second part of *Beowulf* is much gloomier than the first, as noted earlier. The fact that disaster is impending is announced first by an ominous echo: just as Hrothgar and his Danes had lived the good life in Heorot "until their foe started / his persecutions" (200–201), so King Beowulf ruled his people in peace and prosperity "until a usurper came / to rule in the night" (4420–21).[55] Our sense of *déjà vu*—of the alarming parallel between Beowulf's situation and Hrothgar's—increases when we presently learn that now Beowulf's own

> tall meadhall,
> the gift-seat of the Geats,
> greatest of buildings,
>   was in ashes. (4650–53)

And our feeling that things are going badly wrong is deepened even further by what we are told about Beowulf's psychological reaction to the bad news:

> The old ring-giver's
> heart was heavy
> with huge misgivings;
> he wondered if all
>   unwittingly
> he had offended God,
> the Father of heaven,
> by breaking his law;
> his breast seethed
> with sad foreboding,
> as was seldom the case. (4654–64)

His usual steadiness and buoyancy seem to have deserted him.

---

55. The parallel is even more striking in the original, where the same foreboding phrase (*oð ðæt an ongan,* "until a certain one undertook," etc.) is used to announce the beginning of both persecutions (100b, 2210b).

Beowulf naturally decides that he must defend his people against the dragon's fiery depredations.[56] For an old, old man to set out to fight a flying, fire-breathing dragon all by himself is either the height of *fortitudo* or the height of folly, of course, but it is the sort of thing a king must do if he is really a hero. In a sense, therefore, Beowulf has no choice, and his immediate and energetic response to the challenge presented by the dragon stands in pointed contrast to Hrothgar's twelve years of passivity and self-recrimination when he finds himself in a similar situation.

Beowulf's people protest against his determination to fight the dragon and try to restrain him (though we are only told this afterward, lest it cast even the slightest shadow of doubt on the heroic correctness of the king's decision at the moment when that decision is made):

> We could not dissuade
> our magnanimous king
> by any arguments
> or any means
> from going to fight
>   the gold-keeper,
> letting it lie there
> where it had lain for years
> and occupy its mound
> until the end of the world. (6157–66)

No, the hero proceeds on his heroic course with a will that strikes his people as the next thing to willfulness, and they suffer terribly in consequence, losing not only their king but—ultimately—their kingdom. One of them laments, cogently enough:

> Many must suffer
> misery, at times,
> because of one man's will;
> how well we know it! (6152–56)

Yet in spite of their grief over the king's death and their anxiety about what will happen to them as a result, Beowulf's people understand perfectly well both the necessity and the glory of his course of action:

---

56. The dragon can be seen as prophetic or symbolic of the wars that engulf the human world in the second part of the poem, just as Grendel can be seen as prophetic or symbolic of the kin-slayings that play so prominent a role in the first part.

The doom was too strong,
that drove him here,
and he held to his hero's
high destiny. (6167–70)

"He held to his hero's / high destiny"—this excuses any apparent rashness, any willfulness, any overconfidence.

And there is a lot of overconfidence. Beowulf's much-touted *sapientia* seems to be in abeyance for the moment. He reminds us a little of Grendel, fifty years back: he takes it for granted that his record of uninterrupted successes is going to continue. He has every reason in the world to hold this opinion, of course. When he set out to meet the dragon,

he was quite fearless
and discounted the scather's
skill in warfare,
its naked strength.
Had he not, himself,
survived many
violent clashes
and fierce encounters
since those far-off days
when his grip had crushed
Grendel in combat
and his quick courage
had cleansed the hall
of noble Hrothgar? (4694–4707)

*   *   *   *

Consistently successful,
the son of Ecgtheow
had survived every
violent clash
and fierce encounter
until the fatal day
when he went to fight
that winged dragon. (4793–4800)

A long string of successes in the past is no guarantee of success in the present or future, and just as—earlier—the poet had achieved an impressive effect of dramatic irony by counterpointing Grendel's self-confident expectations and his ignorance of the future against our (the audience's) knowledge that tonight he is going to his death, so now Beowulf's overconfidence, based on his past record of triumphs, is counterpointed against repeated assertions that today he is going to die. There is much irony in this, of course, but pathos in equal measure.

In spite of his overconfidence—or alongside it—Beowulf is extremely apprehensive, and when he reaches the dragon's barrow and gazes at it, he has a premonition that this time he will not have his usual good luck:

> Bowed with age,
> Beowulf sat
> on the sad headland
> and said goodbye
>   to his hall-comrades.
> His heart was uneasy
>   and doom-laden,
> death very near
> that would end the days
> of the old ruler. (4833–42)

It is the fact that his overconfidence is qualified by uneasiness and apprehensiveness—it is his two-mindedness as he looks forward to his fight with the dragon—that distinguishes Beowulf so notably from Grendel, who is totally one-minded, totally committed to a single expectation, and therefore reduced to abject terror and despair when things go the way he had no forethought of.

In any event, Beowulf's foreboding heart, "uneasy / and doom-laden" (4838–39),[57] prompts him to embark on a long and moving review of his life and his relations with the Geatish royal house (4851–5015), in the course of which his beloved lord Hygelac—who has been dead for more than fifty years!—is never far from his mind. After this he challenges the dragon and fights it, suffering a terrible and mortal wound. Aware that his death is imminent, he spells out what he regards as the most important aspects of the heroic virtue that he has striven to display throughout his life, the qualities that distinguish him from so many of his less-than-virtuous predecessors and contemporaries (including, of course, the Danish tyrant Heremod, who has already by this time made two and perhaps even three appearances in the poem as the antitype of the hero). Beowulf tells us:

---

57. A more literal translation would be that his spirit was "sad, restless, and set on death" (*geomor*, *wæfre*, and *wælfus* 2419b–20a). Beowulf is oppressed by the mood of "fear and sadness" that was popularly supposed to afflict all living creatures on the day of their death.

> I ruled this people
> for fifty years.
> No foreign king,
> none of the princes
> of neighboring lands,
> dared attack me
> with deadly force
> or wage warfare.
> I waited, in my homeland,
> for the harvest of fate;
> I held what was mine
> but sought no quarrels
> nor swore many
> oaths unjustly.[58]
> For all these things
> my soul is grateful,
> though I am sick to death.
> The Lord of heaven
> will have little cause
> to accuse me of killing
> kinsmen, when life
> has flown from my body. (5464–85)

Subsequently, Beowulf dies in great agony after (apparently) transferring his kingship to Wiglaf, both verbally (through his *verba novissima*) and by conferring on Wiglaf the great neck-ring that symbolizes royal authority (5600–24).

It is a serious mistake to think (as one occasionally reads) that Beowulf meets death defeated by a dragon. He is not defeated; he is victorious. And for so old a man to die so triumphantly and with such heroic energy is a remarkable achievement, the capstone of a great heroic career. Nor is it any real diminishment of this achievement that he has a helper; in fact there is a kind of ancillary glory in Wiglaf's loyalty and in the close cooperation of these two kinsmen in facing this ultimate challenge. While it is true that Wiglaf gives the dragon a disabling—and probably mortal—blow (5393–5403), it is the old king who actually kills it:

> Dazed but conscious,
> Beowulf pulled

---

58. "*Ne me swor fela / aða on unriht*" (2738b–39a). This verse employs understatement (litotes); Beowulf means that he *never* swore oaths unjustly.

a bright dagger,
his sharp war-knife,
from the sheath on his belt
and sliced the smooth-skinned
serpent in half.
Working together
as one, the two
kinsmen had conquered
their common enemy,
Wiglaf fighting
as a warrior should
by his lord's side
in the illustrious king's
last battle,
the last triumph
of his work in the world. (5404–21)

And Beowulf's triumph consists not only in killing a monster that has been ravaging his country and people; it consists equally in the fact that he has been able to "open the hoard" (*hord openian* 3056b), bringing its long-hidden wealth back to the light of day where men can look on it again.[59] He thereby frustrates the design of the "heathen lords" who buried the treasure and hedged it about with lethal spells

so that no man on earth
could come near the hoard
or gain its gold. (6105–7)

It is worth pausing here for a moment to point out that the poet's attitude toward riches and treasure is always ambiguous. He approves of them when they circulate in the bright, daylight world of heroic enterprise, awarded by leaders to their followers as a badge of distinction and a symbol of their worth or value (3799–3805). On the other hand, he views them with deep suspicion when they function as what we might call the "objective correlative" of the

---

59. To be able to look at (*sceawian*) buried treasure, subjecting it to appreciative scrutiny, is the surest indication that it has been recovered for human use. It is not surprising, therefore, that this verb appears in other accounts in Old English poetry of the recovery of buried treasure. It is interesting to note that gazing appreciatively at recovered treasure is a theme that has occurred twice already in *Beowulf* (3373–75, 4569–72).

psychological need for vengeance, symbolically embodying this need and spurring people to vengeful activity (4048–4132). And he has no use at all for treasure when people bury it and try to keep it hidden, thereby inviting the attention of dragon guardians (who are perhaps projections of its malevolent influence). In any event, burying treasure is a completely futile activity,

> for heathen gold
> easily thwarts
> efforts by men
> to hide it forever,
> hard though they try. (5528–32)

All of this contributes to the considerable irony that pervades the end of the poem. A minute or two before his death, Beowulf, lying on the ground mortally wounded, is justly proud of having won a great treasure for his people and sends Wiglaf back into the dragon's mound to fetch a portion of it out into the open for him to look at. But his people have a different idea of what to do with it and decide to commit the whole treasure to the flames of the king's burial pyre (6020–24). The irony is further amplified when they decide to re-inter it with him in his barrow:

> they buried all of it
> back in the ground,
> that unlucky gold,
> where it lives today
> as idle and vain
> as it ever was. (6331–36)

"Idle and vain"—that is the poet's comment on this particular buried treasure and probably (by extension) on *all* buried treasure. Moreover, there is something ominous and even a little frightening about his calculated use of the word "lives" (*lifað* 3167b) in this passage: this is not a verb that is normally used in Old English of inanimate things, and its use here implies that this gold is somehow "alive" and will continue to lurk in the ground, an evil presence waiting for the day when future men uncover it once again, enabling it to charm and enslave them and cause more havoc.

All this, of course, does not diminish or undercut Beowulf's triumph in "opening" the dragon's treasure. And it certainly *was* a triumph, for the poet had told us that

> no man on earth
> could come near the hoard

> or gain its gold
> unless God himself,
> the guardian of men
> and granter or triumphs,
> vouchsafed him safety
> and unsealed the treasure:
> some great hero
> whom God found deserving. (6105–14)

Beowulf is obviously the "great hero" in question, and his being able to "open the hoard" is nothing less than heaven's final seal of approval: he would not have been able to perform the deed

> unless he [had] first obtained
> the gold-granting grace
> of God, the *real*
> Owner of all
> earthly treasure.[60] (6146–50; emphasis added)

Thanks to God's favor, Beowulf escapes the terrible fate in store for those who break the ancient curse on this treasure: confinement forever in some sort of heathen hell (6144–45). His actual destiny is pointedly different:

> his soul left his body
> and went to obtain
> the reward of the just.[61] (5638–40)

Is this the reward of virtue? Yes, of course; but the comment is so brief that it seems almost perfunctory. It does little to alleviate the genuine sorrow we feel about Beowulf's death or to alter our deep sense of the *finality* of that death. It is good to know that Beowulf's soul is in safe hands, but its eternal welfare is not—and has never been—the focus of the poet's interest. And that is hardly surprising: he has made it abundantly clear throughout the poem

---

60. The original is famously obscure (or corrupt) here. This seems the most satisfactory interpretation.

61. It is hard to know how to translate this critically important statement: literally it means, "departed to seek the judgment (or glory) of those who are staunch in the truth" (*soðfæstra dom* 2820b = *iudicium iustorum*). Notice that the word "heaven" or "God's kingdom" or anything of the sort is carefully avoided.

that in spite of the many references to God's continuing management of events on earth, his own concern is with how those events unfold—with what actually happens in this world, the secular world bounded by men's birth and death—and not with "the reward of the just."

In *this* world, virtue is its own reward: the virtue of individual human beings—and the poet does seem to regard virtue as the loftiest goal we can aim for in our lives—guarantees nothing but itself. It certainly does not guarantee the future. As long as Beowulf is alive and in charge of things—during his fifty-year reign—his virtue makes the world a better place in which to live, and he is able to insure peace and justice for his people, making the land of the Geats an oasis of order in a generally disordered Scandinavia. The moment he dies, however, both he and his virtue cease to have any power or exert any force, and nothing can stave off any longer the rush of disastrous events that has been set in motion by his less virtuous predecessors and contemporaries. In the secular context that seems to be the fundamental domain of this poem, virtue *is* its own reward and nothing more. But that does not mean it is any the less worth striving for.

Finally, it seems worth suggesting that in his portrait of Beowulf the poet presents us with his solution to the problem of how one can be a Christian and a warrior at the same time. It must have been a problem that struck at least some of his contemporaries as worth pondering. On the one hand, the message of Jesus in the New Testament is by and large pacifist; on the other hand, complete pacifism was an unrealistic ideal in the dog-eat-dog political world depicted in the poem (and typical of early-medieval society in general). If there is no perfect solution to the problem of interpersonal and international violence, there may at least be some sort of middle way that allows one to live honorably, committed in theory to virtue and nonviolence, but willing in practice to do whatever is necessary to combat genuine evil. Perhaps this is the solution exemplified by Beowulf.

As far as we can tell, Beowulf has no wife, and it is certain that he has no son, since he tells us this himself (5457–63). Is his wifelessness a virtue? Does it originate in some sort of feeling that chastity is a moral excellence, even in secular persons? And is it thus part of some larger strategy to depict Beowulf as a sort of "secular saint"? Or is it, alternatively, a mistake, a fault, or at the very least a regret (as Beowulf himself seems to feel), since his childlessness—his failure to provide an heir and legitimate successor—will lead to disaster for his people? Or is the ambiguity deliberate, part of the poet's ongoing lesson that many things in life are two-sided and double-edged?

Christianity and the Problem of Violence

It is not unlikely that some of the "historical" memories preserved in *Beo-wulf* were transmitted orally for a long period of time in a cultural matrix that was pre-Christian and included memories of the heathen Germanic gods, their stories, and their worship. If poems containing such memories had ever been committed to writing in pre-Christian England—which they were not—they might well have contained scenes showing associations between gods and men that are similar to those in the *Iliad*.[62] Nothing like this is found in *Beowulf* as it has come down to us. Hints or whispers of the heathen Germanic interpretation of life and the universe certainly survive here and there in the poem—Scyld Scefing's ship funeral is an outstanding example—but anything having to do with the heathen gods has been evicted from the tradition that underlies it and replaced by the god known to us today as God.

God enters the poem frequently, often incidentally and almost parenthetically, but never in less than full glory and full control: he is "our Father, the Maker / of times and seasons, / the true Creator" (3220–22).[63] And indeed, it is God's creativity that particularly impresses the *Beowulf*-poet and leads him to produce a splendid passage that shows his familiarity with the creation story in the Book of Genesis, either at first hand or through its brief summary in a famous Old English poem known as "Caedmon's Hymn." In Heorot, as the poet describes it, one can hear

> the harp ringing
> to the song of the singer
> singing the story
> of earth's creation
> ages ago,

---

62. The Old Icelandic "*Sörla þáttur*," which is our most important source for the divine origin of the necklace of the Brosings mentioned in *Beowulf* (2397), paints an almost Homeric picture of gods involving themselves in wars among men, and many other northern sources contain memories from the heathen period that show gods consorting with human beings.

63. Another Old English poem ("Maxims I") makes clear how profoundly this distinguished him from the divinities of the heathen Anglo-Saxons: "Woden made idols; God Almighty created glory, the spacious heavens" (*ASPR* III, 161).

>   how almighty God
>   made this glorious
>   world of wonders
>   washed by the sea,
>   how he set on high
>   the sun and moon
>   as undying lights
>   for dwellers on earth
>   and trimmed the distant
>   tracts of the world
>   with branches and leaves,
>   bringing forth life
>   in every kind
>   of earthly creature. (178–96)

It is being obliged on a daily basis to listen to this beautiful and reverent creation song, as well as to the joyful noises of men living happily in community, that enrages Grendel—outcast (like his ancestor Cain) from human society—and fills him with envy, impelling him to begin his raids against the Danes. It is important to note, in the scene in *Beowulf* (134–96) of which this creation song forms a part, how the poet uses echo-words (or in this case etymologically related words and word-parts) to establish and emphasize what he clearly regards as the very serious and important theme of creation and creativity: we are no sooner told that Hrothgar *scop* ("shaped," i.e., created) the name Heorot for his great hall than we are shown a scene in the hall in which the *scop* ("shaper," i.e., creator, poet) sings about the *frum-sceaft* ("original shaping," i.e., creation) of men, and how God *gesceop* ("shaped," i.e., created) life in all living things.

It is hardly surprising, knowing what we know about the *Beowulf*-poet's structural principles, to find him positioning all this material about beginnings, and about creation, at the beginning of his own creation. It is a little more surprising, perhaps, to see how the material about beginnings and creation (134–228) is shot through with allusions to destroyers and destruction: the future burning of Heorot; the first announcement of Grendel's existence ("A dread demon / who dwelt in the shadows" [171–72]); and then—after the wonderful description of the creation of the universe cited above—the actual appearance onstage of the monster in all his fearfulness. It seems clear from the way the scene is constructed that the poet views creation and destruction, the beginning and the end, *alpha* and *omega,* as inseparable and complementary, like yin and yang, opposed hemispheres of one sphere.

God is omnipotent and omniscient, almighty and all-knowing, and

> God's sovereignty
> over men and their fates
>   has been manifest
> from the beginning of time. (1400–1403)

It is senseless and futile to resist God's power and authority, as we learn from the poet's passing reference to

> that ancient war
> when the angry flood
> swept from heaven
> to slaughter the giants;
> those rebels suffered,
> that race estranged
> from God almighty;
> he gave them their quittance,
> the fate they deserved,
> in those foaming waves. (3377–86)

Similarly, God's omniscience stands in sharp contrast to the very limited knowledge possessed by men, especially their knowledge of the future. The fact that human beings often assume, out of arrogance or ignorance, that they know what is going to happen next, lays them open to all the ironies of reversal and discomfiture. Grendel is so used to having his own way in Heorot, to meeting no serious opposition, that he enters the hall on what will turn out to be his last night in a dangerously unalert and precommitted frame of mind:

> He saw before him
> in the silent hall
> a throng of youthful
> thanes and kinsmen
> lying in their beds.
> He laughed in his heart
> out of pure pleasure:
> he planned to separate
> those sleeping men's
> souls from their bodies
> long before daybreak;
> he looked forward
> to fabulous feasting.
> But fate would forbid him

> to eat people
> ever again
> after that night. (1455–71)

Those last four verses constitute one of a number of passages in this part of the poem in which we (the audience) are told that the assault on the hall will end in disaster for Grendel. He does not know this, of course, and so—in a succession of scenes rich with dramatic irony and even black comedy—we observe the behavior of a monster who is confident in his "knowledge" of the future, agog with pleasurable anticipation, and totally unaware of the possibility that he will soon be quelled. There is a lesson for all of us, here, for human beings are often just as blind—just as vulnerable to being blind-sided—as Grendel is. We must never forget (the poet implies) that we live on a knife-edge of uncertainty and must conduct ourselves accordingly. *Homo proponit* ("Man proposes"), as the saying has it, but *Deus disponit,*

> The Lord disposes
> all things on earth
> and always will;
> foresight, therefore,
> and forethought are best,
> and mental balance,
> since men who inhabit
> this weary war-ravaged
> world experience
> many good things—
> and much evil. (2114–24)

Being aware that the texture of life is mixed, that it contains "many good things— / and much evil," is one of the most important ingredients of "wisdom."[64]

---

64. The original says that anyone who lives in the world for a long time *on ðyssum windagum* ("in these days of strife") will experience *Fela . . . leofes ond laþes* (1060b–62b, "a lot of what is lief and what is loath"). Remarkably enough, the idea of the potential doubleness of experience ("lief" and "loath") is already present in the poignantly ambiguous compound *windagas* of the original, which can mean either "days of strife" or "days of delight" (for the latter meaning see "The Fortunes of Men," *ASPR* III, 155). It is hardly surprising to find this poet taking advantage of homonyms of antithetical meaning when they contribute to his exploration of this particular theme.

Human beings must be prepared for any outcome, good or bad, in any-
thing they undertake; they must be ready to win or lose. Beowulf himself is
fully aware of this. Whenever he utters an obligatory *beot* ("heroic vow")
before going into a fight, he always has the fight's two possible outcomes in
mind. As a young man facing Grendel he is, he claims,

> fully prepared
> to win or to lose;
>   for one of us
> must die, submitting
> to the doom of God. (878–82)

And as an old warrior going into battle against a dragon, he has confidence
in his resolution and his ability to stay the course, but he is careful to make
no promises about anything lying outside his own control, like who will win
and who will lose.

> I solemnly vow
> not to flee a footstep
> but to let fate decide
> our doom as it will,
> our destiny—fate
> and almighty God. (5048–53)

This circumspect attitude toward the future is very characteristic of the hero.
    As has already been noted, the focus of the poem (and the poet) is very
much on the actions and behavior of people in this world, the everyday world
in which men live and move and have their being, hatching their plans and
purposes, enacting their tragedies, suffering their fates. In their lament at
Beowulf's funeral, his closest followers praise him as "the best and wisest /
of kings of this world" (6360–61). The phrase "kings of this world" (*wyruld-
cyninga* 3180b) seems at first to resonate with royal splendor, power, and
glory—and of course it does. But it is also extremely precise and delimiting,
marking for this Christian poet and his Christian audience the boundaries of
the space in which any kind of human action is possible: "*this* world."
    Both the poet and his audience know there are other worlds, and the poet
sometimes mentions them.[65] According to Beowulf, Unferth "will one day

---

65. Hrothgar's description of the uncanny scenery in the neighborhood of Grendel's
pool (2714–28) bears a close resemblance, sometimes even in striking verbal details, to
that of the approaches to hell in one of the ninth- or tenth-century *Blickling Homilies*

roast / shamefully in hell" (1176–77). The most significant of these refer-
ences to other worlds stands close to the beginning of the poem and is so
"doctrinal" that some scholars—probably mistakenly—have refused to be-
lieve it is the work of the *Beowulf*-poet himself, regarding it as an interpo-
lation by a Christian scribe. It begins by describing how Hrothgar's Danes
behave in their despair over Grendel's depredations:

> His men often
> assembled in council,
> seeking a way
> to end Grendel's
> evil attacks
> and sudden onslaughts.
> Sometimes they practiced
> demon worship
> at dark altars,
> offered sacrifice,
> asked the Devil,
> > the soul-slayer,
> to send them help
> in their dreadful need:
> a damnable custom,
> the hope of heathens. (342–57)

This seems to be presented as atypical behavior on the part of the Danes, a
lapse of some sort, and the Anglo-Saxon poet may well have been thinking
of how his own ancestors, during the long process of their conversion to
Christianity, would sometimes turn to old pre-Christian means of warding
off disaster when the new Christian ones appeared ineffectual. It was not that
these ancestors deliberately chose to worship the Christian Devil, of course,
as the above citation seems at first to imply; it was rather that they reverted
to their earlier heathendom, to the worship of pre-Christian gods. But mis-
sionary Christians in England interpreted these pre-Christian gods as the
devils of Christian belief. That is why the poet continues:

(where the description is based on a Latin text, an apocryphal Vision of St. Paul; see
Klaeber, 183). This is one of the very few occasions in which descriptive material in
Beowulf can be shown to be closely related to that in another extant Old English text.
It seems impossible to determine whether the poem is dependent on the homily here,
or the homily on the poem, or both on some common source. But the relationship
certainly provides plenty of food for thought (and speculation) about the intellectual
milieu in which the written *Beowulf* took shape.

Helle gemundon	Hell had possession
in modsefan,	of their erring minds,
Metod hie ne cuþon	they were ignorant
dæda Demend,	of the Light of Life,
ne wiston hie Drihten God,	the Lord almighty,
ne hie huru heofona Helm	and of how to pray
herian ne cuþon,	to heaven's King,
wuldres Waldend.	the God of glory.
Wa bið þæm ðe sceal	Grim is the lot
þurh sliðne nið	of heedless men
sawle bescufan	who hurl their souls
in *f*yres *fæ*þm,	into the clutch of fire,
*f*rofre ne *w*enan,	who cut themselves off
*w*ihte ge*w*endan;	from grace forever!
*w*el bið þæm þe mot	Glorious the lot
æfter deaðdæge	of men who rely
Drihten secean	on the Almighty for peace
ond to *F*æder *fæ*þmum	and who find mercy
*f*reoðo *w*ilnian. (179b–88b)	in the Father's arms. (358–76)

No other passage in *Beowulf* is so full of outright Christian moralizing and Christian doctrine. But there is nothing uncertain or jerry-rigged about it: a lot of skill and effort has gone into its carefully constructed syntactic parallelism, its careful contrast of the auxiliary verbs *sceal* ("must," implying absolute compulsion) and *mot* ("may," implying the need for divine grace), and its elaborate and cunningly rung changes on the alliteration of *f* and *w* (highlighted by boldface italic type). It is one of the most artfully, even artificially, constructed passages in the whole poem, and it certainly serves as a brilliant climax and conclusion for Section II. Its stylistic accomplishment makes one skeptical of the argument that it is by a different poet than the rest of the work.

With the references to Cain and Abel and the derivation of the monsters from Cain, we come to material that shows the poet's familiarity, first- or second-hand, with the Old Testament. He has no discernible interest in Adam or Eve, in their eating the fruit of the forbidden tree that "Brought death into the world and all our woe" (Milton, *Paradise Lost*, Book 1, 3). On the contrary, he seems to attribute "all our woe" to something different, the fact that "Cain cruelly / killed his brother, / his closest kinsman" (2523–25).

> Accursed by God,
>   and with that murder
> marking him, he fled
> to live in the wasteland.

> From his loins sprang
> a monstrous progeny,
> among them Grendel, (2526–32)

as well as all the other evil semihuman creatures who trouble the world, spooks and spirits,

> elves and goblins
> and evil ghouls
> and those bold giants
> who rebelled against God,
> asking for trouble. (223–27)

But Cain's crime is more than just the ultimate source of these unsavory creatures. It is also, for this poet, an archetypal event, the fountainhead of violence among human beings, not only the kin-slayings that fill the pages of the poem, but *all* acts of violence—including warfare—by means of which men kill their brothers, literally or metaphorically conceived. As another Old English poet put it, "Violence [*fæhþo*] came to the race of men a long time ago, when the earth swallowed Abel's blood. This was not an evil lasting only a single day: from those sinful drops huge crime sprang far and wide among men, evil mixed with destruction for many peoples."[66]

The *Beowulf*-poet provides a thorough analysis of violence in the society he depicts, calling attention to its psychological origins and the inadequacy of the society's violence-control mechanisms, and offering, in his presentation of the hero, a model of how individuals can exert a force for nonviolence and peaceful resolution of conflict.

Violence always begets violence. Feud—the modality through which the *lex talionis* ("an eye for an eye, a tooth for a tooth") typically expresses itself—was widespread in early Germanic life and literature, where examples of vengeance and counter-vengeance are legion. In fact the *Beowulf*-poet at one point observes bleakly that vengeance is "the law of the world" (MS *woroldræden* 1142b)—*this* world, of course—and we saw earlier how, in his depiction of the feud between the Danes and the Grendel clan, he documents the fact that feud is often not satisfied with mere tit-for-tat vengeance but tends toward amplification of the scale of retribution.

Violence, in the form of the need and craving for counter-violence—or vengeance—easily seeps through time, imbuing the artifacts of violence from one generation (jewelry, armor) with symbolic meaning that generates

---

66. "Maxims I," *ASPR* III, 163.

violence in the next generation, often enmeshing perfectly innocent victims in its toils (4039–4137).

Violence-control mechanisms practiced by the society depicted in *Beowulf* included solemn public oaths (2213–15), political marriages (4048–57) based on the hope that a bride would be able—or be allowed—to function as a "peace-weaver" (3881), and wergild settlements. In *Beowulf*, all these strategies are shown to be hopelessly ineffective floodwalls against the passionate surges of memory and hatred that fuel vengeance.

The poet's negative attitude toward human violence emerges in a number of ways. The concrete portrayal of human beings shedding other human beings' blood is saved until the grim and bitter final pages of the poem, when we get the sudden shocking picture of the ancient Swedish king Ongentheow waiting to be slaughtered while "streams of blood / poured from a scalp-wound" (5932–33). Especially effective in darkening the picture at the end of the poem are the animal scavengers who prey on dead Geats after a sudden dawn attack:

> it will not be the harp
> that wakes warriors,
> but the wan raven
> cawing over corpses,
> croaking to the eagle
> what fine feeding
> he found this morning,
> gnawing at bodies
> next to the wolf. (6046–54)

These "beasts of battle" are traditional and appear in a number of Old English poems. But only in *Beowulf* are they brought vividly and uncannily to life and imagined as chatting with one another amid the carrion after a great slaughter. The passage makes hideously and repulsively real the fate of the Geats after Beowulf's death; it also very neatly exemplifies the truth of E. G. Stanley's argument that the *Beowulf*-poet "uses the traditional material of Old English verse with an aptness which makes it often seem the fresh product of his mind."[67] We usually lack the comparative materials that would enable us to make judgments about the poet's originality; here, for once, such materials *are* available, and they suggest that he was uniquely and brilliantly inventive in his use of traditional poetic themes.[68]

---

67. E. G. Stanley, "Beowulf," in *Continuations and Beginnings: Studies in Old English Literature,* edited by Eric Gerald Stanley (London: Nelson, 1966), 115.

68. The abundance of comparative material available for the study of compound-formation in Old English poetry has been used to show that the poet was also uniquely

The poet's uneasiness about human violence means that he is always ready to show sympathy for its innocent victims, and it is his compassion for their suffering that provides the tincture of sorrow and melancholy that pervades the poem—the Virgilian note, as it has often been called. It is frequently the fate of women that evokes this sympathy, whether the old Geatish woman at Beowulf's funeral who

> wailed her heart out,
> crazed with terror,
> crying bitterly
> that she dreaded days
> of doom and disaster,
> invading armies,
> violence of troops,
> slaughter, exile,
> slavery, (6302–10)

or the Danish princess Hildeburh, who woke up one morning with plenty of reason "to curse / her wretched destiny" (2153–54),

> when she saw them lie
> slaughtered, kinsmen
> she loved more deeply
> than life or any
> treasure on earth. (2155–59)

Beowulf is not an "antiwar" poem in the modern sense, of course; it is hard to conceive of the existence of such a thing in a society organized as Anglo-Saxon society was, except perhaps among persons who took with absolute literalness the Christian injunction to turn the other cheek. The poet seems to believe that some wars are "just" (for example, the war in which Beowulf avenges the death of his cousin Heardred [4781–92]), and there are clearly places where his sympathies lie more with one contending party than the other (Danes over Frisians; Geats over Swedes). But on the whole he is quite evenhanded in describing the clash of peoples. There is certainly no calling an enemy abusive names or gloating over his discomfiture, the sort of thing we find in "The Battle of Brunanburh" and "The Battle of

---

and brilliantly inventive in coining *new* compounds and thus enriching the diction of Old English verse. See Arthur G. Brodeur, *The Art of "Beowulf"* (Berkeley: University of California Press, 1959), 254–71.

Maldon,"[69] which are poems treating military events that were contemporary with their poets and are very definitely one-sided. The wars that fill the pages of *Beowulf* are so far in the past that no feeling of real partisanship is possible any longer.

What then, as the poet sees it, is the solution to the problem of human violence?

When Beowulf reviews his life as he lies dying, one of the aspects of his virtue that he finds most satisfying to remember is his nonaggressiveness. "I held what was mine," he says, "but sought no quarrels" (5474–75). From the poet's point of view, "seeking quarrels" is a sure recipe for trouble, and a king who engages in this sort of behavior not only risks losing his own life but may be setting up long-term disaster for his people. This is what Beowulf's uncle Hygelac did when he attacked the Franks, apparently with no provocation. A Geatish speaker explains:

> Our feud with them started
> when King Hygelac
> carelessly raided
> the Rhineland coast
> with a marauding fleet
> and harried the Hetware,
> hearth-friends of the Franks.
> They met him in battle
> with a mighty host
> and, far from rewarding
> his forces with plunder
> after a fine triumph,
> our freebooting king
> was slain with his army,
> and since that time
> we have been viewed as foes
> by the Merovingian king. (5826–42)

Even more significant for the ultimate destiny of the Geats is the enmity of their neighbors the Swedes, and the mechanism through which this enmity is made to bear on them is typical of the hopeless tangles created in this society by the proclivity to violence and the "need" for vengeance. When Beowulf is dying he transfers his power and authority to his young kinsman

---

69. *ASPR* VI, 16–20 and 7–16, respectively. (Both these poems, incidentally, contain descriptions of the "beasts of battle" mentioned earlier.)

Wiglaf. Wiglaf is a Swede (5207) whose father Weohstan had killed Eanmund, the brother of the present Swedish king Eadgils.[70] Wiglaf's elevation to the throne of the Geats is an open invitation to Eadgils to invade their land and avenge his brother's death; and this may well provide the background not only for the apprehension of Beowulf's people, at the end of the poem, about a pending Swedish invasion, but also—in *real* history—for the Geats' disappearance as an independent people.

It seems that the only viable antidote to violence and the spreading contagion of destructiveness that it causes is virtuous behavior on the part of individuals: steady self-control and a fixed determination to act in a constructive and nonviolent way whenever possible, the sort of behavior exhibited everywhere in the poem by its hero when he is dealing with other human beings.

* * * *

Beowulf is full, as we have seen, of reverence for God and reference to his power and authority. What is remarkable in a poem so aware of this religious dimension, and so evidently produced by a Christian poet in a Christian culture, is that it does not contain a single reference to Christ. This seems at first very puzzling.

It is not as if the poet was ignorant of the New Testament. His familiarity with its teachings, either directly or through contemporary homiletic writings, is clear in a number of places, most notably perhaps in the passage in Hrothgar's great "sermon" in which the king describes an assault by the Devil and his minions upon a man whose burgeoning pride has left him with no defense against them:

> his heart mounts up
> and haughty thoughts
> quicken within him
> and conscience sleeps,
> the soul's sentry,
> its slumber deepened
> by banal routines.
> Near him the Devil
> creeps with his quiver
> of crooked arrows,
> the warped suggestions

---

70. Presumably this explains why we find Weohstan and his son Wiglaf living among the Geats (5247–48), where they must have felt a lot safer than they did in Sweden.

> of wicked fiends,
> but he has lost his shield,
> and at last he feels
> a shower of sharp
> shafts in his heart. (3479–94)

It seems clear that the ultimate source of this passage is St. Paul's tremendous admonition in his Epistle to the Ephesians (6:11–17), cited here from the Authorized or King James version of the Bible:

11 Put on the whole armor of God, that ye may be able to stand against the wiles of the devil.

12 For we wrestle not against flesh and blood, but against principalities, against powers, against the rulers of the darkness of this world, against spiritual wickedness in high places.

13 Wherefore take unto you the whole armor of God, that ye may be able to withstand in the evil day, and having done all, to stand.

14 Stand therefore, having your loins girt about with truth, and having on the breastplate of righteousness;

15 And your feet shod with the preparation of the gospel of peace;

16 Above all, taking the shield of faith, wherewith ye shall be able to quench all the fiery darts of the wicked.

17 And take the helmet of salvation, and the sword of the Spirit, which is the word of God.

St. Paul's theme of spiritual warfare is fully consonant with the concerns of the *Beowulf*-poet, and the military imagery in which it is expressed fits seamlessly into the poet's own presentation.

His deliberate allusion to Ephesians here jibes with other evidence from the poem to suggest that we cannot claim he was ignorant of the New Testament or its account of Christ's life and mission. Nor can we claim that he lacked the vocabulary to talk about Christ, had he wanted to do so. Anglo-Saxon religious poetry is full of synonyms (*heiti*) for Christ: function-based periphrases like *Hælend* ("the Savior," literally, "the one who heals") and *Nergend* ("the Savior," literally, "the one who preserves"). Enough of these were available to allow Christ to be referred to in any alliterative environment. But the *Beowulf*-poet never uses any of them: he apparently made a deliberate decision to exclude from his poem all direct mention of Christ, the events of his life and death, and his tremendous significance for mankind.

Why did he do this? The likeliest and most satisfying explanation is that although he could not have given an exact date (or even an approximate date) to any of the "historical" events recorded in his poem, he knew they had all happened long before the conversion of his own people to Christianity in the sixth and seventh centuries, and thus in some sort of pre-Christian past. To have mentioned Christ in his account of their doings would have been anachronistic. He seems to have thought of his own ancestors and their relatives in Scandinavia as being like the Hebrews of the Old Testament: monotheists (except when they suffered occasional hankerings after strange gods) but unaware of Christ and his significance. For the *Beowulf*-poet, the invention of this pre-Christian world required a certain disciplined effort of historical imagination. But he has brought it off brilliantly.

With Adam and Eve absent from the picture (along with their "original sin"), and with Christ absent (along with his remission of that sin), we find ourselves in a radically secular world, a world that is—for the most part—morally chaotic and incoherent.

Some characters get their just deserts; others suffer an evil fate that is incommensurate with anything they have done to "deserve" it. It is true that Hrothgar's experiences (and Grendel's, too, for that matter) seem to teach that pride goes before a fall, that "hubris" will inevitably be followed by "nemesis." This is implicit in the narrative at the beginning of the poem, when the completion of Heorot, symbol of Hrothgar's pride and ambition, is quickly followed by Grendel's assaults on it. It becomes explicit later in Hrothgar's magnificent "sermon" (3399–3568), which is in a real sense the ethical center of gravity of the whole poem, and where the king makes the suggestion that the reversal of fortune (*edwenden*) that is so regular a feature of the human condition was in his own case the direct consequence of pride and could even be considered a punishment for it:

> I have held Denmark
> for half a century,
> guarded my people
> in grim battle
> with ash-spear and sword
> from every foe
> on earth, till I thought,
> in the end, I had no
> enemy anywhere
> under the sun.
> Cruel reversal
> came to me here
> in my own kingdom,
> when that ancient fiend
> Grendel usurped
> my gold-roofed throne,

> bringing me years
> of bitter grief
> and thickening despair. (3537–55)

The irony of *edwenden* is cruelly emphasized here by the contrast between
Hrothgar's arrogant belief that he had no enemy "anywhere / under the sun"
and his humbling discovery, when an enemy finally *did* appear, that it ap-
peared on his home turf—"in my own kingdom."

The Poet

The great Christian scholar Alcuin of York (d. 804), who was one of the most
distinguished Latin poets of his day, spent his mature years living across the
English Channel at the court of Charlemagne, to whom he served as a sort
of religious and educational consultant. In 797 he was scandalized to learn
that back in his native England certain monks, during meals in their
monastery refectory, instead of listening in attentive silence to biblical and
patristic readings, were in the habit of hearing poems about the great
Heathobard hero Ingeld—the very same Ingeld who makes an impressive ap-
pearance in one of the digressions in *Beowulf* (4048–4137). Alcuin wrote in-
dignantly to the Mercian bishop Hygebald:

> Let the Word of God be read when the clergy are at their meal. It is seemly to
> hear a reader there, not a harper; to hear the sermons of the Fathers of the
> Church, not the lays of the heathen. For what has Hinieldus [i.e., Ingeld] to do
> with Christ? The house is narrow; it cannot contain them both; the King of
> Heaven will have no part with so-called kings who are heathen and damned,
> for the One King reigns eternally in Heaven, while the other, the heathen, is
> damned and groans in Hell. In your houses the voices of readers should be
> heard, not a rabble of men making merry in the streets.[71]

This passage is of enormous interest since it shows an attitude that is very
different from the *Beowulf*-poet's toward both the vernacular oral poetry of
the Anglo-Saxons and its traditional heroes and stories. Alcuin is unable or
unwilling to dissociate these heroes from the heathen matrix in which they

---

71. *"Beowulf" and its Analogues,* trans. by G. N. Garmonsway and Jacqueline Simp-
son (London: J. M. Dent, 1968), 242.

originally developed and flourished, so when he rejects it, he must reject them too. The *Beowulf*-poet, on the other hand, who knew and clearly loved the old stories, was unwilling to throw the baby out with the bath water and took another tack: semi-Christianization of his Germanic heroic material. "Semi-Christianization" here means the poet's eviction of the heathen gods along with their cults and ritual as functioning parts of a living religion, but the retention of attitudes and values consonant with those of Christianity.

The *Beowulf*-poet is anonymous, so he can only be known to us today through his work. If he was a monk or other professional religious—which is a reasonable hypothesis—he obviously had a great affection for the things and values of the secular world (though his attitude toward them was laced with ambivalence). If he was a chieftain or court poet or itinerant singer wandering, like the fictional bard Widsith, from court to court—another possible hypothesis, though probably a less likely one—he certainly had a deep vein of spirituality.

We know nothing about the poet and nothing specific about his intended audience.[72] That audience could have included cowherds like Caedmon and princes like King Edwin of Northumbria—though not, of course, at the same time. The example of Shakespeare, whose works were sophisticated enough to entertain the "finest spirits" of his age, yet enormously popular among the London apprentices as well, shows that it is not always wise to jump to correlations about literary sophistication and social class in earlier periods. A person reciting or reading *Beowulf* would not have been welcome at a monastery run by Alcuin, but he might very well have found a ready and appreciative audience at Jarrow in the days of the Venerable Bede (who knew a good deal about his people's vernacular poetry and even wrote some himself), and he would certainly have done so at the court of King Alfred the Great a hundred and fifty years later.

So we are reliant on the poem itself for insights into the mind and personality of the man who created it, as well as for any clues about his intentions. Like the singer whom he invents to celebrate his hero's victory over Grendel, he was obviously

> a consummate poet
> who knew and could sing
> numberless tales,
> could relate them in linked

---

72. We *do* know the general contours of his audience, however, thanks to the efforts of Dorothy Whitelock in *The Audience of "Beowulf"* (Oxford: Clarendon Press, 1951).

> language, in words
> arrayed properly. (1736–41)

He had a mind well-stocked with traditional lore and doubtless knew as many tales as the fictive singer Deor (see pp. 184–86). Moreover, he had thought hard about the meaning of his stories and the sometimes complex and conflicting purposes of those who played roles in them. He must have been a keen observer with a thorough understanding of his contemporaries, and a deep insight into their minds and motivations, or he would not have been able to project their behavior so convincingly onto the figures he awakens from the past—so convincingly, indeed, that he often manages to make them *our* contemporaries as well.

The *Beowulf*-poet has a remarkable sensitivity to language, to the resonances and interactions of words, and to the full range of their denotations and connotations, as is apparent everywhere in the poem—never more so than in his extraordinary fertility in compound-formation and his love of thematically relevant wordplay.

He is keenly interested in what constitutes right and wrong behavior, and his yardstick here is mainly—but not exclusively—Christian: the rules for conduct that can be derived from his poem are of universal validity and many of them would appeal to adherents of most spiritual traditions. (An exception, of course, is the hero's—but not necessarily the poet's—ringing endorsement of the vengeance ethic [2768–70].)

In spite of his distance from us in time, the poet's sensibility and way of looking at the world—his *Weltanschauung*—often seem strangely familiar to English speakers, that is, "Northern European" ("Germanic"), not "Mediterranean" ("Greco-Roman"). Hearing or reading his poem we often feel ourselves "at home," in a world of subjectivity, psychological acuity, ready moralizing, and even considerable sentimentality.

He was a sensitive and reflective person with a keen sense of the depth of history, of men's roots and motives stretching far into the past, of societies dying and being succeeded by other societies.[73] He is a pessimist who sees greed, anger, and ignorance operative at all times and places in the human world, the secular world of things, relationships, and politics; he sees tragedy and potential tragedy everywhere. The political world is a world of up-

---

73. The presence in the English landscape all around the Anglo-Saxons of monuments created by the Romans, monuments that evidenced a level of civilization and technology that they themselves would never be able to achieve, made Anglo-Saxons peculiarly sensitive to issues like this, as the poem "A Meditation" so eloquently shows (see pp. 177–83).

heavals, reversals, and betrayals; it offers no safety, no stability, and no certain future. Hence the only way to live life "successfully," to give it dignity and meaning, is to commit oneself to virtue, as Beowulf does. And here, in a conception of heroism that embraces physical strength and prowess, intelligence and wisdom, and a constant readiness to do what one believes to be right and proper, the poet finds his recipe for success in life and death.

It is no surprise that he turns out to be not only what we might call a "realist idealist," but a teacher bent on imparting to his contemporaries a lesson about how to live and die triumphantly. He fashions his central character Beowulf to embody this lesson. He knows that being a hero is not easy: Beowulf had an unpromising boyhood that brought him reproach and shame among his people; he suffered an awful moment of doubt and failure of self-confidence on the very eve of fighting the great dragon; and he died unwillingly and in terrible pain. It was not easy, the poet tells us,

> for the sorely pressed
> son of Ecgtheow
> to relinquish his long
> life in the world,
> destined to dwell
> in a different place,
> like everyone else
> on earth, and surrender
> this brief being. (5173–81)

In his weaknesses as well as his strengths, Beowulf is recognizably "one of us."

The poet, who clearly wants his poem to be a source of instruction as well as entertainment, to combine *utile* and *dulce,* shapes his hero into a model to be imitated by everyone, kings and cowherds alike, each in his (or her) own sphere. The challenges of living life on earth constantly demand heroic behavior of us, the poet seems to say, even if this means no more than getting up early in the morning to feed the pigs, even if it means no less than going out to fight a fiery dragon. It seems likely that the poet of *Beowulf* would have agreed with Robert Louis Stevenson: "You may think this is a hard thing. But did you suppose there is any way in life in which a man is allowed *not* to be a hero?"[74]

---

74. "Address to the Samoan Students at Malua, January, 1890," in Graham Balfour, *The Life of Robert Louis Stevenson* (New York: Charles Scribner's Sons, 1911), II, 227 (emphasis added).

The Meter of the Translation

This translation of *Beowulf* makes no attempt to provide an *exact* replica of the meter of the Old English original, which is a much debated matter in any case, but only a "simulacrum": something similar enough to give a reasonable impression of its characteristic features and qualities. With four important exceptions, the meter of the translation is based on the Sievers/Bliss analysis of the meter of the original, that is, the analysis originally proposed by E. Sievers and later modified in certain respects by A. J. Bliss.[75]

Verses and Lines

The basic metrical unit is the *verse*. Verses range from two to ten syllables in length; most of them are three to seven syllables long. Here is a string of fourteen "normal" verses:

              When I first set out
              on this far adventure
1265   with my faithful thanes,
              I was firmly resolved
              either to end
              the evil plight
              of Denmark forever
1270   or to die fighting
              your ancient enemy,
              either to achieve

---

75. E. Sievers, *Altgermanische Metrik* (Halle, 1893) and A. J. Bliss, *The Metre of Beowulf,* 2nd ed. (Oxford, 1962). The four exceptions are (1) the omission of all verse types involving secondary stress, (2) the elimination of the role played by resolved stress, (3) the introduction of verses of Type F, and (4) the admission of extended anacruses in forestressed verse types A, D, and E. For a complete inventory of the limited number of types allowed in the translation and an illustrative example of each, see the Appendix. For an identification of the type of each of the 6364 verses in the translation, see the free-access Web site http://digital.library.wisc.edu/1711.dl/ Literature.RinglBeowulf. Persons intending to give public readings of this translation, in whole or in part, may want to consult the Web site for guidance and should contact Hackett Publishing Company for permission. Persons interested in the general subject of Germanic prosody will find plenty to chew on in the Appendix in Dick Ringler, *Bard of Iceland: Jónas Hallgrímsson, Poet and Scientist* (University of Wisconsin Press, 2002), 361–84.

                              a mighty victory
                              or to meet death,
       1275   grim and inglorious,
                              in this great wine-hall.

In many modern editions and translations of *Beowulf,* pairs of verses are printed together as *lines,* with a typographical gap separating the two verses of the pair:

               When I first set out   on this far adventure
               with my faithful thanes,   I was firmly resolved
               either to end   the evil plight
               of Denmark forever   or to die fighting
               your ancient enemy,   either to achieve
               a mighty victory   or to meet death,
               grim and inglorious,   in this great wine-hall.

In the surviving manuscript of *Beowulf,* the text is written out as if it were prose,[76] so any modern rearrangement into verses or lines is arbitrary, undertaken by editors and translators in order to highlight certain prosodic features at the expense of others. In the present translation, the individual verses are printed in a single vertical column. This arrangement has the advantage of emphasizing the rhythmic independence of each verse[77] and also enabling

---

76. This practice presented Anglo-Saxon readers with no real obstacle to understanding the metrical structure of the poetry, since this was clearly signposted by the recurrent alliterative patterns (these will be discussed in a moment). In some manuscripts of Old English poetry, additional guidance was provided: individual verses were separated by a simple raised point (*punctus*). Treated in this way, the passage cited in the text would look like this:

when I first set out · on this far adventure · with my faithful thanes · I was firmly resolved · either to end · the evil plight · of denmark forever · or to die fighting · your ancient enemy · either to achieve · a mighty victory · or to meet death · grim and inglorious · in this great wine-hall

77. Bliss presents evidence to suggest that the metrical structure of an individual verse may not be totally independent of the structure of its alliterative companion (135–38). If this is indeed the case, it would be an argument in favor of the line-by-line layout in presentations of the Old English text. It would not, however, have any relevance to the layout of the present translation, in which no *metrical* relationship between two members of an alliterating pair of verses is ever posited.

readers to distinguish at a glance among the three different kinds of verses—normal, light, and heavy—that appear in the translation.[78] It also encourages a more fluent and fast-moving reading of the text than the line-by-line layout (which can sometimes suggest to readers today that Old English poetry was uniformly leisurely and stately—even sluggish—like a good deal of inferior blank verse in Modern English).

Important Note. One consequence of adopting the verse-by-verse layout of the text is that the present translation contains 6364 *verses* instead of the usual 3182 *lines*. This means that to find a corresponding passage in modern editions of the text or other translations, one must *halve* the verse number in the present translation.

Kinds of Verses

The translation contains three different kinds of verses: *normal verses, light verses,* and *heavy verses.*

Normal Verses and Light Verses

A *normal verse* contains two heavily stressed syllables and a variable number of lightly stressed syllables. A *light verse* differs from a normal verse in containing only one heavily stressed syllable. In the translation printed in this book, light verses are distinguished from normal verses by indentation. Here is a string of thirteen normal and light verses:

And now, once again,
noise mounted

1285   in the meadhall,
mirth, revelry,
and proud boasting,
  until presently
Hrothgar decided

1290   to rise and take
his nightly rest;
he knew the enemy
had been waiting to raid
the wondrous hall

1295   all the day long.

---

78. In addition this arrangement has behind it the authority of the Icelandic tradition of printing the eddaic meter *fornyrðislag,* which is cognate with the standard Old English meter of *Beowulf.* See *Bard of Iceland,* 435–36, n. 10.

Both normal verses and light verses can occur at any point in the translation, and their distribution does not reflect the way these two kinds of verses are distributed in the original (where the preference for one kind or the other does not normally appear to have any extra-metrical, or rhetorical, motivation).

Here is the passage again, with heavy (/) and light (x) stresses for a given verse indicated above it:

>   x   /   x   x /
> And now, once again,
>
>   /   /   x
> noise mounted
>
>   x x   /   x
> in the meadhall,
>
>   /   / x x
> mirth, revelry,
>
>   x   /   /   x
> and proud boasting,
>
>   x x   /   x x
> until presently
>
>   /   x   x / x
> Hrothgar decided
>
>   x / x   /
> to rise and take
>
>   x   / x /
> his nightly rest;
>
>   x   /   x   / x x
> he knew the enemy
>
>   x   x   / x x /
> had been waiting to raid
>
>   x   /   x   /
> the wondrous hall
>
>   / x   x   /
> all the day long.

Heavy Verses

Heavy verses are comparatively rare in *Beowulf*. There are only twenty-three in the translation, and all of them occur in exactly the same places as do the twenty-three heavy verses of the original. Heavy verses seem to have been used to underscore important statements (3409–14) or to emphasize emotive aspects of the contexts in which they occur—for example, uneasiness and foreboding (2325–36), or approval and triumph (5989–92). Heavy verses usually—but not always—occur in pairs. Odd-numbered heavy verses contain three heavily stressed syllables; even-numbered heavy verses contain two heavily stressed syllables, like normal verses, but a greater number of anacruses (i.e., lightly stressed introductory syllables) than are permitted in normal verses. In the present translation, heavy verses are distinguished from normal verses by being extended to the left beyond the normal-verse margin. Here is a string of fifteen normal and heavy verses:

        the king of the Geats,
        the heir of Hrethel,
        gave Eofor and Wulf
5985   unwonted wealth
        to reward their valor:
        a hundred thousand
        hides of folk-land,
        farmsteads of fabulous value;
5990   nor could he be faulted for that largess,
        idly censured by others,
        since they had earned it in battle;
        and Eofor got the king's
        only daughter
5995   as a prize for his hearth
        and a pledge of favor.

Here is the passage again, with heavy and light stresses indicated:

  x / x x   /
the king of the Geats,

  x / x / x
the heir of Hrethel,

   x / x x   /
gave Eofor and Wulf

   x / x   /
unwonted wealth

  x x / x   / x
to reward their valor:

```
x  /  x   /   x
```
a hundred thousand

```
   /  x  /   x
```
hides of folk-land,

```
 /   x  x  / x x  / x
```
farmsteads of fabulous value;

```
x   x   x x  /  x  x  x   /  x
```
nor could he be faulted for that largess,

```
/ x  /  x   x  /  x
```
idly censured by others,

```
x    x   x    /   x x  / x
```
since they had earned it in battle;

```
   x  /  x  x  x   /
```
and Eofor got the king's

```
 /  x   /   x
```
only daughter

```
x x  /   x  x   /
```
as a prize for his hearth

```
 x  x   /   x  / x
```
and a pledge of favor.

Alliteration

Structural alliteration—alliteration that occurs in regular recurring patterns and is therefore an element of formal structure—is obligatory in both the Old English original of *Beowulf* and the present translation. It may well be this characteristic feature of Old English verse that the *Beowulf*-poet refers to when he praises Hrothgar's court poet for telling tales "in linked / language, in words / arrayed properly" (1739–41).

The word "alliteration" denotes a correspondence between the initial sounds of heavily stressed syllables, thus *big* and *bat; single, cycle,* and *psychic; quarter* and *akimbo; nebulous* and *Scandinavia; ache, eight,* and *creation.* Note that alliteration involves a correspondence of *sounds,* irrespective of their *spelling;* also that alliterating stressed syllables can occur *within* words as well as at their beginning.[79]

---

79. On a few occasions in the present translation, alliteration reflects the way the

In the present translation, a given Modern English sound normally alliterates only with itself, as in the examples just provided. But there are some special cases:

— any vowel or diphthong alliterates with any other vowel or diphthong, thus

> Otherwise, *ever*
> *a*fter, he is doomed

— each of the following sounds alliterates only with itself, never with any of the others (or with simple *s-*):

> *sh-* (as in "*sh*allow" or "as*s*urance")
> *sk-* (as in "*sk*ull" or "*sq*uare")
> *sp-* (as in "*sp*eed")
> *st-* (as in "*st*urdy")

— the sound [w], however spelled (e.g., whether as in "*w*ant" or as in "on*c*e") alliterates with the sound [wh] (as in "*wh*ite" or "*wh*ale")[80]
— the sound [r] (as in "*r*apid" or "ar*r*est") alliterates with the sound [hr] (as in "*H*r*othgar")

Distribution of Alliterants

In odd-numbered normal verses, either the *first* heavily stressed syllable or *both* heavily stressed syllables alliterate with the first heavily stressed syllable of the even-numbered verse that follows. In even-numbered normal verses, the first of the two heavily stressed syllables—and *only* the first—alliterates with the alliterating syllable(s) of the preceding odd-numbered verse.[81] Thus we find both

---

text is actually pronounced, not the way it is conventionally spelled or syllabicated. For example,

| they *n*ever bring it | or | Moreover, *wr*itten |
| a*n* ounce of profit | | in *r*unic symbols |

80. Here and in the paragraph that follows, the sounds in question are represented in the alphabet of the International Phonetic Association (IPA).
81. The alliteration of weakly stressed syllables is "accidental" and metrically irrelevant.

5	how the *g*reat war-chiefs	[odd-numbered normal verse]
	*g*ained their renown	[following even-numbered normal verse]

and

9	*m*astered the *m*eadhalls	[odd-numbered normal verse]
	of *m*any peoples	[following even-numbered normal verse]

In light verses, which can also—like normal verses—occur in either odd- or even-numbered position, the single heavily stressed syllable alliterates with the alliterating syllable(s) in its companion verse; for example,

143	the *g*ifts *G*od	[odd-numbered normal verse]
	had *gi*ven him	[following even-numbered light verse]

or

87	than the *w*arriors	[odd-numbered light verse]
	who had *o*nce sent him	[following even-numbered normal verse]

In odd-numbered heavy verses, two of the three heavily stressed syllables alliterate with each other. In even-numbered heavy verses, the first of the two heavily stressed syllables alliterates with the alliterating syllables of its companion verse (see 3409–14 in the following example).

Here is a string of normal, heavy, and light verses that illustrates various alliteration patterns:

	As a *k*ing who tries
3400	to en*c*ourage truth
	a*m*ong his people,
	and who re*m*embers days
	*s*unk in darkness,
	I *s*ay this warrior
3405	was *b*orn a hero!
	*B*eowulf, my friend,
	your *f*ame has reached out
	to *f*ar peoples,
	*m*en in re*m*otest regions!

3410   Because you have both *m*ight and wisdom,
       *f*ierceness in *f*ighting and judgment,
       I am not a*f*raid to support you
       *f*ully with my *f*riendly counsels.
       In the *f*uture, I reckon,
3415   you will *b*e your land's
           *b*lessing and hope,
           un*l*ike our *l*ate
           *l*ord Heremod,
           who *b*rought no *b*lessing
3420   but *b*loodshed, grief,
           *d*anger, and *d*eath
           to the *D*anish race,
           the *h*ei*r*s of Ecgwela.
           In his *a*ngry fits
3425   he *k*illed his *c*omrades
           and *c*lose associates
           until *f*orced to *f*lee
              his *f*atherland
           and the de*l*ights of men,
3430   a for*l*orn exile.

It is a serious error to regard the meter of Old English poetry, especially as it is used by the *Beowulf*-poet, as in any sense primitive or clumsy. Nothing could be farther from the truth. Although this meter is based on—and reflects—the ordinary speech patterns and usages of the language, it is a flexible and highly sensitive instrument, ideally suited to the creation and oral delivery of poetry. In spite of its apparent simplicity, it can serve remarkably sophisticated purposes, complementing the poet's frequently brilliant diction. Like that diction, it reflects the sophistication of the aristocratic and courtly milieu that fostered and promoted the poetry.[82]

Furthermore the regularly occurring but constantly varying alliteration sequences of Old English verse are not merely decorative but highly functional, helping to maintain its momentum: this is of great importance in a long,

---

82. We are indebted to Edith Sitwell for one of the most absurd and misleading statements ever made about Old English poetry: "The earliest English poetry of all, with its crude and unskilled thumping, or creaking, alliteration, echoes the sound of those earthy occupations which accompany the work of food-getting" (Edith Sitwell, *A Poet's Notebook* [London: Macmillan and Co., 1943], 59).

action-filled work like *Beowulf*.[83] Moreover, the alliterative requirement gives the text firm formal shape and keeps it from dithering or sprawling. It is not so rigorous, however, that it inhibits the free expression of ideas or obstructs the flow of the narrative. The alliteration, important though it is, rarely calls attention to itself, and rarely becomes obtrusive or even especially noticeable, except in passages where that is precisely the effect intended by the poet.

To get a sense of what the present translation is intended to sound like, consult the free-access Web site, Beowulf: A New Translation for Oral Delivery (http://digital.library.wisc.edu/1711.dl/Literature.Ringl Beowulf). This Web site contains a streamed sound file of the entire text, read by the translator. Also available (as a three-CD set), is a semi-dramatization of the full text, read by the translator and professional actors from the American Players Theatre and the Guthrie Theatre, with music and sound effects. This can be obtained from the University of Wisconsin Press.

---

83. Especially important in this regard is the fact that—both in the original and in the translation—the beginning of new syntactic units is often "out of phase" with (i.e., does not coincide with) the onset of new alliterative pairs, as for example, in two places in the following passage (1679–80 and 1683–84). As a result, a given alliterative pair often straddles separate syntactic units, thereby driving the verse forward:

	Folk-chiefs had traveled
	from *f*ar and near
	to *st*are at a marvel:
1680	the *st*range being
	had *l*eft behind him
	*l*arge, bloody
	*f*ootprints in the ground.
	His *f*ate gratified
	*m*en who followed
	that *m*onstrous spoor.

Appendix

Light and Normal Verse-Types Permitted in the Present Translation, with Examples

The designations of the verse-types are modeled on those in A. J. Bliss's analysis (*The Metre of Beowulf*, Appendix C, Table II, 123–27) and so are the permitted distributions. (Note that all types with secondary stress have been eliminated.) In the three columns on the right, the symbol ✓ shows that a verse of the type in question is permitted in the position indicated: Position *A* is odd-numbered verses with double alliteration; Position *B* is odd-numbered verses with single alliteration; Position *C* is even-numbered verses. In places where the ✓ is replaced by a figure, the figure serves the same purpose and *also* indicates the permitted number of anacruses. (This number has been determined by adding one extra anacrusis to those allowed in forestressed verses of this type according to Bliss's analysis in Appendix C, Table III, 127.)

Heavy (i.e., "hypermetric") verses occur in the translation at the same points that they do in the original (see Bliss, Index, 162). On the structural models for such verses, see Bliss, Appendix D, Table II, 130–33 (but note that these models are drawn from the whole corpus of Old English verse, not just from *Beowulf*).

Verse-Type		Example	Distributions		
			A	*B*	*C*
Light verses					
a1b	x x / x	as your leader (497)		✓	
a1c	x x x / x	if the attacker (2663)		✓	
a1d	x x x x / x	And we are unlikely (5843)		✓	
a1e	x x x x x / x	and could not be dissuaded (1019)		✓	
d1a	x / x x	like icicles (3215)		✓	✓
d1b	x x / x x	than the warriors (87)		✓	✓

Verse-Type		Example	Distributions		
			A	B	C
d1c	x x x / x x	If you are curious (687)		✓	✓
d1d	x x x x / x x	and it was a miracle (1541)		✓	✓
e1b	x x /	on the bench (2381)		✓	
e1c	x x x /	they had been told (2693)		✓	
e1d	x x x x /	though before tonight (1435)		✓	
e1e	x x x x x /	but it was reinforced (1545)		✓	

Normal verses

Verse-Type		Example	A	B	C
1A1a(i)	/ | x / x	moors | and marshes (207)	2	1	2
1A1a(ii)	/ | x / x x	stripped | of ornaments (5522)	1		1
1A1b(i)	/ | x x / x	doomed | and despairing (1700)	3	1	1
1A1b(ii)	/ | x x / x x	grim | and inglorious (1275)	1		
1A1c	/ | x x x / x	now | and in the future (2444)	1		1
1A*1a(i)	/ x | x / x	Glory | in battle (127)	2	1	1
1A*1a(ii)	/ x x | x / x	Herebeald | and Hæthcyn (4867)	1		
1A*1b	/ x | x x / x	diving | through the water (3238)	2		1
1A*1c	/ x | x x x / x	seem senseless. | It was precisely (4923)[84]	1		1
1A*2a(ii)	/ x | x / x x	illness | or accident (3525)	1		
1D1	/ | / x x	high | destiny (6170)	2	1	1
1D*1(i)	/ x | / x x	Swooping | suddenly (3001)	1		
1D*1(ii)	/ x x | / x x	Woe-stricken | warriors (6355)	1		
2A1a(i)	/ x | / x	famous | children (118)	1	1	1

---

84. This verse contains an anacrusis.

Verse-Type		Example	Distributions		
			A	B	C
2A1a(ii)	/ x l / x x	Hrothgar's l sentinel (458)		1	1
2A1a(iii)	/ x x l / x	glorious l treasures (4206)	1		1
2B1-	/ l x /	wet l with blood (2571)		✓	
2B1a	x / l x /	the sun l and moon (188)	✓		✓
2B1b	x x / l x /	will support l their prince (47)	✓	✓	✓
2B1c	x x x / l x /	and on campaigns l abroad (2496)		✓	✓
2B1d	x x x x / l x /	before he embraced l the pyre (5636)			✓
2B2-	/ l x x /	bright l from the forge (610)			✓
2B2a	x / l x x /	his name l was renowned (15)	✓	✓	✓
2B2b	x x / l x x /	to the edge l of the sea (57)	✓	✓	✓
2B2c	x x x / l x x /	I must go back l to the coast (636)			✓
2B2d	x x x x / l x x /	though he was a lad l when I once (744)			✓
2C1-	/ l / x	twelve l winters (296)		✓	✓
2C1a	x / l / x	a dread l demon (171)	✓	✓	✓
2C1b	x x / l / x	of the wide l ocean (90)	✓	✓	✓
2C1c	x x x / l / x	so it is less l likely (675)	✓	✓	✓
2E1a	/ x l x /	mailcoats l and swords (77)	✓	✓	✓
2E1b	/ x l x x /	soaring l to the clouds (153)		1	1
3B1a	x / x l /	the surging l sea (19)	✓	✓	✓
3B1b	x x / x l /	from his father's l hoard (41)	✓	✓	✓
3B1c	x x x / x l /	beneath the solemn l bluffs (421)	✓	✓	✓
3B1d	x x x x / x l /	it was in a frenzy l now (4607)	✓	✓	✓
3B1e	x x x x x / x l /	Although it is a dragon's l style (4550)			✓
3B2b	x x / x x l /	inexperienced l men (4036)			✓

Verse-Type		Example	Distributions		
			A	B	C
3B2c	x x x / x x l /	in that unnatural l hall (3140)			✓
3B*1a	x / x l x /	a creature l of hell (202)	✓	✓	✓
3B*1b	x x / x l x /	you have brought it l to pass (1907)	✓	✓	✓
3B*1c	x x x / x l x /	from the beginning l of time (1403)	✓	✓	✓
3B*1d	x x x x / x l x /	and who was already l at work (1742)		✓	✓
3B*1e	x x x x x / x l x /	because they had assaulted l the Geats (846)			✓
3E1	/ x x l /	fabulous l wealth (73)	1	1	1
3E*1	/ x x l x /	Beowulf l the Geat (2382)	1	1	1
3F1-	/ l /	matched l bays (4327)	✓	✓	✓
3F1a	x / l /	the sweet l mead (991)	✓	✓	✓
3F1b	x x / l /	As the years l passed (292)	✓	✓	✓
3F1c	x x x / l /	if it is fate's l will (559)	✓	✓	✓
3F1d	x x x x / l /	they should have the same l rights (2175)	✓	✓	✓

[Prologue]

We have heard tell
of the high doings
of Danish kings
in days gone by,
how the great war-chiefs
gained their renown,
how Scyld Scefing
shattered his foes,
mastered the meadhalls
10   of many peoples,
conquered their kings.
He came to Denmark
as a lone foundling,
but later he thrived;
his name was renowned
beneath the skies
and kings and kingdoms
across the whale-road,
the surging sea,
20   swore him allegiance,
paid him tribute.
He was a peerless king!
Later the Lord
of life gave him
a son who would someday
succeed him in Denmark,
a pledge to its people:

their plight had moved him,
their time of trial
30   and terrible grief
lacking a leader.
The Lord bestowed
success and honor
on this son of Scyld,
and Beowulf the Dane
could boast a name
known everywhere
   in Scandinavia.
In just such a manner,
40   with generous gifts
from his father's hoard,
a future king
insures that one day
unshrinking friends
will stand by his side
if strife should come,
will support their prince:
it is praiseworthy deeds
that win warriors'
50   willing allegiance.
At his foreshaped hour
Scyld departed,
grey-haired, vigorous,
into God's keeping.
Care-stricken comrades
carried his body
to the edge of the sea,
honoring the wish
he had made when still
60   master of his speech,
he who had so long
held the kingdom.
His ring-beaked ship
was ready to sail,
ice-clad, impatient,
eager for the voyage.

They laid their beloved
lord in its hold,
rested their ring-giver
70   in its roomy hull
near the heel of the mast.
They heaped beside him
fabulous wealth
from far-off lands;
I have never heard
of such magnificent things,
mailcoats and swords
    and mask-helmets
and bright war-shields;
80   on his breast lay many
dazzling jewels
destined to travel
to the far reaches
of the flood's domain.
His men equipped him
with much more treasure
    than the warriors
who had once sent him
wandering the wastes
90   of the wide ocean,
alone and friendless,
a little child.
Finally the Danes
affixed a golden
standard above him,
let the stream have him,
the sea-surge take him.
Their souls were troubled,
numb with mourning.
100   No man on earth,
not even the wisest,
can ever know
or say for certain
who received that cargo.

I

When Scyld Scefing's
ship had set sail,
leaving behind
the land of the Danes,
they crowned Beowulf
110   king in his stead
and for many years
he remained their leader.
His highborn son
Healfdene followed
and ruled in his turn
the realm of Denmark,
fathering four
famous children
who were given by God
120   to this great war-king:
Heorogar, Hrothgar,
Halga the Good,
and a blithe daughter,
the bride of Onela,
sweet bedfellow
of the Swedish king.
Glory in battle
was given to Hrothgar,
fortune in war,
130   so his followers all
obeyed him gladly
and his band of young
comrades increased.
It occurred to him then
to command a mighty
meadhall to be built,
richer and rarer
than the race of men
had ever seen
140   on earth before,
and in that stately hall
to distribute all

the gifts God
  had given him,
except for public land
and people's lives.
They tell us he assigned
the task of building
that marvelous meadhall
150   to many races
from around the earth.
It rose quickly,
soaring to the clouds,
and soon it was finished,
noblest of buildings.
He named it Heorot,
he whose word and will
had wide dominion.
He stood by his vow,
160   distributing gold
from the hoard, while high
overhead the great
wooden rafters
waited for floods
of fire to enfold them,
for the fated day
when the tragic hate
of two in-laws
would flash into flame,
170   into fierce warfare.
A dread demon
who dwelt in the shadows
daily endured
desperate pain,
obliged to listen
to the bright music
of heroes in hall,
the harp ringing
to the song of the singer
180   singing the story
of earth's creation
ages ago,

how almighty God
made this glorious
world of wonders
washed by the sea,
how he set on high
the sun and moon
as undying lights
190   for dwellers on earth
and trimmed the distant
tracts of the world
with branches and leaves,
bringing forth life
in every kind
of earthly creature.
Thus Hrothgar's thanes
reveled in joys,
feasting and drinking,
200   until their foe started
    his persecutions,
a creature of hell.
Grendel, they called him,
this grim spoiler,
a demon who prowled
the dark borderlands,
moors and marshes,
a man-eating giant
who had lived in a lair
210   in the land of monsters
ever since God
    had outlawed him
along with the rest
of the line of Cain.
Abel's murder
had angered the Lord,
who avenged that deed
of violence on Cain,
driving him far
220   from the dwellings of men.
Spooks and spirits
are spawned from his seed,

elves and goblins
and evil ghouls
and those bold giants
who rebelled against God,
asking for trouble.
They earned their reward!

II

When darkness came
230   the demon set out
for the silent hall
to see how the Danes
had bedded down in it
   after their beer-drinking.
They were sound asleep,
sated and carefree
   after the banquet,
a band of warriors
slumbering softly
240   without sorrow or dread.
He attacked them at once
with terrible swiftness,
grimly, greedily
grabbing from their beds
thirty unlucky
thanes of the king,
gloating, glorying
in the grisly deed,
then shambling home
250   with his shameful spoil.
Later, in the grey
light of morning,
his vast violence
was revealed to men.
Weeping was heard
in the wake of laughter,
noises of lament.
Noble Hrothgar,

the best of rulers,
260   sat bowed with grief,
dazed by the dreadful
death of his friends,
while he gazed at the ghastly
gore-spattered track
left by the monster.
That lethal assault
by night was his first,
but the next evening
he again raided
270   the great meadhall
murdering many
men brutally,
prowling pitiless
    and impenitent.
    And afterward
it was easy enough
to find heroes
who preferred sleeping
    in the outbuildings,
280   once the evil fiend's
mayhem was made
manifest to all,
the marks of his malice:
men who escaped
those cruel clutches
found quarters elsewhere.
The ruthless marauder
ravaged Heorot,
one against many,
290   until the wide ale-hall
stood unused at night.
As the years passed
the Danish king
sank deeper in sorrow;
it was a tragic time,
twelve winters.
The ogre's evil
went on so long

that news of his raids
300   was known everywhere,
leaping from land
to land in songs,
how Grendel warred
grimly with Hrothgar,
fought with him fiercely,
feuded season
after sad season,
sought no parley
of peace, no pact
310   with the prostrate Danes,
and was deaf to demands
     for indemnity;
the king's councilors
had no cause to expect
rich reparation
from the ravager's hoard!
Instead the monster
stalked and slaughtered
old men and young,
320   an eerie death-shadow
lurking at night,
lying in ambush
on the misty moors.
Men never know
where wandering fiends
wait in the dark!
And so the sinister
slayer of men
roamed in blackness
330   and reveled in crime,
ravaging the hall,
ranging its shadows
and dim depths
in the dead of night,
for the Lord never
allowed him the joy
of that bright building
in broad daylight.

It was a cruel fate
340   for the king of the Danes,
misery of mind!
His men often
assembled in council,
seeking a way
to end Grendel's
evil attacks
and sudden onslaughts.
Sometimes they practiced
demon worship
350   at dark altars,
offered sacrifice,
asked the Devil,
    the soul-slayer,
to send them help
in their dreadful need:
a damnable custom,
the hope of heathens.
Hell had possession
of their erring minds;
360   they were ignorant
of the Light of life,
the Lord almighty,
and of how to pray
to heaven's King,
the God of glory.
Grim is the lot
of heedless men
who hurl their souls
into the clutch of fire,
370   who cut themselves off
from grace forever!
Glorious the lot
of men who rely
on the Almighty for peace
and who find mercy
in the Father's arms.

III

Thus Healfdene's son
was harrowed by grief,
by sorrow that seldom
380   ceased churning.
Nothing could help him:
the nightly assaults
were too terrible
and too prolonged,
the dark bedevilment
dogging his people.
But at long last,
in the land of the Geats,
Hygelac's thane
390   heard about Grendel.
In that day
of this life
no earthly man
had equal strength
or equal courage.
He asked for a swift
seagoing ship,
said he intended
to visit Hrothgar
400   over the vast waters,
now that the war-king
was in need of help.
Much as they loved him,
men did not try
to dissuade the prince
from his set purpose
but urged him on.
The omens were propitious.
He chose from among
410   his choicest followers
a keen company
of comrades, the bravest
he could find in the land.
With fourteen others,

a seasoned sailor,
he sought out his ship,
leading the way
to land's end.
With little delay
420   they launched the vessel
beneath the solemn bluffs.
Excited mariners
clambered aboard
while currents swirled,
the surf on the sand.
Seamen of the Geats,
laughing with pleasure,
loaded the hold
with burnished swords
430   and bright armor,
then shoved the nail-clinched
ship out to sea.
Spurred by gusts
it splashed and scudded
through the wild waters
like a wind-blown bird,
     until by noon
the next day
the swift vessel
440   had made such headway
that the lookout at last
saw land ahead,
wide sea-cliffs,
windswept, sunswept,
and vast headlands.
The voyage was over,
the sea had been crossed,
and sailors leapt
into the welcome surf
450   and waded ashore.
They moored the vessel,
their mailcoats rustling,
and gave grateful thanks
to God almighty

that their sea-crossing
had been safe and easy.
From rocks up above them
Hrothgar's sentinel,
whose task was to guard
460 and patrol the sea-cliffs,
saw strangers who bore
stout battle-gear
and sturdy war-shields
striding down the gangplank;
he needed to know
who these newcomers were.
Mounting his horse
he made for the beach,
brandished his spear
470 and bluntly challenged
the foreign sailors
with formal words:
"Who are you, you unknown
ironclad men,
alien troops
armed in mailcoats,
bringing your boat
from abroad, crossing
the sounding sea?
480 I have served for years
as coastguard here,
carefully watching
to defend these shores
against foes meaning
to wreak havoc
in the realm of the Danes.
Never before
have unknown sailors
landed on our coast
490 with less concealment,
even though you came
without asking leave
of noble Hrothgar;
never before

have I seen a man
of such eminence
    as your leader
in his lordly mail,
a hero, I think,
500 no hall-sloucher,
    unless he is counterfeit!
Quickly, now, tell me
what land you come from,
before I let you proceed
a league farther
in the land of the Danes—
spies, perhaps!
Suspicious voyagers!
Seafarers! hear
510 my simple thought:
    it would be wise of you—
you would be well advised!—
to tell me instantly
what tribe you come from."

IV

The bold captain
of the band of comrades
quickly replied
in careful words:
    "We are mariners,
520 men of the Geats,
hearth companions
of Hygelac our king.
My father was famous
for his fierce warfare,
a noble chieftain;
his name was Ecgtheow.
He had a long life
and at last he died,
wise and worshipful.
530 War-chiefs of even

modest wisdom
remember him still!
As for us, we have come
in honest friendship,
seeking your king,
the son of Healfdene.
Kindly give us counsel!
We carry important
news for your master,
540 for noble Hrothgar,
though only when we meet
can it all be disclosed,
not before.
You know if the tales
they have told us are true,
the terrible stories
that among the Danes,
when midnight approaches,
some awful monster
550 (but I have only heard
shadowy hints!)
shows his hatred,
gorging on their flesh.
I can give Hrothgar
some useful advice,
young though I am,
how the king and his comrades
can quell this monster,
if it is fate's will
560 that he should find relief,
      consolation
for his long sorrows,
and his dread and despair
are destined to end.
Otherwise, ever
after, he is doomed
to live in anguish,
as long as his great
hall-building stands
570 with its high gables."

The coastguard replied
in careful language
where he sat on his horse:
"A seasoned warrior
has the wisdom to weigh
both words and actions,
to assess their worth.
I perceive clearly
    that you seafarers
580   are sincere friends
of the king of the Danes.
Keep your weapons
and travel onward.
I will teach you the way.
    And I will also
order my men
to guard your vessel
with great vigilance
from foes, where it lies
590   all freshly caulked
with tar on the sand,
until the time comes
when the splendid ship
with its spiral prow
bears the hero
back to his homeland.
So gallant a man,
so great in virtue,
is bound to survive
600   battle unharmed."
Men started moving,
marching inland;
motionless, the ship
lay moored behind them,
tethered tightly.
On top of their helmets,
    above cheek-guards
of chased silver,
bronze boar-figures
610   bright from the forge

protected them.
The troop, advancing
at a smart pace,
soon caught a glimpse
of the hall Heorot,
high and glittering,
Hrothgar's residence,
radiant with gold,
the best, most brilliant
620   building on earth,
lighting the land
for leagues around it.
Pausing, the coastguard
pointed it out
to the keen warband,
so they might more quickly make
their way to its door,
then wheeled his horse
and spoke in parting
630   to the resplendent troop:
"I must leave you here.
May the Lord almighty,
the King and Father,
keep you from harm
in this bold venture.
I must go back to the coast
to hold sea-watch
against hostile fleets."

V

A pathway with stone
640   paving guided
the marching men.
Their mailcoats gleamed,
and the hard rings
of handlocked iron
sang noisy war-songs
as they neared the hall

for the first time
in their fierce array.
Sea-weary sailors
650   unslung their shields
and leaned them slanting
against the long wall.
Mailcoats rustled
as men wearily
sank onto benches,
while their slim spear-shafts
still stood upright,
a stand of ash-trees
grey on top.
660   Those good weapons
were an honor to their owners.
An eagle-eyed sentry
who stood in the doorway
studied them closely.
"What country do you come from
with your curved shields,
your meshed war-shirts
    and mask-helmets,
your iron spears?
670   I am the herald
of noble Hrothgar.
I have never seen
so bold or brave
a band of foreigners,
so it is less likely
that you are landless strays
than valiant adventurers
visiting my king."
The man of the Geats,
680   the mariners' chief,
presently replied
in the pride of his youth:
"In our homeland we sit
at Hygelac's table,
next to our master.
My name is Beowulf.

If you are curious
why I came to Denmark,
I would rather explain
690   to Hrothgar himself,
Healfdene's son,
if the high war-king
will only grant us
an audience."
The other answered,
an eminent Wendel
whose name, Wulfgar,
was known among men
for truth and wisdom:
700   "I will tell Hrothgar
my ring-giver,
ruler of the Scyldings,
about your visit here,
will convey the news
to my king
as you request me to,
and will come back at once
to bring you the reply
my dread master
710   deigns to give you."
He walked rapidly
to where the wise one sat,
immensely old
in the midst of his thanes;
he strode firmly
until he stood at last,
polite and proper,
in his lord's presence.
Wulfgar saluted
720   the war-king of Denmark:
"Mighty Hrothgar!
Men of the Geats
have come to our shores,
cruising the wide
waste of waters.
Warriors call

the leader Beowulf.
My lord Hrothgar!
Their only desire
730   is to ask humbly
    to speak with you,
O splendor of kings.
Do not deny them
their deepest wish!
    In their war-harness
they are worthy, I think,
of a prince's approval.
An impressive youth,
a hero, has led them
740   here to our land."

VI

Hrothgar replied,
ruler of Denmark:
"I recollect him well,
though he was a lad when I once
befriended Ecgtheow
his father, to whom Hrethel,
the Geatish king,
had given his daughter.
Their son Beowulf
750   has sought us now,
looking for a loyal
and reliable friend.
Voyagers of ours,
visiting the Geats,
taking them gifts
and tokens of love,
have told us often,
after returning home,
that the hero's hard
760   hand-grip has in it
thirty men's strength.
I think it likely

that God almighty
has graciously sent him
here to Denmark
to help us in our struggle
against Grendel's attacks.
I will give this youth
wealth in abundance
770   to reward his daring.
Return to them at once
and tell them to enter
and look on my court
of loyal kinsmen.
Let your words warrant
how welcome they are
here in Heorot!"
The herald returned
and said loudly
780   from inside the doorway:
"My sapient lord
has sent me back
to announce that he knows
your noble lineage
and to give such great
and glorious heroes
a loving welcome
in the land of the Danes.
You may now enter
790   his renowned presence
wearing your mailcoats
    and war-helmets;
but leave your lances
and lindenwood shields
outside here to await
the success of your words."
Beowulf stood up,
about him a throng
of tried retainers.
800   He told some of them
to wait there, guarding
    their weaponry;

the rest hurried
under the roof of the hall,
guided by Wulfgar.
Their great-hearted leader
strode to the high-seat,
stood facing it
and spoke, conspicuous
810   in his splendid mail,
the wonderful workmanship
of Wayland the smith:
"Hail, great Hrothgar!
I am Hygelac's thane
and kinsman. Though young,
I have acquired honor
through gallant deeds.
Grendel's outrages
are known everywhere
820   in my native land:
many visiting
merchants have told us
    that nowadays
this magnificent hall
stands idle and useless,
empty of men,
as soon as the sun
has set in the west.
I was urged, therefore,
830   by my own people,
    by the worthiest
and wisest among them,
to come to the court
of King Hrothgar.
They knew my nearly
preternatural strength;
they had watched when I strode,
washed in battle-blood,
from a fight where I fettered
840   five enemies,
butchered some giants
who were bent on mischief,

and slew monsters
in the sea at night;
I slaughtered those foes
because they had assaulted the Geats;
I ground them to gruel.
Now it is Grendel's turn
to feel the fury
850 of my fierce grip,
my lethal wrath.
Lord of the Danes!
Prince of the Scyldings!
I implore you now,
when I have come so far
from my country to ask
your dear indulgence:
do not refuse me
one request,
860 O worthy Hrothgar,
   but allow me,
alone with only
my comrades here,
to cleanse Heorot.
Men have told me
that our murderous friend
scoffs at weapons,
scornful and reckless,
so I swear solemnly
870 that as I seek to deserve
the heartfelt love
of Hygelac my lord,
I will not carry
my noble sword
into battle, but fight
with my bare hands,
fiercely and fearlessly,
fully prepared
to win or to lose;
880   for one of us
must die, submitting
to the doom of God.

The terror master
will try, if he can,
to dine on us Geats
in the dark meadhall
    as easily
as he has always enjoyed
having Danes for dinner.
890   If death should take me,
noble Hrothgar,
you need not give me
a big funeral
or bury my corpse,
for he will have it:
he will haul my bloody
carcass away
crushed in his jaws.
You will not even
900   need to provide me
with meals or a bed
a moment longer.
    If he should slay me,
send Hygelac
the grey mailcoat
that guards my breast,
the work of Wayland;
it was once King Hrethel's.
Well, fate is certain
910   to unfold as it must."

VII

The peerless king
replied: "You have come here
to repay a debt
of past kindness.
Once, in the country
of the Wylfings, your sire
killed Heatholaf,
kindling such a feud

that afterward even
920 his own people
dared not harbor him,
dreading reprisals.
An outcast, exiled
by his own Geats,
he fled to Denmark
to find asylum.
I was barely more
than a boy at the time,
just beginning my reign
930 in this great kingdom;
my older brother,
the heir to the throne,
Healfdene's son
Heorogar the prince,
a heroic youth,
had recently died,
an abler warrior
than I. I settled
your father's feud,
940 freely sending
the Wylfings treasure
over the wide ocean.
I saved your father;
he swore me allegiance.
    It is bitter
to be obliged to tell
anyone on earth
what awful grief
Grendel has caused me
950 with his grim hate-thoughts
and dreadful attacks.
My dear war-band
dwindled as fate
dashed them away
into Grendel's maw.
God, if he wished it,
could easily end
this orgy of death.

Emboldened by beer,
960   my best warriors
would often, emptying
their ale-cups, vow
to wait for Grendel
and his wild onslaught
here in the meadhall
with hard war-swords.
But when the light of dawn
at last appeared,
these spacious walls
970   would be spattered with gore,
the bench-planks splashed
with bloody stains,
the floor dripping.
My faithful band
had shrunk once again,
shamefully butchered.
Now sit at the banquet
and say what you think;
tell us how you hope
980   to triumph over Grendel."
Benches were cleared
in the bright meadhall
    so the seafarers
could sit together;
strong in spirit,
those sturdy warriors
assumed their places.
A servant presently
brought them embossed
990   beer-cups and poured
the sweet mead.
Sometimes the poet
with his ringing voice
would rouse the company
of Danes and seamen
drinking together.

VIII

Unferth, the son
of Ecglaf, was sitting
at the king's feet;
1000   he was court spokesman.
Bristling, he broached
a battle challenge;
Beowulf's unbidden
bold arrival
annoyed him enormously,
since he was never pleased
     when anyone
was honored more
or more highly esteemed
1010   than he was. "Are you
the Beowulf," he said,
"whom Breca defeated
and soundly trounced
in a swimming match?
The pair of you agreed
out of pride and folly
to race in the ocean
at the risk of your lives
     and could not be dissuaded
1020   by a soul on earth,
neither friend nor foe,
from this freakish scheme.
You paddled out
into the pitching waves,
embraced the breakers
in bold folly,
climbed them with arms
crazily flailing
as you slogged through the spray.
1030   For seven nights
the two of you tirelessly
toiled in the icy
billows of winter.
He beat you soundly;

he was much stronger.
In the morning the waves
washed him ashore
in the wild country
    of the Battle-Rams,
1040   from where the brave hero
at last reached his home,
the land of the Brondings,
and his high gift-throne,
where he handed out rings
and swayed his subjects.
The son of Beanstan
scored a great success
and made good his vow.
And thus, though from this
1050   or that fracas
you may, possibly,
have emerged unharmed,
you will find your match,
I fancy, if you wait
here in this meadhall
for a whole night."
The prince of the Geats
replied with a grin:
"Friend Unferth,
1060   fuddled with beer
you've been babbling away
about Breca's deeds.
No one but me
knows what happened.
I have shown more strength
and shared more hardship
in the ocean than any
other warrior.
Breca and I,
1070   when both of us
were mere children,
made an agreement
to wager our lives
in the wintry sea,

to demonstrate our daring.
We did so, too,
brandishing bright
blades in our fists
to fight off whales
1080   in the freezing waves.
Breca could never
have bettered my speed
or swum more swiftly
in the surges, while I
was reluctant to leave him
lagging behind me.
We fought with the flood
for five nights,
swimming side by side,
1090   until a sudden storm
and deep darkness
drove us apart.
Battle-fierce blasts
blew from the north
straight in our faces,
stirring up the depths,
exciting the sea-monsters,
who swarmed to attack me.
But my hard mailcoat
1100   helped me withstand them:
grey and hand-linked,
it guarded my breast
with its thousands of rings,
and thwarted their malice.
Then an obscene sea-beast
seized me, dragging me
down to the deepest
depths of the ocean
fast in its clutches;
1110   but fate was with me
and let me skewer
the loathsome brute
with my iron blade:
I was able to kill

that evil creature
with my own hand.

IX

This only provoked
the other horrors
    into pursuing me;
1120   but I served them all,
right and proper,
with my wrathful blade,
and the nasty things
took no pleasure
in their bestial attempts
to batten on me,
sitting round a feast
    on the sea-bottom.
When morning came
1130   they were mere flotsam
littering the beach,
lulled into sleep
by iron music,
and ever since
they have ceased to be
a serious menace
to sailors at sea.
    The sun came up,
God's bright beacon;
1140   the gale subsided,
and soon I saw
sea-cliffs in the distance,
fair and windswept.
Fate spares warriors
whose days are not numbered
and who do their utmost.
With my mighty sword
I managed to kill
nine sea-monsters.
1150   I have never heard

of so cruel or conclusive
an encounter by night,
nor a man more menaced
in the midnight sea.
But I survived those foes'
venomous assault
and the flood swept me
far, far away,
alone and exhausted,
1160   to the land of the Finns.
I cannot ever
recall hearing
such a tale of triumph
told about you—
your big battles!
Breca has never,
and neither have you,
known such success
in battle (I scorn
1170   to boast of it!)
though it is quite clear
that you killed your brothers,
your own kinsmen:
an evil deed
for which, friend Unferth,
you will one day roast
shamefully in hell,
shrewd though you are.
Son of Ecglaf,
1180   I say to you frankly
that this grim monster
Grendel would never
have wrought such ruin
to Hrothgar, here
in Heorot, if your mind
were half as bold
    or swashbuckling
as you yourself suppose.
But the fiend has learned
1190   to fear no resistance,

no wrath or reprisal
from wretches like you,
no vengeance from the valiant
'Victory Danes.'
He exacts his toll,
he exempts no one
of Scylding blood,
shredding, ripping,
gnawing, knowing

1200   he has nothing to fear
from the nerveless Danes.
But now I will show him
the full fierceness
and fury of the Geats,
how they clear accounts.
And then, tomorrow,
when the sun rises
in the south, clothed
in morning radiance,

1210   men will again
laugh in this meadhall,
delivered from fear."
Hrothgar, the white-haired
ruler of Denmark,
was filled with relief
and fresh hope
that succor was near:
he had seen the hero's
quick resolve

1220   and courage in action.
Warriors relaxed
and the walls echoed
with winsome words.
Wealhtheow, Hrothgar's
queen, adept
at court etiquette,
went round the room,
radiant in gold,
greeting the thanes.

1230   She gave the mead-cup

first to Hrothgar,
the father of Denmark,
bidding him be blithe
  at the beer-drinking
since he was loved by all;
her lord gratefully
took the cup
and turned to the feast.
The highborn lady

1240   of the Helmings next
served each of the thanes,
both old and young,
with mellow mead,
until the moment came
when, circling the room,
she slowly drew near
the bench in the beer-hall
where Beowulf sat.
She greeted the prince,

1250   giving God thanks
that her long-held wish
had at last come true,
that at last she could look
to a living soul
for solace in her sorrow.
The son of Ecgtheow
accepted the cup
with sincere thanks,
then spoke earnestly,

1260   spurred to valor
and burning for battle.
Beowulf replied:
"When I first set out
on this far adventure
with my faithful thanes,
I was firmly resolved
either to end
the evil plight
of Denmark forever

1270   or to die fighting

your ancient enemy,
either to achieve
a mighty victory
or to meet death,
grim and inglorious,
in this great wine-hall."
Pleased with this promise
from the prince of the Geats,
Hrothgar's consort,
1280   radiant with gold,
solemnly returned
to sit by her lord.
And now, once again,
noise mounted
    in the meadhall,
mirth, revelry,
and proud boasting,
    until presently
Hrothgar decided
1290   to rise and take
his nightly rest;
he knew the enemy
had been waiting to raid
the wondrous hall
all the day long,
from the hour of sun-up
until blackest night
blankets the world
and shapes of shadow
1300   come shambling forth
in the dread darkness.
The Danes stood up.
As he left, Hrothgar
saluted Beowulf,
wished him a watchful
and wary stewardship
of the splendid hall,
and spoke these words:
"Never before,
1310   since I knew how to heft

the hilt of a sword,
have I handed control
    of this ale-hall
to anyone but you.
Guard the greatest
of gift-seats well,
be strong and steady—
and stay awake!
If you survive the fight
1320   I vow to reward you
with all the riches
you could ever desire."

X

Royal Hrothgar,
ruler of the Danes,
strode from the meadhall
with his staunch war-band;
he wanted to find
Wealhtheow and share
his consort's couch.
1330   The King of heaven
had given the Danes
a great-hearted hall-guard
to deal with Grendel
and to do Hrothgar
a special service
dispatching giants.
The prince of the Geats
was putting his trust
in his great strength
1340   and in God's favor.
Off came the hero's
iron mailcoat
and hard helmet;
he handed over
his trusty sword
to an attendant thane

and asked him to safekeep
all that war-gear.
Confident, the prince

1350   climbed into bed
and vowed solemnly
in vaunting words:
"I know that my hand
is no less ready
for grim grappling
than Grendel's is.
I disdain, therefore,
to destroy this fiend
with the edge of the sword,

1360   though I easily could.
Adept though he is
in deeds of malice,
    he is ignorant
of iron weapons
and their unique virtues;
we will not, therefore,
duel with swords
if he dares to meet me
in close combat.

1370   When we come together,
God in his wisdom
will grant victory
to whichever of us
    he chooses to."
Beowulf lay down,
burying his face
in a rich pillow,
while around him his troop
of seamen anxiously

1380   sank to their rest.
Not a man among them
imagined he would live
to behold his hearth
or homeland again,
the dear precincts
where his days had begun,

for they knew that here
in this benighted hall
the fiend had slaughtered
1390   far too many
of the men of the Danes.
But almighty God
would give the Geats
the glory, thanks
to one man's strength,
of worsting their foe,
so that all might share
the honor, Geats
together with Danes.
1400   God's sovereignty
over men and their fates
    has been manifest
from the beginning of time.
Now Grendel came
striding the shadows.
The staunch warriors
who defended the hall
had fallen asleep,
all but one.
1410   It was obvious
that the prowling fiend
could not pull men down
to grim destruction
unless God willed it,
since tonight a man
who was not asleep
waited for battle,
watchful and angry.

XI

Now Grendel came,
1420   gliding like mist
across the bleak moorland,
bearing God's wrath.

The merciless monster
meant to ensnare
fresh victims
in the fear-stricken hall.
He strode rapidly
beneath the starless sky
until at last Heorot
1430   loomed before him,
gleaming with gold.
This greedy visit
to the home of the Danes
was hardly his first,
   though before tonight
he had never found
hardier hall-thanes
or harder luck.
Now Grendel came,
1440   grim and joyless,
to the entrance door.
Its iron, fire-forged
bolts shattered
at his bare touch.
Raging and ravenous
he wrenched open
the mouth of the building
and his monstrous feet
trod on its precious
1450   tile-covered floor;
in the eerie dark
his eyes darted
rays of raging
red hellfire.
He saw before him
in the silent hall
a throng of youthful
thanes and kinsmen
lying in their beds.
1460   He laughed in his heart
out of pure pleasure:
he planned to separate

those sleeping men's
souls from their bodies
long before daybreak;
he looked forward
to fabulous feasting.
But fate would forbid him
to eat people
1470   ever again
after that night,
for there lay Hygelac's
kinsman, alert
and carefully watching
   how the murderer
meant to proceed.
The monster was not
minded to dawdle
1480   but swooped suddenly
on a sleeping man;
slobbering with greed
he slit him open,
guzzled the blood
gushing from his veins
and gulped down great
gobbets of flesh;
he polished him off
completely, hands
and feet included.
1490   The fiend stepped closer,
stretching his stealthy
steel-clawed fingers
toward a still figure
who stirred suddenly
   and braced himself,
then sat bolt upright
and grabbed Grendel's
groping forearm.
The ruthless marauder
1500   realized at once
that he had never met
another man

anywhere on earth
with such awesome strength
in his ten fingers;
but the terror that froze
his heart was of no
help in escaping.
Frightened now, he longed
1510   to flee to the darkness
of his devils' den;
this dreadful encounter
was nothing like those
he had known before!
Beowulf recalled
his boasting words
at last night's banquet;
he leapt to his feet
and grasped Grendel
1520   in a grip of steel.
Fingers shattered
as the fiend made
a lunge for the doorway,
longing to get clear;
the ogre intended,
if only he could,
to flee to the fens;
his fingers, he knew,
were in his foe's power.
1530   It was a fateful trip
the twilight prowler
had taken to Heorot!
The crashes and cries
coming from the hall
filled the Danes with dread,
like draughts of bitter
and baleful beer.
Both combatants
were blind with fury.
1540   The building shuddered
and it was a miracle

it managed to survive,
withstanding the shock
instead of collapsing,
   but it was reinforced
and firmly braced
outside and in
with iron, the work
of master smiths,
1550   though the mead-benches trimmed
with gold were shattered
into glum wreckage
(I have heard it said)
during that hostile clash.
How could the builders
of Heorot imagine
that any man
by any means
   could damage it,
1560   adorned with ivory,
could ravage and ruin it,
unless raging flames
should someday swallow it?
The sounds grew louder,
pulsing eerily;
panic and dread
harrowed the Danes
who heard the noise,
the wild wailing
1570   through the wall of the hall,
the ghastly screams
of God's enemy,
the horrid captive
of hell keening,
howling in defeat,
held by Beowulf.
A man with more
might was not living
in those days
1580   of this world.

XII

The noble hero
had no intention
of letting the monster
leave the meadhall:
he valued that vicious
violent life
at next to nothing.
And now, at last,
Beowulf's men
1590   brandished their swords
and tried to protect
their protector's life
with their own dear blood,
if only they might.
But how could those hardy
heroes have known,
as they swung their bright
swords and crowded
the evil creature
1600   on every side,
straining to strike him,
that their strokes were useless,
that no weapon
known among men,
no iron on earth
could ever touch him:
with his magic spells
he had made them all blunt
and thus useless.
1610   And therefore his death
on that day
in this world
was destined to be vile,
and his damned spirit
to fall afterward
into fiends' clutches.
The scourge who had slain
such scores of victims

with mirthful murderous
1620   mind in his feud
with God, now perceived
with gathering dismay
that his vast body
availed him nothing,
    now that Hygelac's
hard-bitten nephew
held him by the hand.
Their hatred for each other
was boundless. And now
1630   the brute's shoulder
could stand the enormous
strain no longer;
his muscles gave way
and massive stress
snapped his sinews.
Success in battle
was given Beowulf
and Grendel fled,
mortally hurt,
1640   to his marsh hideout,
his dismal abode,
doomed and despairing;
he knew that his hours
were numbered and felt
death upon him.
The Danes, however,
were filled with delight
when the fight was over.
Wise and worshipful,
1650   the warrior prince
who had come from afar
had cleansed the great
hall of Hrothgar.
The hero was pleased
with his night's labors;
he had now fulfilled
the mighty promise
he had made the Danes,

ending their years
1660   of agony
and wreaking ready
and rough vengeance
    for the violence
and vast cruelty
they had suffered so long,
as could be seen by them all
when the noble Geat
nailed Grendel's
arm and shoulder,
1670   all of the monster's
hideous grip,
to Heorot's gable.

XIII

In the morning, they say,
many warriors
gathered together
at the great meadhall.
Folk-chiefs had traveled
from far and near
to stare at a marvel:
1680   the strange being
had left behind him
large, bloody
footprints in the ground.
His fate gratified
men who followed
that monstrous spoor
and saw how he stumbled,
sad and stricken,
dying, defeated,
1690   dragging agonized
lagging footsteps
to the lair of sea-beasts,
where the waves were all
awash in blood,

their red surges
reeking and steaming
and heaving, hideous
with hot gore.
He died joylessly,
1700   doomed and despairing,
forfeited life
   in his fen-refuge,
and hell swallowed
his heathen soul.
Mounting their horses,
men headed
home from the water
in high spirits,
elated and laughing,
1710   light-hearted youngsters
riding side by side
with seasoned thanes;
they talked of the hero's
spectacular success,
saying that neither
to the south nor the north
nor anywhere else
   on earth, beneath
the wheeling sky,
1720   did a warrior live
wiser or worthier
of a wide kingdom,
though they meant with this
   no diminishment
of great Hrothgar,
their gracious king.
Sometimes they raced
their swift horses,
hardy warriors
1730   in high spirits,
where the woodland ways
were wide and the tracks
safe and easy;
sometimes a thane

of the king's would perform,
a consummate poet
who knew and could sing
numberless tales,
could relate them in linked
1740   language, in words
arrayed properly,
and who was already at work
blazoning Beowulf's
brilliant achievement,
composing a poem
of praise, skillfully
weaving its web.
This word-smith repeated
all the tales
1750   he had ever heard
      about Sigemund
the son of Wæls,
striking stories
of struggle and feud,
wickedness, wide
wanderings, stories
that no one knew
but his nephew, the young
Fitela, who heard
1760   frequent accounts
of his uncle's old
exploits and feats
when the two kinsmen
traveled together,
slaying numerous
savage giants
with their swift swords.
Sigemund later,
      after his death,
1770   possessed undying fame:
beneath grey cliffs
the great champion
had fought a dragon
who defended a hoard.

He slew the creature
by himself, performed
the feat entirely
without Fitela's help,
swinging his sword
1780 with such savage force
that it skewered the great
scaly horror
and its deadly point
sank deep in the rock.
Swiftly, in the sequel,
the son of Wæls
plundered the dragon's
priceless treasure
to his heart's content,
1790 heaping his ship
    with beautiful
bright ornaments;
meanwhile the monster
melted away
    into sludge-puddles.
Sigemund's courage
    was so absolute
that in after years
he was remembered by men
1800 as the most exalted
of princely exiles
    after the pitiful
death of the Danish
despot Heremod,
betrayed by his own
tribe to the Jutes
and murdered at once.
Mental anguish
had crippled Heremod:
1810 he became, in the end,
an evil burden
to his own people,
who were enraged by his wrathful
and erratic deeds,

his lawless ways.
He lost the hearts
of loyal followers
who looked to him for help,
who thought that their prince
1820   would thrive in virtue,
inherit the great
high-seat of his father
and lead Denmark.
But he lost their hearts
when sin and sorrow
usurped his mind;
   whereas Beowulf
won the unbounded love
of each of the Danes
1830   and all mankind.
Sometimes the horsemen
measured sandy paths
on their dark-hued steeds.
The day wore on
and by mid morning
a mob of chieftains
had gathered at Heorot
to gaze at the tokens
of Grendel's defeat.
1840   Great Hrothgar
himself, the gracious
soul of Denmark,
came to join them
with a crowd of thanes,
and Wealhtheow his queen
walked by his side
down the meadhall path
with her maiden train.

XIV

Hrothgar made a speech
1850   when he reached the hall

and stood on its steps,
staring upward
at the golden roof
and Grendel's arm:
"Let us give thanks
to God our lord
for his might and mercy!
How much I suffered
from Grendel! But God,
1860 the great Protector,
can work wonder on wonder
on wonder forever!
It is a long time
since I lost hope
that anyone on earth
could ever assuage
my grief and anguish,
when this great building
stood here empty
1870 and stained with blood
and my men were all
unmanned by terror,
my closest and wisest
counselors and friends
truly perplexed
how to protect his hall
from ghouls and goblins.
With God's assistance
this foreign prince
1880 has performed a task
that we, with our deep
wisdom and cunning,
attempted in vain.
Whatever woman
gave birth to this man
of battles may say
with strict truth,
if she is still alive,
that the God of old
1890 showed her great honor

when she bore that child.
Beowulf! Henceforth
I aim to love you
as my own son!
Never forget
this new relationship,
ablest of heroes!
Where I command,
  you will have everything
1900   you could ever desire.
I have often bestowed
armlets of gold
on lesser men
and less deserving,
weaker in war.
With wisdom and valor
you have brought it to pass
that your bright glory
will live forever.
1910   May the lord God
favor and befriend you
in future years!"
The son of Ecgtheow
swiftly replied:
"I engaged in the fight
with great good will
and fought fiercely,
unfazed by Grendel
and his wicked strength.
1920   I wish, my lord,
you could look with your eyes
on his lifeless corpse,
stained horribly
with streams of blood!
My plan for the battle
was to pin him down
with bold embraces
on a bed of death,
where his life would ebb
1930   loathsomely away

unless the monster could find
some means of escaping.
God did not give me
the grace to hold him,
for I failed to clutch
the fiendish creature
tightly enough,
and he was too quick
lunging from my grasp,
1940　　though he left his hand
behind, in his headlong
haste, and his arm
and shoulder too.
　　　But the shade-stalker
could not prolong his life,
his lethal existence,
by such a sacrifice
and has since died,
crushed by sins
1950　　and clasped in hell-chains,
compelled to submit
to painful bondage,
to fetters of flame,
befouled with crimes
and dreading the great
day of judgment,
when God will justly
give him his wages."
Unferth the son
1960　　of Ecglaf was silent,
much less inclined
to mocking speech
when, thanks to the hero,
the thanes of Hrothgar
saw the huge trophy
on Heorot's gable,
the fiend-like talon.
　　　The fingertips
of the heathen foe's
1970　　horrible claw

were like nails,
like enormous spikes
of iron or steel,
and everyone agreed
that no weapon
known among men,
no matter how sharp,
could have made a wound
on that hand hanging there,
1980   horrid with gore.

XV

Hundreds of hands
were helping now,
men's and women's,
making the beer-hall
ready to host
a royal banquet.
Gold tapestries
gleamed on the walls,
webs of beauty,
1990   wonders for men
who like looking
on such lovely things.
The building had been badly
battered within,
though braced with iron
bands, and the hinges
wrenched from the door-posts;
the roof alone
stood there intact
2000   when, stained with sin,
the defeated fiend
fled, hoping
to avoid his doom.
But evading death
is no easy task
(let anyone try it!)

since every creature
the earth brings forth
with soul and senses
2010   necessarily comes
to the place appointed
    and prepared for it,
where it sleeps soundly
in its silent bed
and the feast of life
is finished at last.
The hour was at hand
for old Hrothgar,
Healfdene's son,
2020   to host the banquet.
I have never known
the noble Danes
clamor so loudly
in their king's presence;
jubilant thanes
enjoyed their carouse,
while right in their midst
the royal kinsmen
Hrothgar and Hrothulf
2030   reveled together,
draining many
deep bowlfuls
in blithe fellowship.
The benches of Heorot
were filled with friends;
the faithful Danes
had not learned, yet,
to love treachery.
Soon the famous
2040   sword of Healfdene
was brought to Beowulf,
and a banner of gold
to mark his triumph,
a mailcoat and helmet;
men looked on
as that marvelous blade

was given to the prince,
who gladly accepted
a brimming mead-cup
2050   without blushing for shame
at rewards unworthy
of warriors' praise.
I cannot recall
a king giving
four such treasures
filigreed with gold
to other men
    at the ale-drinking!
Up on the helmet
2060   was an iron ridge
that would bear the brunt
of blows to the head,
so that hard showers
of hostile missiles
could not harm the hero
when, holding his shield,
he strode forward
to strike down foes.
On orders from Hrothgar
2070   eight war-horses
with bridles of gold
were brought inside
the wide wine-hall;
one of them bore
a saddle, jeweled
    and sumptuous,
the rich war-seat
of Hrothgar himself,
Healfdene's son,
2080   when he headed his troops
and prepared them for war;
his prowess in battle
    had been unfailing
when he fought in the van.
The lord of the Danes
lovingly bestowed

both these treasures,
battle-gear and steeds,
on Beowulf the Geat,
2090 bade him enjoy them.
Thus did Hrothgar,
there in Heorot,
reward the warrior
with wealth and horses,
ornate treasures,
and no one wishing
to utter truth
will ever reproach him.

XVI

Next, in the meadhall,
2100 the munificent king
gave some old heirlooms,
exquisite treasures,
to Beowulf's band
of bold followers,
and promised besides
to pay compensation
in gold for the one
Grendel had murdered,
as he meant to murder
2110 many others,
if that great hand-grip
and God's wisdom
    had allowed him to.
The Lord disposes
all things on earth
and always will;
foresight, therefore,
and forethought are best,
and mental balance,
2120 since men who inhabit
this weary war-ravaged
world experience

many good things—
and much evil.
Old Hrothgar,
who an age ago
had fought to support
his father Healfdene,
was served at the feast

2130   with song and story:
harp music rang
through the high rafters
when the court poet
recounted the tale
of Finn the Frisian
and the fierce Danish
champion Hnæf,
who with his choice war-band
was attacked by Finn

2140   on a trip to Frisia.
The fair Hildeburh,
Finn's consort
and Hnæf's sister,
had no need to praise
the truth of the Jutes
when her two loved ones,
her son and brother,
were slain together
by wrathful swords.

2150   What a bereaved lady!
When daybreak came
the daughter of Hoc
had reason to curse
her wretched destiny,
when she saw them lie
slaughtered, kinsmen
she loved more deeply
than life or any
treasure on earth.

2160   The attack left Finn
with just a handful
of his Jutish troops,

too few by far
to defeat Hengest,
the Danish leader
after the death of Hnæf,
or end the stand-off
by ousting the Danes
    from their entrenchment.
2170   So terms were offered:
        that a hall
and high-seat should be cleared
for the Danes who survived;
that in the days ahead
they should have the same rights
as the sons of the Jutes;
and that Finn the Frisian,
Folcwalda's son,
should treat them daily
2180   to treasure in abundance,
giving Hengest's men
handsome presents
of burnished gold
in the banquet hall,
presents as lavish
as it was his practice to give
his Frisians and Jutes
to fire their courage.
A pact of peace
2190   was promptly sealed
by both parties.
Brave but fated,
Finn gave Hengest
firm guarantees
that he would treat the Danes
with tact, wisdom
and noble restraint,
and that no Frisian
would endanger the pact
2200   by deed or word,
nor, moved by malice,
would mock the Danes

for living in allegiance
to their lord's killer,
since fate had clearly
forced them to do so.
If, however,
any Frisian
should ever mention
2210   the old conflict,
then the sword's edge
must settle matters.
A solemn oath
was sworn and treasure
was brought from the hoard.
The body of Denmark's
lost champion
was laid on the pyre,
where the eye could behold
2220   iron helmets
emblazoned with golden
boar images,
bloody mailcoats,
and, battered and torn,
a mound of corpses,
for many had died.
Hildeburh asked
that her hapless son
should be lifted up
2230   to lie by Hnæf,
that his corpse should be burnt
to cold ashes
by his uncle's side.
She uttered a lament
as his loved body
was laid on the pyre.
Soon ruddy flames
roared at the foot
of the black barrow,
2240   while blood spurted
from reopened wounds
or oozed from gashes

and heads melted.
The hungry flames
battened greedily
    on the battle-dead
of both peoples;
their bloom was extinguished.

XVII

The followers of Finn
whom the fight had spared
returned bitterly
to towns and high
halls throughout Frisia.
But Hengest stayed on,
remaining with Finn
    that murder-stained
unhappy winter,
homesick and filled
with pain, but unable
to put out to sea
in his ring-prowed ship:
it was raging with storms
and winter winds,
its waves frozen
until next spring
should renew the world,
that noble season
that never failed
to appear to men
at its proper time—
and does so still.
The dark days passed
and the earth turned green;
the exile's heart
thirsted to depart,
but his thoughts dwelt less
on the voyage ahead
than on revenge and a grim

2250

2260

2270

end to the quarrel.
2280   In his innermost heart
he treasured hatred
for the treacherous foes
and longed for vengeance,
the law of the world,
itching for battle
every morning
when he girded on
grey Hunlafing,
his trusty weapon,
2290   the terror of the Jutes.
And so came the day
when swords drawn in anger
put an end to Finn
in his own meadhall,
when Oslaf and Guthlaf
openly complained
about the foul attack
that followed their arrival,
and about monstrous wrong.
2300   Men were unable
to restrain their rage,
and straightway the floor
was flooded with blood,
Finn slaughtered,
the king in his court,
and his queen taken.
The elated Danes
loaded their ships
with the vast riches
2310   of the vanquished king,
hall furniture
and heaped-up gems,
countless treasures.
They carried the lady
Hildeburh home
in their heaving ships,
restored to her people.
The story was finished;

the poet fell silent
2320   and applause resounded
amid cries of the feast.
Cupbearers poured
wine from flagons
and Wealhtheow strode forth,
graceful in her golden necklace,
to where the great co-rulers,
Hrothgar and Hrothulf, were sitting
in unruptured friendship,
uncle and eminent nephew;
2330   and there sat Unferth the spokesman,
fast by the feet of Hrothgar,
for they had faith in Unferth,
    in his great spirit,
though he had given no quarter
once, in war, to kinsmen.
And now Wealhtheow was speaking:
    "Giver of treasure,
my great consort!
Drain this beaker,
2340   drink and be merry!
My splendid lord,
speak to these Geats
with friendly words,
as is fit and proper;
    and be liberal,
lavish with the goods
that you now possess
from near and far.
    They have told me
2350   you intend to adopt
this hero as your son.
Heorot has been cleansed,
our jubilant hall,
so enjoy good fortune
as long as you can;
but leave the kingdom
to your own children,
your heirs, when death

finally comes.
2360   I have faith that Hrothulf,
your loyal nephew,
will look on our two
youngsters with love
if you, most gracious
and dread sovereign,
should die before he does.
I trust he will treat
our two children
with mildness and mercy,
2370   remembering
the warmth and kindness
with which we treated him
when he was himself
a helpless child."
She approached the place
where her princelings sat,
Hrethric and Hrothmund,
around them a throng
of Danish youths
2380   and, drinking between them
on the bench,
Beowulf the Geat.

XVIII

She handed the hero
a huge beaker
with liberal thanks,
lovingly gave him
two armlets
of twisted gold,
a gorgeous robe,
2390   and a great neck-ring,
one of the worthiest
ever worn on earth;
I have never known
a nobler treasure

under high heaven
since Hama carried
the torque of the Brosings,
twinkling with jewels,
to the fair stronghold,
2400   when he fled the cunning
evils of Eormenric
for endless gain.
Noble Hygelac,
the nephew of Swerting,
lost that neck-ring
on his last campaign,
rallying round
the royal standard,
defending his plunder.
2410   Fate had crossed him;
arrogant and rash,
he had asked for trouble
by raiding the Frisians,
recklessly taking
the ring with him
across the rolling sea.
He died there swinging
his desperate shield,
and his grey mailcoat
2420   and that great neck-ring
fell afterward
into Frankish hands,
when warriors of less
worth plundered
the field where corpses
of defeated Geats
held lifeless sway.
There was loud applause
and Wealhtheow spoke
2430   before the waiting court:
"Dear Beowulf,
duly enjoy
these great treasures,
this gold-trimmed robe,

this precious collar.
Prosper always,
glorying in strength,
and give these boys
your wise counsel.
2440   Rewards will follow.
You have brought it to pass
that brave men will praise you
near and far,
now and in the future,
wherever wide headlands
and windbeaten capes
are washed by the sea.
Warrior prince,
may your days be blest!
2450   From the depths of my heart
I give you these gifts.
Be good to my boys
and act in their interest,
triumphant hero!
Everyone here
honors his comrades
and loves his lord
with a loyal heart;
the nation is united
2460   and its noble thanes
drink merrily
and do as I bid them."
She returned to her place.
Intrepid warriors
drank wine and boasted;
not one of them guessed
what fate had in store,
the fearful doom
that would drag them down
2470   when darkness fell
and Hrothgar withdrew
to his royal couch
   to refresh himself,
while a force of his thanes

lay down in the hall
as they had done in the past,
piling their bedclothes
and pillows on the benches.
One of that weary
2480   warrior band
was destined and doomed
to die that night.
Lightly they hung
their lindenwood shields
next to their heads,
and near the bench
of each warrior
you could easily see
his boar-crest helmet,
2490   his bright mailcoat,
his ashwood spear;
it was always the Danes'
rule to be fully
ready for combat,
both in peacetime at home
and on campaigns abroad,
whenever their king
needed their help.
    They were a proper
2500   and praiseworthy folk.

XIX

The warriors dozed.
One of them paid
dearly for that,
a daily occurrence
when Grendel frequented
the gold-decked hall,
reveling in wrong
until he reaped his reward
and was slain for his sins.
2510   But soon it was clear

and known everywhere
that another fiend
had come to avenge him,
to requite the Danes
for his grisly death:
Grendel's mother,
a monstrous female,
who mourned and raged
in her foul den
2520   in the fenlands, the black
bottomless abyss
that had been her home
since Cain cruelly
killed his brother,
his closest kinsman.
Accursed by God,
   and with that murder
marking him, he fled
to live in the wasteland.
2530   From his loins sprang
a monstrous progeny,
among them Grendel,
the outcast fiend
ambushed in Heorot
by a wakeful man
waiting for trouble;
when the raging foe
reached out to grab him,
he relied for help
2540   on his limitless strength
and the grip of steel
God had armed him with;
his faith in the Lord's
favor and love
was steadfast, and thus
he destroyed the foe,
who fled in a frantic
frenzy, his life
ended, his joys
2550   over forever.

But the mother
of mankind's enemy
was living still
and longing to strike
a vigorous blow
to avenge her child.
She went to Heorot
where warriors slept
throughout the building.
2560   The instant she stormed
inside it, the Danes
suffered a dreadful
reversal of fortune:
her violence was less
than Grendel's only
in degree, as women's
might is less
than men's when battle
surges and weapons
2570   with slashing blades
wet with blood,
the work of sword-smiths,
hack swine-figures
on helmets facing them.
Weapons were again
wielded in Heorot
by shouting men
and shields brandished,
   though the troop
2580   had no time to put on
helmets and mailcoats
when the horror struck.
The moment she knew
men had seen her
she wanted to slip
away to safety.
Snatching up a thane
with her slashing claws,
she fled in panic
2590   to her fen-refuge.

The man she murdered
was the most esteemed
of all Hrothgar's
intimate friends,
    a magnanimous
and noble chieftain,
butchered in his bed.
Beowulf had left
when the feast was finished;
2600   the famous Geat
had been allotted his night's
lodging elsewhere.
Going from the hall,
Grendel's mother
caught sight of the hand
of her son and took it.
What grim barter
that gold-hall had witnessed,
lives of loved ones
2610   lost in a deadly
game of swapping!
The grey old king,
royal Hrothgar,
was ravaged by grief
when he learned of his loss,
that his beloved friend
and dear comrade
was dead, murdered.
At once Beowulf
2620   the warrior Geat
was brought to his bedchamber.
In the bleak light
of that disturbed morning
he strode briskly,
surrounded by comrades,
to where Hrothgar sat,
anxious to learn
if he would ever see
a change for the better
2630   after this chilling news,

and as the worthy prince
walked steadfastly
forward with his friends,
the floorboards thundered.
He saluted the king
politely, asking
if he had slept soundly
or if something was wrong,
considering this strange
2640   summons at dawn.

XX

"Wrong?" said Hrothgar,
ruler of the Danes,
"is something wrong?
Sorrow is renewed
for all Denmark!
Æschere is dead,
the older brother
    of Yrmenlaf,
my counselor, confidant,
2650   and closest friend,
the faithful comrade
who fought at my side
in bloody battles
when boar-standards clashed,
tossing in tumult;
whatever a good
soldier should be,
such was Æschere!
A sudden marauder
2660   has slaughtered him, brought him
death in Heorot.
I do not know
    if the attacker
has returned home,
glutted with feeding,
but she has grimly avenged

your daring deed
of the day before,
when you slew Grendel
2670   with sudden hand-grip,
paying him back
for preying so long
on my loyal thanes.
He lost the fight;
but now in requital
another monstrous
visitor has come
to avenge her kinsman
and boost the blood-toll
2680   of our baleful feud,
as is all too clear
to anyone who once
enjoyed Æschere's
generous bounty
and whose heart is now heavy.
The hand lies dead
who gave in abundance
the gifts you longed for!
I have heard men say,
2690   my hall-comrades,
keen counselors
    and countrymen,
        they had been told
that two such beings,
hideous, horrible,
haunted the moors,
wandering fiends.
One of the pair,
as far as they ever
2700   could figure out,
had a woman's form;
the wicked creature
who shared her exile
had the shape of a man
but was huge, much huger
than human beings.

For countless years
he has been called Grendel.
Nothing at all
2710   is known of his father
   or if any
ogres like him
were born before him.
The bogs are their home,
a waste world
of windswept crags
and wolf-haunted hills
where the wild torrent
drops down
2720   to depths in the earth
unknowable by men.
It is not far,
measured in miles,
to that menacing place.
Fringing the pool
are fast-rooted trees,
their clawlike limbs
covered with ice.
At night you see something
2730   unnatural there,
flames in the water!
No fleshly man
has dared to explore
that dark abyss.
When the high antlered
heath-stepping stag
is pursued by hounds
and seeking cover,
he will stop and make
2740   a stand on the bank
sooner than plunge
in those sullen waves
and swim to safety.
What a sinister spot!
When stormy winds
stir up the depths,

moist exhalations
mount to the skies
until the air turns black
2750   with icy rain
and the heavens weep.
Help us, Beowulf,
for you are our hope!
You have yet to behold
the wild wasteland
where one can find
that sinful demon—
seek it if you dare!
I will give you a trove
2760   of golden treasure,
undreamt of wealth,
as I did before,
if you vanquish the fiend
and survive the battle."

XXI

Beowulf replied:
"You must bear this sudden
misfortune patiently.
It is far, far better
to avenge a friend
2770   than vainly mourn him.
Each of us comes
to the end of life
here on earth;
let him who can
earn himself fame
with honor, the best
    memorial
once a man is dead.
Get to your feet now!
2780   We will go at once
to follow the fiend's
foul kinswoman.

I promise she will find
no place of concealment
in the depths of the earth
or in deep forests
or in gulfs of the sea,
go where she will!
 Be resolute,
2790   Hrothgar, and show
the splendid composure
 I expect from you."
Joyfully the king
jumped to his feet,
giving thanks to God
for those thrilling words.
They bridled a horse
with a braided mane
for royal Hrothgar,
2800   who rode forward
surrounded by comrades
with ready shields.
They glimpsed the footprints
of Grendel's mother
far and wide
along the forest tracks,
saw the spoor of the fiend
where she sped onward
over murky moors
2810   and mist-shrouded hills,
clutching the lifeless
corpse of the best
and most courageous thane
in Hrothgar's Denmark.
The dauntless Geat
with some Danish scouts
was always in the lead
as the armed squadron
struggled over steep
2820   stone-covered slopes
or threaded its way
through thin defiles

where they walked warily
one at a time,
while slimy sea-beasts
slithered into holes.
Suddenly they saw
sinister trees
growing crookedly
2830   against grey boulders.
Blood-streaked billows
boiled beneath them,
weltered in gore.
And what did they find
on the brink of that pool,
bringing them grief,
bringing them great
bitterness of mind,
what did they find there
2840   with woe and fear
and anguish, what
but Æschere's head?
Warriors stared
at the waves heaving
with hot gore,
while their horns bleated
urgent battle-calls.
Everyone sat.
They watched as weird
2850   water dragons
    and sea-serpents
slid through the waves
or basked in the sun
on bluffs near the water,
cruel creatures
of the kind that wreck
sailors and ships
at sun-up, out
on the high seas.
2860   When they heard that bright
hubbub of horns
they hurried away,

surprised and panicked.
The prince of the Geats
wounded one of them
    with a war-arrow;
the fire-hard point
transfixed its vitals
with fine effectiveness—

2870   and fatally: it swam
slower and slower,
disabled by death.
Deftly the men
dragged it to shore
with barbed boar-spears,
beached it, hoisted it
high on the windy
headland, a weird
wave wanderer;

2880   warriors stared
at the baleful thing.
Now Beowulf put on
    his fighting-gear,
unafraid of death.
His wide war-corselet,
woven by hand,
splendid and supple,
must explore the depths;
it was fashioned with skill

2890   to defend his body
    so that enemies
    could not injure him
nor the malice of foes
menace his life.
The helmet gleaming
on his head, adorned
with silver, must sink
through swirling waves
to stir up the bottom

2900   of that strange abyss;
it was all reinforced
with iron bands

forged by smiths
of a former age,
emblazoned and embellished
with boar images
protecting its owner
from the touch of weapons.
The hero counted
2910 on help from the sword
Hrunting, the blade
Hrothgar's spokesman
Unferth lent him
in this hour of need,
   a preeminent
ancient treasure,
its iron edges
etched with poison-twigs
and baptized in blood;
2920 in battle it had never
failed anyone
who flourished it boldly
and dared to indulge
in desperate war-play.
This was far from the first
fierce struggle
the splendid weapon
was expected to win,
and when Unferth, son
2930 of Ecglaf, handed
his blade to a far,
far better swordsman,
he chose to forget
his challenge while drunk
of the night before.
He did not himself
have any appetite
for undersea combat
and thus lost his chance
2940 of lasting fame,
   which was totally
untrue of the other,

of Beowulf, once
he bound on his armor.

XXII

The son of Ecgtheow
said in parting:
"O sorrowing king!
Son of Healfdene!
Graciously recall,
2950   as I go to perform
this special service,
what we spoke of before,
    that if I should die
    while daringly
acting in your interest,
you would afterward play
the part of a father
toward a departed son.
Dread Hrothgar!
2960   If death takes me,
protect and cherish
my trusting companions,
my sorrowing thanes,
and send Hygelac
the great treasures
you gave me yesterday;
when he looks on those gifts
the lord of the Geats,
the son of Hrethel,
2970   will see at once
that I found favor
with a friend and enjoyed
his loving bounty
as long as I could.
And let Unferth,
that illustrious man,
have my own weapon,
my heirloom blade

full of swirling designs;

2980   with his sword Hrunting
I will do great deeds
or die trying."
At once then, without
waiting a moment
for pause or parley,
the prince of the Geats
leapt in the water
that lapped beneath him.
While he dove downward

2990   the day slipped by,
but at last he made out
the loathsome bottom.
She saw him at once,
the obscene creature
who had controlled the sea's
terrible depths
for a hundred years:
a human being
raiding her monstrous

3000   realm from above!
Swooping suddenly,
she seized the hero
in cruel clutches,
but her claws failed
    to injure him;
the iron rings
of his mail ensured
that she might not pierce
that linked war-shirt

3010   with her long talons.
Reaching the bottom,
the raging sea-wolf
bore Beowulf
to her bloody lair,
holding him so tight
that he was helpless to wield
a weapon, no matter
how wildly he tried;

3020

and meanwhile many
amazing sea-creatures
attacked his armor
with tusks and fangs,
sorely assailing him.
Soon he noticed
they had entered an eerie
undersea hall
where the turbid waves
could not touch him at all,
while high overhead

3030

a hollow vault
kept out the water.
How uncanny it was
that a blazing fire
    should be burning there!
But its light let him see
the loathsome she-wolf
of the ocean depths.
He instantly struck her
an awesome blow

3040

with all his might:
he let Hrunting
play a loud war-tune
    on her skull,
but discovered then
that the keen weapon
could not harm her;
its famous edges
failed Beowulf
in his hour of need,

3050

though always in the past
    it had been successful
when swung against hard
helmets and mailcoats.
Here, however,
the famous weapon
failed shamefully.
Wholly undaunted,
Hygelac's nephew

fixed his mind
3060 on feats of valor;
throbbing with anger
he threw down the sword
with its steel edges
and strange patterns
so it rang on the ground.
He reckoned now
on his sure hand-grip—
which shows how a man
must act, if he aims
3070 to earn glory,
rightly despising
risks and reversals.
Prompt and pitiless,
the prince of the Geats
grabbed the shoulder
of Grendel's mother;
raging with wrath
he wrestled her down,
fierce and relentless,
3080 and she fell to the earth.
She was quick to requite him
    with a counterblow,
lashing out lethally
with her long talons.
Weary, exhausted,
the warrior stumbled,
lost his footing
and lurched to the ground.
She drew the bright-edged
3090 dagger at her belt
and straddled her guest,
striving to avenge
her only child,
and only his closely
woven mailcoat,
the war-dress on his shoulders,
stopped her knife
    from destroying him.

3100
The son of Ecgtheow,
the slayer of Grendel,
would doubtless have died there
deep underground
if that marvel of meshwork
made by Wayland
had failed to protect him
and if the Father of all,
God in heaven,
had not given him help,
ordering the outcome
3110
with evident justice,
since Beowulf once more
bounded to his feet.

XXIII

His eye, darting
eagerly about,
glimpsed a heavy sword
hanging on the wall,
a massive weapon
made by the giants,
huger than any
3120
human being
besides himself
could swing in battle,
forged in the giants'
fabulous smithy.
The slayer of Grendel
seized it by the hilt
and flourished it fiercely,
fighting for his life;
he swung the snake-patterned
3130
sword forcefully
and hit the sea-hag
on her hideous neck,
smashing her spine;
the sword drove on

through her doomed body
and she dropped to the ground.
His blade dripping blood,
Beowulf rejoiced.
He noticed, now,

3140   in that unnatural hall,
fire burning
fierce as the sun,
heaven's candle.
Hygelac's thane
hastily searched
the whole area,
keeping to the walls
and clutching the sword
tightly by the hilt:

3150   he trusted its edges
to work his will
and wanted to give
Grendel a final
grim requital
for his killings on more
occasions than one,
that murderous first
midnight visit
when he slew Hrothgar's

3160   soldiers and thanes
brutally in bed:
he bolted down
fifteen retainers
who had been fast asleep,
then fled to the fens
with fifteen more,
a horrid booty.
The hero had given
that cruel foe

3170   his quittance in Heorot,
a fatal injury,
and found him now
dead in bed,
drained forever

of his ruthless strength.
The rotten carcass
burst open
when Beowulf struck it
a last blow

3180   and lopped off its head.
Soon the Danes
sitting up above
on land with Hrothgar
and looking at the waves,
saw that the surges
of the sea were turning
a ghastly red.
Grey-haired counselors
blindly assumed

3190   that Beowulf was dead;
they said men would never
see him again
walking in triumph
to wait on Hrothgar,
their ancient king;
they all thought
the she-wolf of the deep
was sure to have killed him.
In late afternoon

3200   they left the headland,
care-stricken comrades,
and the king with them,
their bountiful lord.
But Beowulf's men
stayed there, heartbroken,
staring at the water,
longing to look
on their lord but never
imagining they would.

3210   Meanwhile, down below,
that gigantic blade
had begun to melt
in the demon's blood,
dripping to the earth

like icicles
at the end of winter,
when the Lord loosens
the ligatures of frost
that fetter the waves,

3220   our Father, the Maker
of times and seasons,
the true Creator.
Beowulf disdained
to bear from that place
any of the spoils
lying all around him
except for Grendel's head
and the golden hilt,
ancient and awesome;

3230   it was all that was left
of that huge sword,
so hot was the blood,
so poisonous the fiend
    who had perished there.
When Beowulf saw
that both his enemies
were dead, he swam upward,
diving through the water.
The ocean depths

3240   had been exorcised,
cleansed of evil,
when the cruel fiend
left this transient
and delusive world.
Soon Beowulf,
swimming steadily,
breached the surface,
bearing the great
burden of booty

3250   he was bringing to land.
His men ran to meet him,
a tumultuous throng
of thanes, rejoicing
and thanking God

that they saw him again,
safe among them.
They unbuckled their lord's
bloodstained mailcoat
and white helmet,
3260   while the waters drowsed,
curdling thickly,
clabbered with gore.
Frolicking fearlessly,
footsoldiers trooped
from that fateful tarn,
following the now
familiar track;
mettlesome youths,
four of them, lugged
3270   the fiend's severed
unsightly head
from that seaside cliff,
a taxing business
for the two pairs of men
chosen to carry
the chilling burden
to the tall meadhall
trussed to their spears.
Soon they neared
3280   the sumptuous building,
fourteen exulting
foreign warriors
marching together,
in their midst their lord,
pacing the well-known
path to Heorot.
At last the illustrious
leader of the Geats,
honored by his acts,
3290   entered the precincts
of the hall itself
to hail the king.
The demon's head
was dragged by its hair

and dumped on the floor
where the drinkers sat,
a dreadful sight
for the Danes and their queen;
they gazed in terror
3300   at the grisly thing.

XXIV

The triumphant son
of Ecgtheow spoke:
"Soul of Denmark!
Son of Healfdene!
We deliver the spoils
you look on here,
our gage of success,
with great satisfaction.
I almost lost
3310   the undersea duel:
it was neck or nothing,
and not without plenty
of fearful peril.
The fight would have ended
grimly—and swiftly—
if God had not stood by me!
This excellent sword,
Unferth's Hrunting,
could not help me at all
3320   in that hard struggle,
but the Omnipotent,
who never fails
to guide the friendless,
gave me succor:
I saw an ancient
sword hanging
beside me on the wall
and seized it at once.
Later, when luck
3330   allowed me, I smote

the two who lived there.
Torrents of hot
battle-blood blackened
the blade of my sword,
burning it up,
but I bore off the hilt.
　　I had avenged
the violent deaths
of so many Danes

3340　and meted out justice.
I swear to you solemnly,
you can sleep in Heorot
safely now, you
yourself, your thanes,
and all the people
of your entire folk,
yeomen both old
and young; you need not
dwell in daily

3350　dread of attack
and death from the quarter
you did before."
There was joyful applause,
and the giant hilt
passed from the peerless
prince of warriors
to Hrothgar, the best
of rulers; it passed
　　into the keeping

3360　of the king of the Danes
after demons had died,
that dread monster
Grendel, the foe
of God himself,
　　and his murderous
mother; it passed
　　into the possession
of the most exalted lord
of the present world,

3370　the prince of kings,

known everywhere
   in Scandinavia.
Hrothgar studied
the rare treasure
   attentively;
it portrayed scenes
from that ancient war
when the angry flood
swept from heaven
3380   to slaughter the giants;
those rebels suffered,
that race estranged
from God almighty;
he gave them their quittance,
the fate they deserved,
in those foaming waves.
Moreover, written
in runic symbols,
in letters of gold
3390   inlaid in the shaft,
was the name of the smith
whose enormous skill
had wrought that weapon
with its writhing designs
long ago.
At last the son
of Healfdene spoke
and the hall fell silent:
"As a king who tries
3400   to encourage truth
among his people,
and who remembers days
sunk in darkness,
I say this warrior
was born a hero!
Beowulf, my friend,
your fame has reached out
to far peoples,
men in remotest regions!
3410   Because you have both might and wisdom,

fierceness in fighting and judgment,
I am not afraid to support you
fully with my friendly counsels.
In the future, I reckon,
    you will be your land's
    blessing and hope,
    unlike our late
    lord Heremod,
    who brought no blessing
3420   but bloodshed, grief,
    danger, and death
    to the Danish race,
    the heirs of Ecgwela.
    In his angry fits
    he killed his comrades
    and close associates
    until forced to flee
      his fatherland
    and the delights of men,
3430   a forlorn exile.
    Although God the giver
    had granted him strength
    above all other
    earthly champions,
    a baneful crop
    of bloodthirsty thoughts
    took root in his soul;
    morose, close-fisted,
    he grudged gift-giving
3440   to gain men's praise,
    and both king and country
    came to disaster
    and long-lasting grief.
    Learn from this, my friend!
    Be open handed!
    For your own dear sake
    I tell you this tale.
    It is truly strange
    in what unlike portions
3450   the Lord of heaven,

the absolute Owner
  of everything,
parcels out property,
power, and wisdom.
Sometimes he lets
a successful man's
fancy revel
in fulfilled desire,
lets him possess
3460   in the land of his birth
the pride and pleasure
of power over others,
gives him might and dominion,
making the world
so subject to his will
that he himself never dreams
in his crass folly
it can come to an end.
He bathes in abundance,
3470   not a bit troubled
by age or illness;
anxious worries
do not darken his mind,
nor dangerous threats
from spears, but all things
conspire to pamper
his needs, and he knows
of nothing worse,

XXV

until his heart mounts up
3480   and haughty thoughts
quicken within him
and conscience sleeps,
the soul's sentry,
its slumber deepened
by banal routines.
Near him the Devil
creeps with his quiver
of crooked arrows,

the warped suggestions
3490 of wicked fiends,
but he has lost his shield,
and at last he feels
a shower of sharp
shafts in his heart.
The wealth and the lands
he once enjoyed
seem cramped to him now
and he covets more;
he gives no gifts,
3500 he gives no thought
to evils ahead,
     and all because
God once gave him
some gaudy honors!
At last the body
lent to him briefly
ages and decays,
and after its death
his heaped-up wealth
3510   is inherited
by some spry youngster
who spends it lavishly,
refuses to hoard it
in fear and trembling.
So be on your guard,
Beowulf my son,
and sincerely seek
something better,
eternal gains!
3520 And turn from pride!
O strong warrior,
prestige in the world
is brilliant but brief;
in the blink of an eye
illness or accident
will end your life,
or raging flames
or roaring waters

or the stroke of steel
3530   or streaking arrows
or bitter old age;
or your bright eyes
will dim and darken
and Death, that even
stronger warrior,
will strike you down.
I have held Denmark
for half a century,
guarded my people
3540   in grim battle
with ash-spear and sword
from every foe
on earth, till I thought,
in the end, I had no
enemy anywhere
under the sun.
Cruel reversal
came to me here
in my own kingdom,
3550   when that ancient fiend
Grendel usurped
my gold-roofed throne,
bringing me years
of bitter grief
and thickening despair.
Thanks be to God,
the Lord everlasting,
I have lived long enough
to gaze at this grim
3560   and grisly head
with my old, old eyes
after all that strife!
Sit in your seat now
and savor the feast;
tomorrow, my friend,
when morning comes,
we will share many
shining treasures."

3570

The prince of the Geats
was pleased and strode
at once to his place
as the war-king asked.
And now another
magnificent feast
was served in Heorot
to the assembled thanes.
They drank deeply,
and when dark enclosed them
like a huge helmet

3580

the hearth-comrades rose.
White-haired Hrothgar,
the wise monarch,
knew bed was waiting,
and Beowulf too,
the noble Geat,
was in need of rest,
fatigued by the toils
and travails of the day.
The way was shown him

3590

by one of the stewards,
a trustworthy retainer
who attended to all
the wants and wishes
warrior sailors
used to know
in years gone by.
    The great-hearted
guest slept soundly,
the long rafters

3600

looming above him,
until the black raven,
blinking with dew,
heralded the dawn,
happy and exultant.
As brightness gathered
the band of Geats
were anxious to depart,
eagerly ready

3610

to leave for their homeland;
their leader, too,
fretted to return
to his far-off ship.

He arranged
for Hrunting's return
to Unferth, the son
of Ecglaf, gave him back
his precious sword
with appropriate thanks
for the loan of that old

3620

reliable weapon,
that friend in combat;
he refrained, out of tact
and wisdom, from faulting
the weapon's performance.
His followers by now
were fully armed,
impatient to depart.
The prince of the Geats,
the pillar of Denmark,

3630

approached the high-seat
to bid goodbye
to the best of kings.

XXVI

Beowulf addressed
broad-realmed Hrothgar:
"We far travelers
from a foreign land
want to inform you
that we wish to go home
to Hygelac our lord.

3640

Here in Denmark
we found a warm welcome
and were well entertained.
If, in my lifetime,
there is any way

for me to merit
more of your love
  than hitherto,
I will hasten at once
to sail to Denmark
3650   and serve you again.
If word should reach me
over the wide ocean
  that your neighbors
  are annoying you,
as those dread demons
did in the past,
I will bring thousands
of brave warriors
when you need their help.
3660   I know that Hygelac,
the lord of the Geats,
my loving uncle,
though young in years,
will yield to my entreaties
and second my wishes
so that I may sail here again
with a force of men,
a forest of spears,
or any other
3670   aid you may need.
And if your son Hrethric
should someday resolve
to visit my country,
he can avail himself there
of a wealth of friends;
worthy travelers
win the worthiest
welcome abroad."
Hrothgar replied,
3680   ruler of Denmark:
"God in his wisdom
gave you, my son,
these knowing words.
I have never heard

such masterful speech
from a man so young.
Your might is matchless,
your mind agile,
your talk full of wisdom.
3690   In times to come,
if unlucky chance
or the lot of war,
sword or spear-point
or sickness should take
your youthful king,
and you should survive
the death of your uncle,
I doubt that your race
of able mariners
3700   could ever find
a hardier hoard-keeping
hero than you
to make their leader,
if your mind is allured
by land and lordship.
The longer I know you,
Beowulf my friend,
the better I love you.
Thanks to your valor
3710   the thanes of our two
nations, my Danes
and your noble Geats,
will live in friendship,
and the long terror
of warfare cease
that they once suffered.
While my power endures,
peace shall prevail
and gifts be exchanged
3720   as a gage of the love
and trust uniting
our two nations,
while gift-laden ships
glide past the sea-cliffs

and plunging gannets.
Your people have always
treated friend and foe
with firmness, constancy,
and all honor
3730   in the ancient way."
From his high gift-throne
Healfdene's son
gave twelve outstanding
treasures to his friend,
wished him safety
on the wind-tossed sea,
and begged him to quickly
come back to Denmark.
The royal scion
3740   of a race of kings
kissed Beowulf
his comrade, and then
embraced him warmly;
his beard streamed
with tears as he pondered
      the alternatives:
that they might and might not
meet each other
again on this earth,
3750   gallant chieftains;
more likely not.
The lord of the Danes
was fond of his guest,
so fond that he shed
those tears of passion,
though he tried to check them;
suppressed longing
for the peerless youth
was burning in his blood.
3760   But Beowulf turned
from the weeping king
and walked buoyantly,
pleased with his treasures,
to the place where his ship

rode at anchor,
ready for its master.
His men spoke of Hrothgar
   admiringly:
a prince who had been
3770   the pride of warriors
until struck down
by stern old age,
that stronger warrior
who strikes down everyone.

XXVII

Heading for home
in their hand-linked mail,
hale and happy,
the hardy war-band
arrived at the seashore.
3780   Hrothgar's coastguard,
who had watched them come,
watched them depart,
hailing them now
with no hint of challenge
but with sincere friendship,
saying, as he met them,
how warm and loving
a welcome they would get,
triumphant heroes,
3790   from their own people!
The ring-beaked ship,
at rest on the sand,
was hastily crammed
with horses and war-gear,
mailcoats and helmets;
its mast towered
over rich treasures
from Hrothgar's hoard.
Beowulf bestowed
3800   on the brave coastguard

a gold-chased sword
that would give him prestige
and immense honor
   on the mead-benches
in coming years.
Then the curve-prowed ship
sought the deep sea
and left Denmark behind,
sail fluttering
3810   as it swung from the yard,
halyards straining,
hull creaking.
A spanking breeze
sped the vessel
onward, the agile
ocean courser
with tight-lashed strakes;
it tossed in the rollers
restlessly, its prow
3820   ringed with sea-foam,
until at last they saw
the land of the Geats,
the hills of home,
and their hurtling ship,
cuffed by the sea-breeze,
crunched in the sand.
The harbor master
had been holding watch,
peering out to sea,
3830   patiently waiting
for the heroes' return;
he hurried at once
to tether their sea-steed
tightly on the beach
with cables and hawsers,
so the crashing surf
might not smash it loose
and sweep it away.
The prince ordered
3840   the precious cargo

to be hauled from the hold.
Hard by the shore
was the hall of his lord,
Hygelac the king,
the son of Hrethel,
who sat there feasting
with his noble friends
next to the sea-wall.
He lived splendidly
3850   at that palatial seat
with Hygd his consort,
Hæreth's daughter,
a woman wise
and well accomplished
beyond her years;
though young in winters,
she was gentle and just
and generous with gold,
never grudging
3860   magnificent gifts
to her loyal thanes,
unlike Modthrytho,
a queen infamous
for the crimes of her youth.
Except for her lord,
not a single thane,
no matter how brave,
was man enough
to look on her face
3870   by the light of day;
if he did, he knew,
dread hand-forged
fetters would soon
be fastened upon him,
and swiftly thereafter,
after his sudden arrest,
a deadly blow
from the damascened sword
would close his account.
3880   But a queen should never,

a peace-weaver,
though peerless in beauty,
lay plots or scheme
to deprive a man
of life and light
for an alleged insult.
King Offa,
the kinsman of Hemming,
put a stop to it all:
3890   the story told
over the ale-cups
is that afterward
she was free of such faults,
when her father had once
married her off,
admired and arrogant,
to Offa, the young
and eminent king,
and she had sailed the wide
3900   seas to his court
to join him there.
Gentled and tamed,
she dwelt for the rest
of her days in the world
loved by her people,
lauded for virtue,
and deeply attached
to her dear husband,
who was hailed as a hero
3910   (I have heard it said)
and highly esteemed
by the whole race
of earthly men;
for Offa was known
to be free with gifts,
fierce in battle,
honored and admired
among his own people
and everywhere else.
3920   Eomer his son

was a hero too,
Hemming's kinsman,
grandson of Garmund—
a great warrior.

XXVIII

Beowulf strode
with his band of comrades
along the sand-hills
lining the seashore.
The sun shone brightly
3930   in the southern sky,
candle of the world.
Quickening their pace,
they hastened onward
to the high stronghold,
where they learned that the young
lord of the Geats,
the excellent king,
Ongentheow's slayer,
was holding court.
3940   Hygelac was brought
the news of his noble
nephew's return,
was told that the youthful
protector of his men,
his brave followers,
had come back alive,
hurrying home
unharmed by war.
He quickly gave orders
3950   to clear the benches
and make all ready
for the oncoming guests.
Valiant Beowulf,
survivor of battles,
saluted his lord
with loyal words,

then seated himself
beside the king,
kinsman by kinsman.
3960 The queen of the Geats,
Hygd, the daughter
of Hæreth, showed
her sincere love
by serving mead
to the heroes in hall,
while Hygelac the king
asked courteous questions
of his comrade in arms,
curious to know
3970 the course of their adventures,
what fates had befallen them
in their far travels:
"What deeds did you do,
my dear Beowulf
 when you suddenly
decided to cross
the salt ocean
in search of battle,
slaughter at Heorot?
3980 Did you successfully
find a cure
for the famous ills
of royal Hrothgar?
I was racked with fears,
alarmed and anxious;
I lacked confidence
 in your ability;
I begged you constantly
not to encounter
3990 that pernicious fiend,
but to leave the Danes
alone to settle
their grudge against Grendel.
Now God be thanked
that I see you safe,
sitting next to me."

The son of Ecgtheow
said in reply:
"Noble Hygelac!
4000   It is no secret
        that there was a meeting
between me and Grendel,
        nor that his wickedness
met its well-deserved end
in the very place
where he had vexed the Danes
through so many years
of misery and grief.
I avenged them all,
4010   those vicious attacks,
and none of Grendel's
obnoxious kin
will have cause to boast
of our clash by night,
no, not the oldest
of the nasty brood,
filthy with sin!
When I first entered
that great gift-hall
4020   I greeted Hrothgar.
Healfdene's son
heard in my speech
both worth and wisdom,
the weight of my mind,
and asked me to sit
between his own two sons.
What numbers of thanes!
I have never seen,
anywhere on earth,
4030   such ample delight
of assembled men!
Sometimes the queen,
the people's pledge
of peace, poured mead,
inspiring the young
inexperienced men

with exotic gifts
before resuming her seat;
sometimes Hrothgar's
4040   slender daughter
would serve the older,
more seasoned retainers
in the high hall;
I heard them call her
bonny Freawaru
when she brought them their drink
in goblets of gold.
This girl is pledged
to Ingeld, the son
4050   and heir of Froda,
the Heathobard king
so unhappily slain
in a clash with the Danes,
and canny Hrothgar
means for that marriage
to mark the end
of old enmities.
But even when a bride
is beautiful and young,
4060   the bloody spear
is rarely idle
once a ruler is killed,
and when Ingeld walks
through that ancient hall
with his happy bride,
he and every
Heathobard there
will hate and resent
her attendants: Danes,
4070   entertained like friends,
but wearing familiar
weapons and jewels,
well-known heirlooms
that had once belonged,
while hands could still hold them,
to the Heathobards' sires,

[XXIX–XXX]

until they led away
to a lost battle
their own lives
4080   and their allies' too.
An old warrior,
eyeing those treasures
    at the mead-drinking,
remembers comrades
slaughtered by spears
and his soul is bitter.
With grim goading
he begins to poison
the thoughts of a young
4090   thane of Ingeld's,
rekindling cruel
conflict, whispering:
    'Do you recognize
your reverend father's
weapon, the one
he wore to battle,
marching beneath
    his mask-helmet
to that dread meeting
4100   where the Danes killed him?
They trounced our troops
and controlled the field
after our war-chiefs had died
and Withergyld fallen.
Now a child
of that pernicious race
struts past our benches,
striding jauntily,
wearing—flaunting!—
4110   the well-known sword
which is yours by right,
my young comrade!'
The old man persists
in urgings like these,

calling for vengeance
until it comes at last,
and the woman's thane
welters in blood,
paying with his life
4120   for the past actions
of his sire. The sudden
assassin escapes,
with his near perfect
knowledge of the country.
Soon both parties
break their agreement,
the oaths of earls;
Ingeld's fury
     is unleashed
4130   and his love for his wife
grows cooler, chilled
by curdling sorrow.
I conclude, therefore,
that this compact between
Heathobards and Danes
is highly unstable
and not to be trusted.
But now I must tell you
more about Grendel,
4140   mighty Hygelac,
     so you may know
with what naked strength
and savagery we fought.
When the sun, the jewel
of heaven, had set,
the hellish creature
came prowling stealthily
to pay us a visit
where we held watch
4150   in the high meadhall.
Quickly he killed
my comrade Hondscioh,
quietly asleep
closest to the door,

a girded hero;
Grendel devoured
my faithful friend
with foaming jaws,
swallowed him whole
4160   at a single gulp.
The demon, his teeth
dripping with gore,
had little longing
to leave, to slip
out of the building
empty handed,
so he stepped toward me
and stretched out his hand,
agog with greed.
4170   A glove was hanging
from his belt; it was big
and bloodstained, closed
by cunning clasps
and craftily stitched
from dragon skins
by devilish skill.
Plainly he planned
on popping me,
who had done him no harm,
4180   in that dread game-bag,
another victim.
But it was not to be,
and I rose to my feet
raging with fury.
It would take too long
to tell you, my king,
how he paid the full
price for his crimes
and how my actions there
4190   brought honor to your people,
Hygelac my lord!
He hurled himself from me,
prolonging his life
for a little while

but leaving behind him,
as he lunged away,
his right arm,
wrenched from its socket
when he sought in despair
4200   the safety of the marshes.
When day dawned
the Danish king
rewarded my work
with wonderful gifts,
with gold and jewels,
glorious treasures,
where we feasted in hall
like friends, surrounded
by mirth and music.
4210   Mighty Hrothgar
knows legends and songs
from long-gone times:
sometimes he would play
sweet melodies
on his sounding harp,
sometimes sing songs
sorrowful but true;
sometimes he would tell
astonishing stories,
4220   strange but moving;
and sometimes the old
sad-hearted king,
mastered by age,
would lament his youth
and broken strength,
his breast surging
with immense sorrow
as he remembered the past.
We sat in the hall
4230   the summer-long day,
dining and drinking
until darkness came
again to mankind
and Grendel's mother,

whose son had been slain
   so savagely,
was ready to wreak
red vengeance
and assault the hall.
4240   She soon picked out
a victim in Heorot
and avenged her child,
ending the life
   of Æschere,
the king's closest
confidant and friend.
When day dawned
the Danes bewailed
   their inability
4250   to burn the corpse
of their fellow thane
on a funeral pyre,
for she had borne it to blind
abysses of ocean,
the depths of the sea,
in her devil's embrace:
the gravest, grimmest,
most grievous sorrow
old Hrothgar
4260   had ever known.
In his anguish of mind
he asked me again,
as I valued your life,
to venture mine,
risking destruction
in a rash duel
beneath the pitching waves;
he promised to reward me.
It is well known, now,
4270   how I went to fight
the ghastly guardian
of the great deep;
how we grappled together
in grim combat;

how at last my blade
lopped off the head
of Grendel's mother
in her gloomy hall;
how the sea turned red;
4280   how I swam upward
after a narrow escape
(I was not yet doomed);
and how once again
wise Hrothgar,
Healfdene's son,
gave me handsome gifts.

XXXI

His customs were kingly,
his court noble,
and I found no lack
4290   of fitting rewards:
the highborn son
of Healfdene gave me
ornaments as rich
as any I could hope for.
And here, now, my lord,
Hygelac my king,
I give them all to you,
since every benefit
I have ever received
4300   I owe to you,
my closest and kindest
kinsman on earth."
He bade men bring in
the boar-head standard,
the great helmet,
the grey mailcoat,
the splendid sword
and spoke as follows:
"Hrothgar, the wise
4310   ruler of Denmark,

gave me this war-gear
to give to you,
but told me I should first
tell its history.
These weapons, he said,
had once belonged
to the high war-king
Heorogar the Dane,
who grudged the gift

4320 of the gear to his son,
to lord Heoroweard,
loyal though he was.
Use it with joy,
my young master!"
It is said that four
swift-footed horses,
matched bays,
marvelous steeds,
brought up the rear;

4330 Beowulf gave them
to the king, which is how
a kinsman should behave,
not weaving
nets of malice
 for a kinsman,
cruelly scheming
to harm a comrade.
Hygelac's nephew
was loyal and true

4340 and loved him dearly,
and each thought only
of the other's good.
I heard that the hero
gave Hygd the great
glorious gold necklace
he got from Wealhtheow,
and three horses,
thick-maned and graceful,
with bright saddles;

4350 her breast was adorned

long afterward
by that lustrous gift.
And so, with unceasing
sapience and strength,
the son of Ecgtheow
sought after fame
and pursued glory.
His soul was untroubled;
he hewed down none
4360   of his hearth companions,
but guarded the gifts
God bestowed on him
with skill and greater
discretion than any
warrior on earth.
Once, in his boyhood,
the thanes of his people
had thought him useless
and King Hrethel
4370   had declined to give him
approval or praise
through presents at mead;
they all looked on him
as an idle youth,
a lazy princeling.
He lived to see
this judgment reversed
and enjoy respect.
And now Hygelac
4380   the munificent king
ordered men to fetch
an heirloom of Hrethel's,
radiant with gold;
in the realm of the Geats
there was no sword
more renowned than it.
Beowulf was brought
this blade and confirmed
in his ancestral estates,
4390   seven thousand

hides of land
and a high gift-throne.
Both of them, the king
and Beowulf, had land
   in that country,
the king much more,
the whole kingdom,
since he was higher in rank.
It would come to pass
4400   in the cruel wars
of the harsh future,
when Hygelac was dead
and his son Heardred
had been slain in combat,
bravely thrusting
his battered shield
against savage hordes
of Swedish foes
who had invaded his land
4410   and vanquished his troops,
hacking the nephew
of Hereric to death—
it would come to pass
that the crown of the Geats
became Beowulf's.
He was king of that realm
for fifty years,
befriending its people
and serving their interests,
4420   until a usurper came
to rule in the night,
a raging dragon
who guarded a gold-hoard
in a great barrow
on the rim of the heath,
reached by a path
secret and obscure.
But someone had found it,
had approached the mound
4430   and prowled round the treasure,

hurriedly grabbing
a huge goblet
and then dashing away.
When the dragon found
    it had been robbed
by some rascally thief
while sound asleep,
it soon let the whole
neighborhood know
4440   how annoyed it was.

XXXII

But theft had not entered
the thoughts of the man
who robbed the ring-hoard
and enraged its keeper:
a fugitive slave,
fleeing from his master
because of heinous deeds
and hoping to escape
a bad whipping,
4450   he had bolted inside,
seeking refuge.
This sudden intruder
had hardly entered
the hollow darkness
when he saw the huge
slumbering form
of the dread dragon
and darted away
as fast as he could,
4460   filching the goblet
in mindless terror.
There were many such
elegant ornaments
in that underground vault,
the vast legacy
of a vanished race.

A heart-heavy man
had hidden them there
in a bygone age
4470   while brooding darkly
on those dear treasures.
Death had taken
all his kinsmen
in earlier days,
and this lone relict
of a lost people,
this watcher of the hoard,
awaited it too,
aware he could keep
4480   his wealth for only
the blink of an eye.
The barrow stood ready
on a wide headland
at the water's edge,
secured against thieves
by cunning artifice.
The keeper of the rings
carried inside it
armful after armful
4490   of opulent jewels
resplendent with gold,
then spoke these words:
"Keep, O earth,
this kingly wealth,
since men may not have it.
They mined it from you
in days that are gone;
now death and battle
have claimed them forever,
4500   calling away
my sweet comrades;
they have seen the last
of mirth in the hall.
Not a man is left
to brandish a sword

or burnish a mead-cup;
all have gone elsewhere,
eminent heroes.
Now the stout helmet
4510   must be stripped clean
of its plates of gold:
the polishers sleep
who once furbished
    the war-bonnet;
and the staunch mailcoat
that sturdily endured
the crash of battle
    must not accompany
its owner farther:
4520   those iron rings
are barred from embarking
on that bleak last journey
by their master's side.
The music of ringing
harps is still;
the hawk no longer
swings through the rafters,
nor does the swift stallion
paw the courtyard:
4530   imperious death
has silenced a world
of sentient beings."
So he mourned
    in solitude
for all the others,
anguished and grieving
day and night,
until death's surges
hushed his heartbeats.
4540   The hoard was discovered
unguarded and open
by a great dragon,
a smooth-skinned serpent
in search of a grave-mound,

winging its fiery
way through the night
enveloped in flame,
a violent portent
for dwellers on earth.

4550   Although it is a dragon's style
to hunt out hoards
of heathen treasure,
they never bring it
an ounce of profit.
This fierce, furious
fire-breathing reptile
had been guarding its mound
of gold in the earth
for three hundred years

4560   when the thief robbed it
and roused its wrath.
When he had rifled the mound
and taken the goblet,
the terrified slave
carried the golden
cup to his master,
earning a pardon
for old offenses.
His astonished lord

4570   studied the treasure;
seldom in his life
had he seen such a thing.
Meanwhile the drowsing
monster awoke;
sniffing the ground,
it soon picked up
the scent of the stranger,
who had sneaked too close
to the dragon's head,

4580   a dangerous act;
but a man whose death
    is not mandated,
and whom God guards

and guides, can survive
dozens of dangers.
The dragon combed
the area anxiously,
avid to know
whose foot had approached it
4590   while it was fast asleep.
Sometimes, enraged,
it circled the whole
far-flung fastness, searching,
but it found no one
in that wilderness;
it was wild with anger
and wanted vengeance.
Once it went back
to look for its goblet
4600   and learned that someone
had dared to ransack
its darling treasure,
its hidden gold-hoard.
It could hardly wait
for dusk to descend,
indignant and impatient;
it was in a frenzy now,
fiercely resolved
to repay its foes
4610   with poison and flame
for taking its cup.
When twilight came
it was delighted;
it left the barrow
and soared skyward
in search of battle.
Its onslaught would have
an ill beginning
for the folk in that land
4620   and be followed at once
by an ill ending
for their ancient king.

XXXIII

The despoiler was soon
spitting out flames
and burning down buildings,
bringing men death
and enormous dread;
it had no intention
of leaving anything
4630   alive in that country.
These vast depredations
of the venomous worm
left wide tracts
of wasteland, showing
how whole heartedly
it hated the Geats
and strove to destroy them,
streaking back home
to its big barrow
4640   before break of day,
leaving wreckage and reeking
ruin everywhere.
It trusted its war-strength
and its towering mound
to protect it from harm;
that trust deceived it.
Beowulf was brought
these baleful tidings,
was told that his own
4650   tall meadhall,
the gift-seat of the Geats,
greatest of buildings,
    was in ashes.
The old ring-giver's
heart was heavy
with huge misgivings;
he wondered if all
    unwittingly
he had offended God,
4660   the Father of heaven,

by breaking his law;
his breast seethed
with sad foreboding,
as was seldom the case.
The scather, meanwhile,
had scorched the entire
coastline with fire,
crofts, villages,
courts, and castles;
4670   and the king of the Geats,
the prince of his people,
pondered gloomily
    how to avenge himself.
He devised, in the end,
a shield of iron
and showed his royal
smiths how to make it;
he had seen at once
that a shield of wood
4680   was sure to fail him
in a fight against fire.
The fierce-hearted king
was approaching the end
of his present life,
his sojourn on earth,
and so was the dragon,
who had lain on its gold
so long a time.
The stern war-king
4690   disdained to attack
his flying enemy
with a force of men,
a clutch of companions;
he was quite fearless
and discounted the scather's
skill in warfare,
its naked strength.
Had he not, himself,
survived many
4700   violent clashes

and fierce encounters
since those far-off days
when his grip had crushed
Grendel in combat
and his quick courage
had cleansed the hall
of noble Hrothgar?
And had he not wrought revenge
that was highly praised
4710   when Hygelac his lord,
the son of Hrethel,
was slain leading
his raid on Frisia?
The ruler of the Geats,
the father of his folk,
had been felled in battle
by blows of the sword,
but Beowulf escaped,
performing a famous
4720   feat of swimming,
cleaving the waves
while carrying thirty
suits of mail
on his sinewy arm.

    The Hetware
could hardly boast
of their short-lived charge
with shields held tight
while fighting on foot;
4730   few of them survived
Beowulf's attack
to go back to their homes,
whereas Ecgtheow's son
triumphantly swam
through the ocean waves
to his own people.
There Hygd, the widow
of Hygelac, offered
to give him the throne,
4740   for she had grave doubts

that Heardred her child
could hold the country
against foreign hosts,
now that his father was dead.
But she sought in vain
to persuade the valiant
son of Ecgtheow
to usurp his youthful
cousin's kingdom
4750   or covet its throne
or allow the Geats
to elect him king;
but he guided the boy
in governing the land
until he reached manhood
and could reign on his own.
Then Ohthere's sons,
Eanmund and Eadgils,
exiles from Sweden,
4760   asked for asylum
in the realm of the Geats;
they were rebels, in flight
from Onela their uncle,
the ablest sea-king
and ring-lord ever
to rule the Swedes,
a highborn hero.
Heardred was killed
helping those rebels:
4770   Hygelac's son
obtained a reward
for his hospitality
when the Swedes slaughtered him.
No sooner was he dead
than Onela returned
to his own kingdom,
allowing Beowulf
to lead the Geats
and ascend their throne—
4780   an exceptional king.

XXXIV

In later years
he lived to see vengeance
for his kinsman's death;
he became a friend
to Eadgils, the other
of Ohthere's sons,
and supported his play
for power in Sweden
with vigorous aid,
4790   avenging Heardred
on cold battlefields
and killing Onela.
Consistently successful,
the son of Ecgtheow
had survived every
violent clash
and fierce encounter
until the fatal day
when he went to fight
4800   that winged dragon.
Burning with anger,
Beowulf set out
with eleven men
to look for the monster.
He had been told by now
how the trouble began,
the grim grievance:
the guilty cup
had come to his hands
4810   from the cowardly wretch
whose stealth and terror
had started everything,
and the thief himself
was the thirteenth man
in that picked war-band,
a prisoner, forced
against his wishes
to guide their footsteps.

He soon recognized
4820   the sinister mound,
the huge barrow
hard by the shore
of the surging sea;
inside was a hoard
of gems and jewels
jealously guarded
by the old serpent,
angrily coiled
beneath its earth-wall.
4830   It was no task
for a timid man,
obtaining that gold!
Bowed with age,
Beowulf sat
on the sad headland
and said goodbye
to his hall-comrades.
His heart was uneasy
and doom-laden,
4840   death very near
that would end the days
of the old ruler,
ransack his soul's
ring-hoard and sunder
life and body;
in a little while
the king's spirit
would quit his flesh.
The son of Ecgtheow
4850   said to his companions:
"I survived, in my youth,
volleys of spears,
many battles;
I remember them all.
    When I was seven
my sovereign took me
from Ecgtheow my father
into his own household.

Good King Hrethel
4860   guided and loved me,
gave me handsome gifts
and upheld our kinship.
Though a callow lad
at his court, I never
had any less honor
than his own children,
Herebeald and Hæthcyn—
or Hygelac my lord.
The eldest, Herebeald,
4870   met an early death
through dark misadventure,
accidentally slain
by Hæthcyn his brother,
who hit and killed him
with a badly aimed
bolt from his hornbow:
he missed the target
and murdered his kinsman,
a brother his brother
4880   with a bloody dart.
The crime was committed
within the clan itself,
    unavengeable,
the victim dying
    unatoned for:
tragic for Hrethel,
whose plight was like that
of a poor old man
who must see his son
4890   swing on the gallows,
and whose sole comfort
is singing a dirge,
a doleful lament,
while the dark raven
gnaws at the body
    and he knows himself
helpless to help,
hampered by age.

4900

When morning comes
he is reminded again
of the loss of his heir.
He has little desire
to father a second
unfortunate child
in the world of men,
now that one, his first,
has been deprived of deeds
by the power of death.
He looks with sorrow

4910

on his loved one's seat,
the waste wine-halls
and windswept courts,
silent and joyless;
they sleep in their graves,
the horsemen, the heroes,
and the harp is still,
the revelry that once
rang round the walls.

XXXV

He crawls into bed,

4920

crying bitterly,
the one for the other;
his wealth, his estates
seem senseless. It was precisely
the same with Hrethel,
whose hollowing heart
heaved with sorrow
for Herebeald his son.
How could he make
the offender pay

4930

for his fatal deed?
How show hatred
to Hæthcyn, the son
he no longer loved
because of his luckless mistake?

Wretched, irresolute,
old Hrethel chose
simply to die
and seek God's light,
bequeathing to his heirs
4940   his country and his people,
as a leader should
when he leaves this world.
Soon there was warfare
between Swedes and Geats
and battles fought
by both peoples
over restless seas,
after Hrethel had died
and the sons of the king
4950   of Sweden, Ongentheow,
proved wild and warlike,
unwilling to live
in peace with the Geats;
but they plowed our seas
and struck at our people
near Storm Mountain.
My two relatives
taught them a lesson,
defeating their forces
4960   in a famous campaign,
though the older of my uncles
paid the ultimate price,
forfeiting his life,
for this fight brought death
to Hæthcyn my kinsman.
    But Hygelac,
my other uncle,
wrought an apt vengeance
with naked steel
4970   the next morning,
when Ongentheow was slain
by Eofor, a Geat
whose mind was inflamed
with remembered wrongs;

his savage sword-blow
smashed the helmet
of the king of the Swedes
and he crashed to the ground.
I always repaid
4980   my own lord, Hygelac,
for his countless gifts
with courage in battle
and a grateful sword.
He granted me many
lands and lordships
and had little need
to look for retainers
who would be less faithful,
giving money
4990   to Gepid hirelings,
swashbuckling Swedes,
or swordsmen from Denmark.
I fought always
in the front rank,
the foremost of his foot-troops,
and I firmly intend
to battle like that
while this blade lasts,
which has often been my ally,
5000   early and late,
since the day I slew
Dæghrefen, flower
of the Frankish troops,
in front of the hosts.
He wanted to plunder
Wealhtheow's neck-ring
and carry it off
to the king of Frisia,
but he died in our deadly
5010   duel instead,
the standard bearer
of the stout-hearted Franks,
untouched by the sword:
my terrible bear-hugs

hushed his heartbeats.
Here, however,
it is my worthy blade
that must win us the hoard.”
Beowulf made
5020   his battle vows
for the last time:
“I outlived storms
of strife in my youth
and am still ready,
though feeble with age,
to fight valiantly
and gain glory,
if this grim monster
dares venture
5030   from its den to meet me!”
Now Beowulf said
goodbye to his men
for the last time,
saluting each
of his noble thanes:
“I would not fight
this foe with the sword
if I could find a way,
with all honor
5040   and in all fairness,
to deal with a dragon
as I did with Grendel.
But here I expect
hot battle-fires,
blasts of venom,
and must bear a shield,
swathed in armor.
I solemnly vow
not to flee a footstep
5050   but to let fate decide
our doom as it will,
our destiny—fate,
and almighty God.
My mind is resolved

to forgo vaunts
against this grim spoiler.
    My warriors,
you must await what will come,
standing here steadfast
5060   in your steel mailcoats,
watching to see
which of us survives
disenabling wounds.
It is not your task,
nor meet for man
except me alone
to contest the strength
of this terrible worm.
I shall gain glory
5070   and gaze on its treasure
with my own eyes,
or else it will kill me,
ending the reign
of your ancient king."
Beowulf rose
brandishing his shield,
helmet on his head,
and hurried in his armor
toward the stone rampart,
5080   still confident
in his renowned strength.
He was no coward!
But now this hero,
so nobly born,
survivor of so much
violent conflict,
such fierce encounters
where foot-troops clashed,
saw stone arches
5090   standing before him,
spewing forth streams
of splashing flame
and noxious fumes.
No man on earth

could enter that doorway
and open the hoard
without passing through
those poisonous flames.
Livid with anger,
5100   the lord of the Geats
let a bold war-cry
burst from his lungs;
it entered the mound
and echoed inside it,
ringing loudly
in its rocky depths.
The hoard-keeper, hearing
a human voice,
twitched with fury;
5110   the time was past
for friendly parley.
First came a scorching
blast from the barrow,
the breath of the monster,
its angry war-flame;
the earth shook.
The warrior, watchfully
waiting outside,
swung up his shield
5120   to receive the foe,
whose hate-swollen heart
hurried it out
to kill the intruder.
Quickly Beowulf
unsheathed Nægling,
his sharp sword,
an ancient heirloom;
each of those two
mighty ones meant
5130   mischief to the other.
Tensely leaning
against his tall shield,
the warrior watched
as the worm tightened

into close coils;
the king waited.
Uncoiling in a flash,
the creature launched itself,
streaking toward the stranger
5140 with destruction. His shield
offered protection
to the old war-king
for less time
than he liked or hoped,
where he found he was fighting
his first battle
in which fate was unfriendly
and refused to give him
quick victory.
5150 The king of the Geats
swung his ancestral
sword, striking
the brindled horror,
but its blade failed him
badly in battle,
biting less deeply
      than the peril
of the prince demanded,
harried and harassed.
5160   The hoard-keeper
fumed with resentment
when it felt the blow
and spat out flames;
the sparks flew flashing
a long way off.
The lord of the Geats
could not boast of success,
for his blade had failed him,
his trusty war-sword
5170 had betrayed him at need,
as it should never have done.
It would not be easy
for the sorely pressed
son of Ecgtheow

to relinquish his long
life in the world,
destined to dwell
in a different place,
like everyone else
5180   on earth, and surrender
this brief being.
After a breathing space
they engaged again,
those grim combatants,
the dragon attacking
with redoubled rage
   and the ring-giver,
his reign over,
suffering sorely
5190   in the searing flames.
He could hope for no help
from his hand-picked troop:
instead of staunchly
standing beside him,
flocking to defend him,
they had fled to the woods
   to save themselves,
except for a single thane
who was racked with grief,
5200   for a right-thinking man
can never undo
the knots of kinship.

XXXVI

Wiglaf was his name,
Weohstan his father's;
he was agile and bold,
Ælfhere's kinsman,
and a Swede by birth.
Seeing Beowulf
encased in his war-mask
5210   and overcome by heat,

he recalled the gifts
the king had given him,
the wealthy lands
   of the Wægmundings,
the lands that had once
belonged to his father.
He knew his duty
and could not hold back,
but lifted his yellow
5220   lindenwood shield
and wielded the sword
that had once belonged
to Eanmund the exile,
Ohthere's son.
Wiglaf's father
Weohstan had killed
that friendless wanderer
in fierce combat
and had carried the spoils,
5230   the crested helmet,
the mailcoat, the sword
made by giants,
to Onela, Eanmund's
uncle, who gave him
his nephew's armor
and did not protest
that the bloody corpse
was his brother's son.
Weohstan cherished
5240   that war-gear for years,
the sword and mailcoat,
until his son Wiglaf
was as swift a swordsman
as himself, then gave him
the armor and many
other treasures
in the land of the Geats,
where they lived at the time,
when he was near death.
5250   Never before

had the proud youngster
been proved in combat
or swung a sword
by the side of his chief.
But his faith did not falter,
nor did his father's blade
flinch in battle,
as the firedrake learned
when the two foes
5260   tested each other.
Filled with anger
toward his false comrades,
Wiglaf shouted
words of reproach:
"I remember once
    at the mead-drinking,
while we swilled his beer,
how we solemnly vowed
to the great chieftain
5270   who gave us rings
that we would pay him back
for these precious gifts,
this dazzling war-gear,
if danger should ever
approach him. Today
he picked us out
from among his troops,
    imagining
we were loyal friends,
5280   and loaded us with gifts
because he thought us all
thanes he could trust,
honor-bound men,
though it was always his hope,
as king of the country,
to accomplish this feat
all alone,
for all our sakes,
    since he was aware
5290   of the wonderful deeds

he had done in the past.
Now the day has come
when our noble lord
needs the support
of good companions.
We must go forward
to help our leader
while this heat torments him,
this grim firestorm.
5300 God knows
it would be far better
that flames should devour me
than that I should outlive
my lord and master.
We would be cowards
to carry our shields
home to the loved ones
at our hearths, unless first
we slay this dragon
5310 and save the life
of our beloved king.
It would be little thanks
for all we owe him
if only he
of the folk of the Geats
should fall in battle,
suffer and die,
so I will assist him here
and we will share mailcoat,
5320 shield, and broadsword."
He strode through the smoke
to stand by his lord,
his helmet gleaming
and hailing him loudly:
"Beowulf! My king!
Be bold and resolute!
You vowed in your youth
with vaunting words
that as long as you lived
5330 you would let no chance

for glory slip by you!
In this great contest
   you must unflinchingly
defend your life
with undiminished strength—
and with me to help you!"
These bracing words
had barely been uttered
when the fearful worm
5340   came flying toward them,
swooping from the sky
for a second attack.
Loyal Wiglaf's
lindenwood shield
was consumed in a flash
except for its boss,
and his linked mailcoat
gave little protection.
He crept gratefully
5350   beneath the king's great
iron-forged shield
when his own had been burned
by those baleful flames.
Beowulf, incensed,
swung his gleaming
sword Nægling
with astounding strength,
striking the dragon
on its naked skull.
5360   But Nægling shattered;
   that excellent
ancient weapon
failed its master,
for his fate was such
that iron blades
and edges could never
help him in combat;
his hand was too mighty,
   we have been told,
5370   overtaxing the strength

of every weapon
he had ever borne
   against an enemy.
They all failed him.
Meanwhile the murderous
monster unwound
its loathsome coils
and launched a third
grievous assault
5380   when it got the chance.
Cruelly it clamped
the king's neck
in its bestial jaws
and Beowulf's life-blood
spurted from his veins
and splashed on the ground.

XXXVII

We have heard that then,
in the high-king's need,
faithful Wiglaf
5390   put forth the strength
and huge courage
that were his by nature.
He was ardent and eager
when he aided his king;
ignoring the dragon's
enormous head,
he smote its soft
smooth underside,
singeing his hand
5400   when he swung the sword,
but driving it deep
in the dragon's gut,
damping its fires.
Dazed but conscious,
Beowulf pulled
a bright dagger,

his sharp war-knife,
from the sheath on his belt
and sliced the smooth-skinned
5410   serpent in half.
Working together
as one, the two
kinsmen had conquered
their common enemy,
Wiglaf fighting
as a warrior should
by his lord's side
in the illustrious king's
last battle,
5420   the last triumph
of his work in the world;
for the wound the ancient
grave-dwelling worm
had given him started
to swell and swelter
and soon he felt
inside his body
surges of venom
boiling and seething.
5430   Beowulf staggered
to a slab in the wall
and sat heavily.
He stared at the earth-hall,
saw the stone arches
supported on pillars
that propped it within,
this broad barrow
built by giants.
Meanwhile Wiglaf,
5440   moved by pity,
hurriedly splashed
handfuls of water
on his king, injured
and covered with blood.
When the kindly youth
had unclasped his helmet,

Beowulf spoke,
braving the pain;
he was well aware
5450   that the wound had brought him
to the end of his life
and all enjoyment
of earth's riches,
to the end of his long
days and doings;
now death was waiting.
"How gladly," he said,
"I would give this war-gear
to my heir, if only
5460   I had ever been blessed
with a son who might reign
in succession to me
in the realm of the Geats.
I ruled this people
for fifty years.
No foreign king,
none of the princes
of neighboring lands,
dared attack me
5470   with deadly force
or wage warfare.
I waited, in my homeland,
for the harvest of fate;
I held what was mine
but sought no quarrels
nor swore many
oaths unjustly.
For all these things
my soul is grateful
5480   though I am sick to death.
The Lord of heaven
will have little cause
to accuse me of killing
kinsmen, when life
has flown from my body.
Faithful Wiglaf!

Go now, and enter
these grey stone walls
to the treasure!
5490   The serpent lies here
robbed of its riches,
rigid in death.
Do not delay, Wiglaf,
if I am to look on those heaps
of gems and jewels
and enjoy a glimpse
of the golden hoard,
so that after gazing my fill
on its immense wealth
5500   I may with more ease
relinquish both life
and this land I have ruled."

XXXVIII

I have heard that at once,
hearing these words,
the son of Weohstan
was swift to obey
his lord and master's
last wishes.
As he entered the mound
5510   in his iron mail,
he passed the place
where the prince was sitting
and saw beyond it
the serpent's lair,
its home and hoard
with their huge riches:
gold was glittering
on the ground nearby
and on all the walls;
5520   ancient goblets
stood there moldering,
stripped of ornaments,

unpolished for ages;
proud mask-helmets,
old, rust-eaten,
arm-rings galore.
The hoard had been opened,
for heathen gold
easily thwarts

5530   efforts by men
to hide it forever,
hard though they try.
Good Wiglaf
saw a great standard
blazing in the gloom
above the ring-hoard,
its gold streamers
gleaming brilliantly;
its light let him

5540   look at the treasure
untroubled by fear
of the terrible worm,
asleep from sword-wounds
outside the barrow.
At last, I have heard,
this lone warrior
rifled the contents
of that rich grave-mound,
grabbing up all

5550   the golden trophies
his soul could desire
and seizing the standard,
brightest of banners.
A blow from the sharp
iron dagger
of his old king
had killed the creature
who kept those treasures
for a span of years,

5560   spewing out flame
and fire at midnight
in defense of its gold

until the destined day
when death took it.
Worried and anxious,
Wiglaf went back
outside, eager
to see if perhaps,
on the slab of stone
5570   beside the entrance
    where he had left
his beloved chief,
he would still find him
strong and conscious.
As he approached the king
with the precious spoils
he saw Beowulf
swimming in blood
and near death.
5580   He renewed his efforts
to waken him with water
until, weak and faint,
there burst from his breast
some broken words
as he gazed at the gold
in grief and agony:
    "I am grateful
to God almighty,
the Keeper of heaven
5590   and King of glory,
for the lordly goods
I look on here,
and the grace to gain
such gifts for my people
    before the day
of my death arrived.
I have paid the price
for these priceless things,
life itself.
5600   Look faithfully
to the people's needs;

my part is finished.
Bid my thanes,
after burning my corpse,
build a barrow
on a bluff near the sea,
wide-walled and high
on Whale Headland,
as a remembrance of me
5610   among my people;
in centuries to come
sailors will call it
Beowulf's barrow
when their boats come home
from far journeys
on the fog-grey sea."
The king carefully
unclasped from his throat
his great neck-ring
5620   and gave it to Wiglaf;
he handed his helmet
and hard mailcoat
to the young thane
and told him to use them well:
"My loyal Wiglaf,
you are the last of our race,
    the Wægmundings.
War and ruin
have swept my kinsmen away
5630   at the decree of fate,
awesome warriors,
and I must follow them."
These labored words
were the last to issue
from Beowulf's breast
before he embraced the pyre
and its searing flames;
his soul left his body
and went to obtain
5640   the reward of the just.

[XXXIX]

Wiglaf was woebegone,
watching next to him,
seeing his lord
sink to the ground
and die in his sight,
enduring terrible
death agonies.
The dragon lay
beside him, its days
5650 of soaring over;
the coiled creature
had come to the end
of guarding hoards
of gold in the earth.
Blades of iron
beaten by hammers,
hard and biting,
had hewn it down;
that wide-flying worm,
5660 wounded to death,
had sunk to the ground
beside its treasure
and would skim no more
through the sky at midnight,
sporting in the air,
displaying itself,
proud of its riches;
it had plunged to earth,
killed by the old king's
5670 courage and daring.
They say it is seldom
seen to happen
that a great hero
gains the victory,
daring though he is
in deeds of valor,
if he vies with the breath
and venom of a dragon

or rifles its treasure

5680   with courageous hands
while the worm is at home,
awake and alert,
in its dark barrow.
Death was the price
Beowulf paid
for that bright ring-hoard;
king and monster
came to the end
of life together.

5690   In a little while
the scrimshankers
came skulking from the woods,
ten cowardly
traitors who had all
lacked the courage
to lift their spears
in their prince's last
most pressing danger
and who now bore their shields

5700   ignobly back
to where their leader
lay in the dust;
they waited there, ashamed,
for Wiglaf to speak.
He sat exhausted
by the side of his lord,
fiercely sprinkling
his face with water;
but no matter how much

5710   his mind was bent
on keeping life
in the king's body,
he was helpless to change
the hero's destiny:
God's judgments
governed men's fates
in those days of old
and do so still.

Soon the fainthearts
5720   received their answer
from the grieving youth,
and it was grim and hard;
Wiglaf the son
of Weohstan spoke,
frowning with disfavor
on the faithless crew:
"Our ancient king
often gave us—
heroes while in hall!—
5730   helmets and mailcoats,
the finest treasures
he could find for his men
anywhere on earth,
armor like the brilliant
well-wrought war-gear
you are wearing right now.
Anyone with any
inkling of truth
must freely admit
5740   that he found, in the end,
when threatened with death,
that he had thrown away
the love and the gifts
he lavished on you!
He could hardly boast
of you hearth companions!
But God the giver
of glory allowed him,
acting alone
5750   with only his dagger,
to take vengeance
on his terrible foe.
I myself could give
only small support
in that storm of strife,
but strove even so,
overtaxing my strength,
to protect my kinsman,

and the foe grew feebler
5760   when it felt my blow,
the flames darted
less fiercely from its head.
Too few defenders
flocked to his side
when our prince stood
in peril of his life.
From this day forward,
therefore, your kinsmen
will be given no gifts,
5770   no gold, no war-gear,
no renown by our kings;
they will never receive
gems or jewelry
or enjoy the right
to have and hold
inherited land,
when the country learns
of your cowardly flight,
that deed of dishonor.
5780   Death is better
for any man
        than infamy!"

XL

He told a horseman
to take the news
to the camp on the cliff-top,
where the king's army,
soldiers with their shields,
had sat anxiously
the whole day through,
5790   their hearts suspended
in fitful balance
between fear of his death
and hope of his life.
The herald who carried

the news up the bluff
was not reluctant
to tell his terrible
tidings but shouted:
"The lord Beowulf,
5800   our illustrious king
and loving leader,
is lying dead,
grievously killed
by the great dragon.
Next to him lies
the enormous foe,
slain by his dagger.
His sword was powerless,
though potently swung,
5810   to pierce the armor
of that wicked worm.
Wiglaf, the son
of Weohstan, sits
weeping beside him,
the living beside
the lifeless warrior,
and his heart is heavy
as he holds death-watch
over friend and foe.
5820   I fear that our poor
people will suffer
the plagues of war
when our ruler's death
reaches the ears
of the Franks and Frisians.
Our feud with them started
when King Hygelac
carelessly raided
the Rhineland coast
5830   with a marauding fleet
and harried the Hetware,
hearth-friends of the Franks.
They met him in battle
with a mighty host

and, far from rewarding
his forces with plunder
after a fine triumph,
our freebooting king
was slain with his army,
5840   and since that time
we have been viewed as foes
by the Merovingian king.

　　And we are unlikely
to be left in peace
by our neighbors the Swedes,
for we know to our grief
how Ongentheow their king
made an end of Hæthcyn,
Hrethel's successor,
5850   　　at Ravenswood,
when our fiery prince
in his foolish pride
rashly invaded
their realm with his troops.
Old Ongentheow,
Ohthere's father,
proud and impetuous,
made him pay for that;
he killed the marauder
5860   who had kidnapped his wife,
the wrinkled old queen,
and robbed her of her jewels,
his heir Ohthere's
and Onela's mother.
His levies pursued
the leaderless Geats,
who hoped by fleeing
to hide themselves deep
in dark Ravenswood
5870   after the death of their king.
Raging, Ongentheow
surrounded the forest
with his vast army,
vowing destruction

to the helpless Geats
the whole night through,
swearing that at sun-up
some would be butchered
with iron swords
5880   and others hanged,
breakfast for the birds.
But break of day
brought returning hope
to the terrified Geats,
when they heard from afar
Hygelac's war-horns
and trumpets blowing
as the intrepid prince
rode fearlessly up
5890   to reinforce his troops.

XLI

Cruel evidence
of the clash that ensued
between Swedes and Geats
was seen everywhere,
how those proud peoples
competed in hatred.
Old Ongentheow,
angry and bitter,
fell back baffled
5900   with his band of comrades,
hoping for safety
on higher ground.
He had heard men praise
Hygelac's prowess
and daring in war;
he doubted his own
power to defeat
the prince and protect
the wealth of his kingdom,
5910   its women and children,

from attacking troops,
so he retreated at once
behind a high earth-wall.
Hygelac was quick
to pursue the Swedes;
his excited troops
stormed the stronghold
and his standards were soon
pouring implacably
5920   through that place of refuge.
Old Ongentheow,
angry and grizzled,
was brought to bay
by bright sword-blades;
the fearsome Swede
was forced to acknowledge
the sword of Eofor,
the son of Wonred.
Eofor's brother,
5930   eager young Wulf,
had struck him already,
and streams of blood
poured from a scalp-wound,
but pain did not daunt him,
the intrepid old Swede;
he returned the stroke,
whirling instantly
toward Wulf his assailant,
and bashed him with a brutal
5940   blow in exchange.
It hewed through his helmet
and hammered his skull
so that Wulf the son
of Wonred staggered,
tried in vain
to return the blow,
then lurched to the ground
lathered in gore;
that angry stroke
5950   had injured him badly,

but his life was spared
by lenient fate.
While he lay bathed in blood,
his brother Eofor
let his massive blade
made by the giants
hew the giant
helm of Ongentheow
above his ancient shield;
5960   the old Swede
died instantly
and dropped to the ground.
A huddle of Geats
hurried at once
to assist Wulf
when they safely could,
when the Swedish troops
had been swept from the field.
Eofor plundered
5970   Ongentheow's corpse,
stripping the king
of his steel mailcoat,
his high helmet,
his hard-hilted sword.
The bloody spoil
was brought to Hygelac,
who received it with thanks
and swore to give Eofor
dazzling rewards,
5980   which he did, too,
when they came back home;
the king of the Geats,
the heir of Hrethel,
gave Eofor and Wulf
unwonted wealth
to reward their valor:
a hundred thousand
hides of folk-land,
farmsteads of fabulous value;
5990   nor could he be faulted for that largess,

idly censured by others,
since they had earned it in battle;
and Eofor got the king's
only daughter
as a prize for his hearth
and a pledge of favor.
And here is the root
of the hatred and rage
to soothe whose seethings,
6000   I sadly fear,
the Swedes will soon
seek to destroy us,
when they learn that our lord
and leader is dead,
the war-chief lifeless
who once preserved
the hoard and homeland
of hapless Hrothgar
from monstrous foes
6010   after much slaughter;
he delivered the Danes
and later persevered
in noble deeds.
But now let us hurry
to look on the place
where our lord lies dead,
then bear his lifeless
body solemnly
to the funeral pyre.
6020   Fabulous treasures
will melt with him there,
measureless riches,
the wonderful hoard
he won by dying.
Bracelets and rings
bought at the cost
of his precious blood
must perish by fire.
Flames will consume them,
6030   and his friends will not wear

those rings in remembrance
nor radiant maidens
clasp those circlets
round their comely throats;
instead they will often,
stripped of jewelry
and with woe in their hearts,
wander exile-paths,
now that our leader
6040   has renounced laughter
and the mirth of men.
Many a spear-shaft
will be grabbed in dismay
on grey mornings
numb with frost;
it will not be the harp
that wakes warriors,
but the wan raven
cawing over corpses,
6050   croaking to the eagle
what fine feeding
he found this morning,
gnawing at bodies
next to the wolf."
The speaker ended
his speech and neither
what he said of the past
nor saw in the future
was much mistaken.
6060   Mournfully, the Geats
all went trooping
under Eagle Bluff
to see the marvel;
their souls were weeping.
At last, lying there
lifeless on the sand,
they beheld their lord,
the hand that had once
given them gold,
6070   their great leader;

the king of the Geats
had come to the end
of the world, dying
a wondrous death.
As they neared the spot
they noticed something
even more wondrous,
the monstrous serpent
lying beside him,
6080   loathsome and mottled,
its skin seared
and scorched by the flames,
fifty fearful
feet long
where it lay on the ground.
While it lived, it was fond
of soaring at night,
then swooping back
to its noisome den;
6090   now it was dead;
it had guarded its last
gold-hoard on earth.
Standing beside it
were stoups and flagons,
dishes, drinking-horns,
and damascened swords,
thinned by rust
and their thousand years
of lying idle
6100   in the lap of the earth.
Moreover those rareties
and relics from the past,
those treasures of gold,
were protected by spells,
so that no man on earth
could come near the hoard
or gain its gold
unless God himself,
the guardian of men
6110   and granter of triumphs,

vouchsafed him safety
and unsealed the treasure:
some great hero
whom God found deserving.

XLII

It was manifest
that the man who hid them
had been crossed in his hope
of keeping those riches
hidden forever;
6120   now a hero had died,
killed by a dragon,
before cold iron
hushed its heartbeats.
It is hard to know
what will bring the end
of a brave chieftain
when all his hours
on earth are numbered,
his days of drinking
6130   with dear kinsmen.
It was so with the king
when he sought out the worm,
the cruel dragon;
he was quite unaware
of the doom that would soon
bring death upon him.
For the heathen lords
who hid that treasure
had cursed it, decreeing
6140   until the crack of doom
that anyone aiming
to own those riches
would be punished without pity,
imprisoned among idols
and fettered in hell-chains,
unless he first obtained

the gold-granting grace
of God, the real
Owner of all
6150   earthly treasure.
Wiglaf the son
of Weohstan spoke:
"Many must suffer
misery, at times,
because of one man's will;
how well we know it!
We could not dissuade
our magnanimous king
by any arguments
6160   or any means
from going to fight
   the gold-keeper,
letting it lie there
where it had lain for years
and occupy its mound
until the end of the world.
The doom was too strong
that drove him here,
and he held to his hero's
6170   high destiny.
The hoard has been opened
at hideous cost!
I stood in its midst
and stared at the treasure,
the glory of gold,
when I got the chance;
but venturing inside
that vast earth-hall
is a grim business,
6180   so I grabbed a random
and hurried armful
of hoarded gold,
clasped it to my chest
and carried it out
to show my master.
He was shaken by pain

but still conscious
and striving to speak,
though sick and dying.

6190   He said I should greet you
and tell you to build
a tall grave-mound
to cover his ashes
and keep his memory
alive in our hearts;
for our lord was the best
warrior on earth
and the worthiest king,
as long as he lived

6200   his life among us.
But now let us make
another journey
inside the barrow
to see those riches,
that golden treasure;
I will guide your steps
and lead you to stacks
of lustrous gems,
piles of jewels.

6210   Let the pyre be ready
by the time we return
from our trip inside,
so we may carry our dear
comrade and lord,
our worthy master,
to where he will rest
in the long keeping
of everlasting God."
Sadly, then, the young

6220   son of Weohstan,
the bold warrior,
bade his companions,
    a multitude
of men of the Geats,
to fetch firewood
from far and near

for Beowulf's pyre.
"Now blistering flames,"
he said, "must consume

6230   our sovereign lord,
who so often stood
in the iron storm
when swarms of missiles
swept from bowstrings
and flew over shields,
while feathered shafts
followed arrowheads
and performed their duty."
Weeping, the son

6240   of Weohstan next
summoned seven
soldiers from the host,
the worthiest he knew,
    and went with them,
the eighth in the group,
to enter the mound;
he strode in the lead,
stalwart and bold,
a blazing torch

6250   burning in his hand.
It seemed needless
to decide by lot
who should ransack
that heathen wealth,
when they saw no sign
of the serpent and gold
covered the ground
without its keeper in sight;
they had no regrets

6260   when notable treasures
were carried outside.
They kicked the dragon
    over the sea-cliff,
let the surf take it,
the flood enfold
that fatal hoard-guard.

Fantastic treasures
of twisted gold
were piled on a cart,
6270 and the prince, the white-haired
warrior, was borne
to Whale Headland.

XLIII

There the men of the Geats
made for their ruler
a funeral pyre
of fabulous splendor,
hung with helmets
and hollow shields
and bright mailcoats,
6280 as Beowulf had asked;
amidst these marvels
his lamenting thanes
laid the body
of their beloved king.
The wind died away
when warriors kindled
a bright death-fire
on that bare headland,
and murky wood-smoke
6290 mingled with weeping
rose over roaring
rust-colored flames
as they burned their way
through bone and marrow,
turning them to ash.
With tears and laments
men remembered
their mighty king,
while with hair bound tight
6300 and heaving breast
a woman of the Geats
wailed her heart out,

crazed with terror,
crying bitterly
that she dreaded days
of doom and disaster,
invading armies,
violence of troops,
slaughter, exile,
6310   slavery. Heaven
swallowed the smoke.
Sick with foreboding,
the men of the Geats
made a grave-mound
visible at sea
for vast distances,
and were done in ten
days constructing
Beowulf's barrow.
6320   They built a wall
enclosing his ashes,
crafted it as well
as their most masterful
masons could devise.
Riches of gold
and rings were heaped
in its hollow vault,
the whole treasure
Beowulf's thanes
6330   had borne from the hoard;
they buried all of it
back in the ground,
that unlucky gold,
where it lives today
as idle and vain
as it ever was.
Slowly, then, twelve
sons of princes
rode on horseback
6340   around the barrow,
lamenting their leader
in mournful lays;

they complained of their plight
but praised the king,
applauded his virtue
and prowess in war,
were generous in judgment,
just as retainers
should always be,
6350   honoring their lord
with worthy love
and words of praise
when fate leads him
forth from the body.
Woe-stricken warriors
wept for Beowulf,
along with his hearth-friends
and loyal thanes.
He had been, they said,
6360   the best and wisest
of kings of this world,
kindest to his people,
most open handed,
most eager for praise.

People and Places in *Beowulf*

(The figure in square brackets following each entry is the number of the verse in which the name first appears.)

Abel Old Testament figure, son of Adam and Eve, killed by his brother Cain. [215]

Ælfhere A kinsman of Wiglaf. [5206]

Æschere A counselor and intimate friend of Hrothgar, killed by Grendel's mother. [2646]

Battle-Rams A people living in the area of Romerike in southern Norway. [1039]

Beanstan Father of Breca. [1046]

Beowulf (1) **Beowulf the Dane:** Son and successor of Scyld Scefing. He is to be distinguished from Beowulf the Geat, the hero of the poem. See Genealogy of the Danish Royal House (p. xxviii). [35]

(2) **Beowulf the Geat:** Son of Ecgtheow and nephew of Hygelac. The hero of the poem. His mother was a daughter of the Geatish king Hrethel. See Genealogy of the Geatish Royal House (p. xxviii). [686]

Breca A prince of the Brondings, son of Beanstan. [1012]

Brondings Name of a tribe; it is not known where they lived. [1042]

Brosings In ancient Scandinavian legend, the Brosings (*Brísingar*) were fire-dwarfs who made a magnificent golden necklace for the goddess Freyja. [2397]

Cain Old Testament figure; the son of Adam and Eve who killed his brother Abel. In *Beowulf* he is presented as the progenitor of giants and monsters (including Grendel). [214]

Dæghrefen A warrior of the Franks, killed by Beowulf the Geat. [5002]

Danes A Scandinavian people, inhabitants of Denmark. [93]

Danish See Danes; Denmark. [3]

Denmark	An early Scandinavian kingdom that consisted of the territory of modern Denmark plus the southern portion (*Skåne*) of present-day Sweden. [12]
Eadgils	A Swedish prince (later king), son of Ohthere. After Ohthere's death, the Swedish throne was seized by his brother Onela, but Eadgils later gained it for himself with the help of Beowulf the Geat. See Genealogy of the Swedish Royal House (p. xxviii). [4758]
Eagle Bluff	A seaside cliff in the land of the Geats. [6062]
Eanmund	A Swedish prince, son of Ohthere, killed by Weohstan, the father of Wiglaf. See Genealogy of the Swedish Royal House (p. xxviii). [4758]
Ecglaf	Father of Unferth. [998]
Ecgtheow	Father of Beowulf the Geat. Like Weohstan and his son Wiglaf, Beowulf's loyal follower and successor, Ecgtheow was a member of the family (or tribe) of the Wægmundings, which appears to have had interests in the realms of both the Swedes and the Geats. See Genealogy of the Geatish Royal House (p. xxviii). [526]
Ecgwela	An otherwise unknown Danish king. [3423]
Eofor	A warrior of the Geats, slayer of the Swedish king Ongentheow. [4972]
Eomer	Son of Offa. [3920]
Eormenric	A king of the Ostrogoths, notorious in later Germanic legend for his covetousness and treachery. [2401]
Finn	A king of the Frisians. [2135]
Finns	Lapps (*Sami*) living in the northern part of Norway (*Finnmarken*). [1160]
Fitela	Nephew of Sigemund. [1759]
Folcwalda	A Frisian king, father of Finn. [2178]
Frankish	See Franks. [2422]
Franks	A powerful Germanic people who occupied much of the territory of present-day France and Germany. [5012]
Freawaru	Daughter of Hrothgar, betrothed to Ingeld, a king of the Heathobards. [4045]
Frisia	A Germanic kingdom extending northward toward Denmark from the mouth of the River Rhine. [2140]
Frisian	See Frisia; Frisians. [2135]

Frisians	A Germanic people, inhabitants of Frisia and closely allied to the Merovingian Franks. [2187]
Froda	A king of the Heathobards, father of Ingeld. [4050]
Garmund	Father of Offa. [3923]
Geatish	See Geats. [747]
Geats	A Scandinavian people who once occupied much of the southwestern portion of present-day Sweden. Their kingdom appears ultimately to have been absorbed into that of their powerful neighbors the Swedes, as foretold—by implication—toward the end of *Beowulf*. [388]
Gepid	See Gepids. [4990]
Gepids	An East Germanic people closely related to the Goths.
Grendel	A cannibalistic giant descended from Cain. He ravaged the Danes and their hall Heorot until he was killed by Beowulf the Geat. [203]
Guthlaf	A follower of the Danish leader Hnæf. [2295]
Hæreth	Father of Hygd, the queen of Hygelac. [3852]
Hæthcyn	A king of the Geats, the second son of Hrethel, killed in a battle with the Swedish king Ongentheow. See Genealogy of the Geatish Royal House (p. xxviii). [4867]
Halga	Youngest son of the Danish king Healfdene and father of Hrothulf. See Genealogy of the Danish Royal House (p. xxviii). [122]
Hama	A Germanic hero associated with the Gothic kings Theoderic and Eormenric. According to a thirteenth-century Scandinavian source, he ultimately repented of his sinful life and entered a monastery, bestowing his possessions upon it. [2396]
Healfdene	A Danish king, son of Beowulf the Dane and grandson of Scyld Scefing. See Genealogy of the Danish Royal House (p. xxviii). [114]
Heardred	A king of the Geats, son and successor of Hygelac. After Heardred's death at the hands of the Swedes, his cousin Beowulf became king of the Geats. See Genealogy of the Geatish Royal House (p. xxviii). [4403]
Heathobard	See Heathobards. [4051]
Heathobards	A Germanic people, enemies (and perhaps neighbors) of the Danes. [4076]

Heatholaf	A warrior of the Wylfings. [917]
Helmings	The people of Wealhtheow, Hrothgar's queen. [1240]
Hemming	A kinsman of Offa and Eomer. [3888]
Hengest	A follower (and later the successor) of the Danish leader Hnæf. [2164]
Heorogar	A Danish king, eldest son of Healfdene and father of Heoroweard. See Genealogy of the Danish Royal House (p. xxviii). [121]
Heorot	The name of the great hall built by the Danish king Hrothgar, ultimately destroyed by fire during hostilities between the Danes and the Heathobards. Danish chroniclers consistently locate the hall of the Scylding kings at Lejre, Zealand, and the remains of three great halls have now been found at that site. [156]
Heoroweard	A Danish prince, son of Heorogar. See Genealogy of the Danish Royal House (p. xxviii). [4321]
Herebeald	A prince of the Geats, eldest son of Hrethel, killed by his brother Hæthcyn. See Genealogy of the Geatish Royal House (p. xxviii). [4867]
Heremod	A Danish king infamous for stinginess and treachery, possibly the last member of the dynasty of kings that preceded Scyld Scefing and his descendants. [1804]
Hereric	Brother of Hygd, the queen of the Geatish king Hygelac, and therefore the uncle of Heardred. [4412]
Hetware	A Frankish people living somewhere south of the mouth of the River Rhine. [4725]
Hildeburh	Sister of the Danish leader Hnæf and wife of the Frisian king Finn. [2141]
Hnæf	A Danish chieftain, son of Hoc and brother of Hildeburh, slain during a visit to his sister's husband Finn in Frisia. [2137]
Hoc	A Danish chieftain, father of Hildeburh and Hnæf. [2152]
Hondscioh	A warrior of the Geats and companion of Beowulf, killed by Grendel. [4152]
Hrethel	A king of the Geats, father of Hygelac and maternal grandfather (and foster father) of Beowulf. See Genealogy of the Geatish Royal House (p. xxviii). [746]
Hrethric	A Danish prince, older son of Hrothgar and Wealhtheow. See Genealogy of the Danish Royal House (p. xxviii). [2377]

Hrothgar	A Danish king, second son of Healfdene. It is during his reign that the monster Grendel terrorizes the Danes until killed by Beowulf the Geat. See Genealogy of the Danish Royal House (p. xxviii). [121]
Hrothmund	A Danish prince, younger son of Hrothgar and Wealhtheow. See Genealogy of the Danish Royal House (p. xxviii). [2377]
Hrothulf	Son of Halga and nephew of Hrothgar. Later Scandinavian sources imply that after Hrothgar's death he assumed the Danish throne, excluding Hrothgar's sons Hrethric and Hrothmund. See Genealogy of the Danish Royal House (p. xxviii). [2029]
Hrunting	The name of Unferth's sword. [2911]
Hunlafing	The name of Hengest's sword. [2288]
Hygd	Hygelac's queen. [3851]
Hygelac	A king of the Geats, youngest of the three sons of Hrethel; husband of Hygd and father of Heardred. Beowulf the Geat is his nephew, the son of his sister. See Genealogy of the Geatish Royal House (p. xxviii). [389]
Ingeld	A king of the Heathobards, son of Froda; betrothed to Hrothgar's daughter Freawaru. [4049]
Jutes	A Germanic tribe living in mainland Denmark (Jutland). It is just possible that the word *eotenas*—in the original of verses 1806, 2145, 2187, and 2290—should be translated "giants" instead of "Jutes." [1806]
Jutish	See Jutes. [2162]
Merovingian	See Merovingians. [5842]
Merovingians	A dynasty of Frankish kings.
Modthrytho	A beautiful but evil queen, who was "tamed" by Offa. [3862]
Nægling	The sword of Beowulf the Geat. [5125]
Offa	A king of the Angles while they still lived on the continent, before their migration to sub-Roman Britain; married to Modthrytho. [3887]
Ohthere	A Swedish king, older son of Ongentheow; father of Eanmund and Eadgils. See Genealogy of the Swedish Royal House (p. xxviii). [4757]
Onela	A Swedish king, younger son of Ongentheow; married to the daughter of the Danish king Healfdene. See Genealogy of the Swedish Royal House (p. xxviii). [124]

Ongentheow   A Swedish king, father of Ohthere and Onela, killed by Eofor (a follower of Hygelac). See Genealogy of the Swedish Royal House (p. xxviii). [3938]

Oslaf   A follower of the Danish leader Hnæf. [2295]

Ravenswood   A forest in Sweden. [5850]

Rhineland   The area watered by the River Rhine. [5829]

Scandinavia   The part of northern Europe inhabited by the Danes, Geats, and Swedes. [38]

Scyld   See Scyld Scefing. [34]

Scyld Scefing   "Scyld the son of Scef," founder of the dynasty of Danish kings of which Hrothgar represents the culmination in terms of political power and glory. Scyld's descendants and successors, and sometimes the Danish people as a whole, are called Scyldings. It is possible that Scyld came to the throne after a period of anarchy caused by the exile and death of Heremod. See Genealogy of the Danish Royal House (p. xxviii). [7]

Scylding   See Scyldings. [1197]

Scyldings   An alternate name for the Danes, derived from the name of their great king Scyld Scefing. [702]

Sigemund   Son of Wæls. A famous hero of the Germanic peoples (*Sigmundr* in Old Norse sources). [1751]

Storm
  Mountain   A hill in the land of the Geats. [4956]

Sweden   The kingdom of the Swedes. [4759]

Swedes   A Scandinavian people. [4766]

Swedish   See Swedes; Sweden. [126]

Swerting   Uncle of Hygelac. [2404]

Unferth   Son of Ecglaf; the official spokesperon (*þyle*) at Hrothgar's court. It is possible that this figure's name is really Hunferth, which is how the manuscript regularly spells it, though it always alliterates with vowels and is thus regularly emended by editors to Unferth. [997]

Wægmundings   The people (or family) to which Beowulf the Geat, Weohstan, and Wiglaf belong. [5214]

Wæls   Father of Sigemund. His name in Old Norse sources is *Völs* and his descendants are called *Völsungar* (Volsungs) after him. [1752]

Wayland   The famous semidivine smith of Germanic legend. [812]

Wendel	The Wendels were a Germanic tribe who lived in what is now Vendelsyssel in North Jutland (Denmark). [696]
Weohstan	Father of Wiglaf and slayer of the Swedish prince Eanmund. [5204]
Whale Headland	Site of Beowulf the Geat's burial mound. [5608]
Wiglaf	Son of Weohstan; a Geatish warrior and kinsman of Beowulf. [5203]
Withergyld	A warrior of the Heathobards. [4104]
Wonred	A Geat, father of Eofor and Wulf. [5928]
Wulf	A warrior of the Geats, brother of Eofor. [5930]
Wulfgar	Hrothgar's herald and door-keeper at Heorot. [697]
Wylfings	A Germanic tribe who lived in the neighborhood of the Danes and the Geats, probably somewhere south of the Baltic. [916]
Yrmenlaf	A Dane, the younger brother of Æschere. [2648]

Three Shorter
Old English Poems

These poems are included here for the light they shed on various aspects of Beowulf *and its background.*

"The Fight at Finnsburg"

The text is preserved in an eighteenth-century copy of a lost Anglo-Saxon manuscript. It is a fragment describing what happened in Finnsburg prior to the point at which the *Beowulf*-poet picks up the story (in verse 2133). While on a visit to Frisia, the Danish leader Hnæf, along with his second-in-command Hengest and their followers, are treacherously attacked in their hall at night by the forces of the Frisian king, Finn.

It is difficult to harmonize the two Old English versions of the incident in all their details, which is hardly surprising when we realize that we are dealing with independent tellings of different portions of an (originally) oral tale. The fragment is valuable not only for filling in an otherwise unknown part of the story, but also for offering a vivid glimpse of heroic life and action in all their unmoralized immediacy—very unlike what we get in *Beowulf*, with its focus on the collateral suffering of Hildeburh (Hnæf's sister and Finn's wife). It has been said that there is more sheer delight in battle in this little piece than in *Beowulf* with all its wars, and the direct, fast-paced style of "Finnsburg" is certainly far removed from the reflective, elegiac, sometimes even introspective style of *Beowulf*.

For the text of the Old English original, see *The Anglo-Saxon Poetic Records* VI, 3–4.

". . . gables burning."
But Hnæf cried, "No,

it is none of these—
not day dawning,
nor a dragon in flight,
nor this great guest-hall's
gables burning,
but warriors with weapons,
wolves howling,
10   birds screeching,
and bloody spears
demolishing shields.
The moon is gleaming
as it wanders in clouds,
and woe-laden deeds
must crown this cruel
conflict of peoples!
Wake up at once,
    my warriors!
20   Grab up your shields,
gather your courage,
and fight fiercely
in the front of war!"
His gold-adorned thanes
girt on their swords;
warriors strode
to one of the doorways
with swords unsheathed—   .
Sigeferth and Eaha—
30   while Ordlaf and Guthlaf
went to the other door
and Hengest himself
hurried behind them.
Guthere restrained
Garulf outside,
lest he risk his life
and rich trappings
in the first onslaught
at that fateful door
40   where warriors were waiting
who wanted to take them;

but the lad cried out
loudly, asking
in the hearing of all,
who held the door.
"Sigeferth the Secgan,"
came the swift reply,
"a valiant adventurer,
survivor of many
50   desperate fights.
Death or glory—
whichever you want—
you may choose here!"
Then wrathful sword-blows
rang through the hall
and the hollow shields
held in men's fists
flew into fragments.
The floor-planks dinned
60   and Guthere's son
Garulf went down,
the first of Finn's
followers to die—
though shoals of others
soon shared his fate,
a ruck of corpses.
Ravens were circling
swift and sable-hued,
and swords flashing
70   as if Finnsburg were all
on fire in the night.
I have never heard
of noble retainers—
a mere sixty!—
mightier in war,
nor of men who repaid
mead more faithfully
than the companions of Hnæf
repaid theirs!
80   They fought fiercely
for five days,

those hearth comrades—
and they held those doors!
Then a wounded thane
went from the battle,
saying his mailcoat
was slit and shattered,
his helmet holed
and his harness torn.
90   His anxious leader
asked him at once
how those embattled troops
were bearing their wounds,
or whether anyone . . .

"A Meditation"

This poem is untitled in the manuscript (The Exeter Book) in which it has been preserved. It is often given the title "The Wanderer" by modern editors, but it covers so many bases and contains so many loose ends—and is so apparently disjointed—that a title referring to only one of its two central themes or images is bound to be somewhat misleading. These themes are the desolation of a lordless man and a ruined Roman city: poignant examples of personal loss (the death of friends and loved ones) and public loss (the extinction of cities and empires). These constitute the evidence provided by the poet for his gloomy vision of "this dark life" (*þis deorce lif*). The two themes are related: both of them show how bleak and hopeless life in the world is if what protects and nurtures one is lost—a loving and generous liege lord on the one hand, and a city with its internal support systems and external walls on the other. With these two striking examples of impermanence, the speaker in the poem contrasts the stability of God, which he hopes to attain. Thus the problem faced in the poem and the solution it offers are quite similar to those in the familiar hymn, "Abide with Me":

Change and decay in all around I see,
O Thou who changest not, abide with me.

"A Meditation" may have been written in the first half of the tenth century. It is included here because of the light it sheds on the intellectual, philosophical, and spiritual milieu of *Beowulf*. Indeed, the worldview that often seems to permeate *Beowulf* becomes fully explicit here, and one can even imagine the poem uttered by a follower of Beowulf after the king's death and the dissolution of his kingdom. Moreover, "A Meditation" is a magnificent piece in its own right, and one that takes a deep, steady, unblinkered look at the human condition.

For the text of the Old English original, see *The Anglo-Saxon Poetic Records* III, 134–37. For a thorough treatment of all aspects of the work, see the exhaustive edition of T. P. Dunning and A. J. Bliss, *The Wanderer* (New York: Appleton-Century-Crofts, 1969).

> "A lone man often
> looks for favor,
> for the mercy of God,
> though his mind is troubled
>   and it is his lot
> to lash with his oars
> the icy seas
> of exile, its far-flung
> frostbitten paths.

10 Fate is unrelenting."
> So spoke the earth-stepper,
> sadly recalling
> desperate wars
> and the death of kinsmen:
> "How often, early
> every morning,
> I lamented my fate!
> There was not a man alive
> to whom I dared confide

20 my deepest feelings—
> what was in my heart.
> I have always known
> it is a very great
> virtue in a man
> that he keep his thoughts
> closely concealed,
> thoroughly disguised,
> think what he may;
> for a distressed mind

30 cannot withstand fate,

nor a vexed spirit
provide much comfort—
which is why warriors
who want glory
keep a sad heart
sealed in their breasts.
Like many others,
I had to mask my thoughts
when, as often chanced—
40   exiled from my homeland,
far from my kinsmen—
I was filled with heartache,
after the evil hour
when earth covered
my liege in darkness
and I left him behind
and wandered, woe-struck,
over wintry seas,
hoping to find
50   a hall, whether far
or near, to acknowledge me
and a noble chief
who might—having known
my master in the past—
have no fear of befriending
my friendlessness. Only
a man familiar
with misery knows
how cruel a comrade
60   care always proves
for someone without
a soul to confide in:
his portion is exile,
not precious rings,
an icy breast,
not earthly glory.
He recalls comrades
and costly presents,
how among the youths
70   his master gave him

generous gifts . . .
that joy is done with!
A man who has long
missed his gold-giver's
nurturing love
knows how often,
when sorrow and sleep
besiege his spirit
and hold his heavy
80   heart in their thrall,
he dreams that he sees
his dead master,
clasps and kisses him
and cradles head
and hand in his lap,
which is how he showed him
fealty and friendship
in more fortunate days.
When he wakes at last
90   the wanderer sees
before him nothing
but fallow waves,
splashing seabirds
spreading their wings,
hail mingled
with hoarfrost and snow.
The hurt in his heart
                is heavier
after that sweet sight,
100   and sorrow is renewed
when his mind imagines
familiar faces,
hails them happily
and hungrily scans them.
Those phantoms of friends
soon fade into darkness,
and their fleet spirits
fail to bring him
their well-known voices—
110   so woe is doubled

for one who must send
his weary heart
on frequent journeys
over the frozen waves.
Therefore I marvel
that in this world
my soul does not grow
somber and dark
when I ponder men's
120   impermanence,
how swiftly heroes
are swept from the hall,
young hearth-thanes,
and as the years pass
how the earth itself
ages and decays.
Wisdom is only
won after many
winters in the world's kingdom.
130   A wise man is patient,
neither hot tempered
nor hasty of speech,
neither pliable
nor impetuous,
neither glum nor giddy
nor greedy for riches,
nor prone to voicing
premature vows.
A man must refrain
140   from making promises
until his restless mind
is really certain
where its lurching thoughts
are likely to take him.
A wise man knows
how weird it will be
when the world's riches
lie waste, just as now—
almost everywhere
150   on earth—you can see

wind-blown, desolate
walls standing,
snow-swept ramparts
slick with hoarfrost.
The wine-halls crumble,
the wealthy builders
lie silent and joyless;
their soldiers fell
defending the wall,
160   and when fighting ceased
the bodies were scattered:
birds carried one man
piecemeal out to sea;
pitiless wolves,
grey and greedy,
gorged on another;
a blubbering friend
buried yet another:
the Creator of men
170   emptied this city
and quenched its people's
cries, until the ancient
stronghold of giants
stood deserted.
A person who wisely
ponders these ruins
and deeply meditates
this dark life,
remembering the many
180   merciless wars
of ancient times,
will ask, 'Ah, where
are the heroes and the horses
and the high gift-seats?
Where the benches, the banquets,
and the big hall-joys?
Oh mirthful mead-cups!
Oh mail-clad troops!
Oh gallant princes!
190   How their glory passed,

annulled by darkness
as if it had never been!'
Now the silent wall
with its serpent-shaped stains
is all that remains
of that absent host;
its builders were slain
by bloody spears,
by scudding missiles,
200   by inscrutable fate—
and now their ramparts are raked
by raging winds,
by harsh blizzards
that hobble the earth
in deep drifts
while darkness lowers
and night-shadows fall
and the north sends out
howling hailstorms
210   to harass mankind.
Woe is wide-flung
in the world, where fate
alters everything
under the heavens:
here riches die;
here relatives die;
here a man dies;
here his messmates die—
earth's foundations
220   are all out of kilter!"
So spoke the sage in private
where he sat reflecting:
"Men should be modest and faithful
and not make their sorrows
known or name them in public
until—in their need for solace—
they have seen how to slake them.
It is well with those who seek salvation,
favor from our Father in heaven,
230   where we have a fortress forever."

"Deor"

In this poem, untitled in The Exeter Book manuscript, an imaginary poet named Deor displays his familiarity with various Germanic legendary figures and their stories. All the stories involve individuals who suffered and survived a time of grief and hardship, and by recounting them the poet hopes to find consolation and hope in his own misery: he has been dismissed from his post as court poet of the Heodenings and replaced by a more talented rival named Heorrenda.

"Deor" is useful for suggesting the expertise in Germanic legend that was expected of a professional poet in Anglo-Saxon England, and it shows the same interest and imaginativeness in deploying this expertise that we find in *Beowulf.*

Wayland is the semidivine smith of Germanic legend who is mentioned in *Beowulf* (907). The story of his tragic involvement with King Nithhad and his daughter Beadohild is told in full in Scandinavian sources, most notably the eddaic "Lay of Wayland" ("*Völundarkviða*"). The story of the love of Mæthhilde and Geat is known from Icelandic and Norwegian ballads. Theodric is probably the Merovingian Frankish king of the same name, and Eormanric (who also appears in *Beowulf* [2401]) was a famous ruler of the Ostrogoths, remembered in Germanic tradition as a treacherous tyrant.

The use of a refrain like the one in "Deor" is very rare in surviving Old English poetry. For the text of the original, see *The Anglo-Saxon Poetic Records* III, 178–79. For further information about the poem, see the edition by Kemp Malone, *Deor,* 4th ed. (New York: Appleton-Century-Crofts, 1966).

> Sitting beside
>   his serpent-rings,
> Wayland knew woe
> and wintry misery;
> his companions were pain
> and passionate longing,
> and the master smith
> grew familiar with grief
> after King Nithhad
> cast him in prison,
> binding in chains
> a better man.
> —That sorrow passed
> and this may too.

10

Beadohild was less
bothered by the deaths
of her two brothers
than by her terrible plight,
    once she knew
20   there was no doubt
        that she was pregnant.
She was appalled and scared
and too dazed to decide
what to do next.
—That sorrow passed
and this may too.

We have heard of the hapless
heartbroken sighs
of woeful Mæthhilde,
30   the wife of Geat,
how her care-crossed love
kept her from sleeping.
—That sorrow passed
and this may too.

For thirty years
Theodric controlled
the Mærings' city
as men knew well.
—That sorrow passed
40   and this may too.

We have heard of the hard
heart of Eormanric,
the wolfish master
of the wide empire
of the Goths.
What a grim king!
Many a man
sat mourning secretly,
waiting for woe

50   and wishing frequently
        his realm would one day
        be wrested from him.
        —That sorrow passed
        and this may too.

        You sit in your sorrow,
        severed from joy,
        your soul darkening,
        and sometimes you think
        your load of woes
60   will last forever.
        You should then reflect
        that in this world
        God is always
        going about,
        granting some men
        glory and honor,
        allotting others
        lives of misery.

        Concerning myself
70   I may say this:
        I was hall-poet
        of the Heodenings, once,
        and dear to my master.
        Deor was my name.
        I remained in his favor
        for many years
        until Heorrenda—
        that honey-tongued poet—
        was granted the great
80   and goodly lands
        my worshipful lord
        had once given me.
        —That sorrow passed
        and this may too.

Suggestions for Further Reading

Note: Particularly important or useful titles are preceded by an asterisk.

The Manuscript

Kiernan, Kevin S. *Beowulf and the Beowulf Manuscript.* Rev. ed. Ann Arbor: University of Michigan Press, 1996.

*Zupitza, Julius, and Norman Davis. *Beowulf: Reproduced in Facsimile from the Unique Manuscript British Museum MS. Cotton Vitellius A.xv.* 2nd ed. Early English Text Society No. 245. London: Oxford University Press, 1959.

Editions

* *"Beowulf" and "The Fight at Finnsburg."* 3rd ed. Edited by Fr. Klaeber. Boston: D. C. Heath, 1950.

Heyne-Schückings "Beowulf." 18th ed. Edited by Else von Schaubert. Paderborn: Verlag Ferdinand Schöningh, 1963.

"Beowulf" with the Finnesburg Fragment. 3rd ed. Edited by C. L. Wrenn, fully revised by W. F. Bolton. London: Harrap, 1973.

"Beowulf": An Edition with Relevant Shorter Texts. Edited by Bruce Mitchell and Fred C. Robinson. Oxford: Blackwell Publishers, 1998.

Meter

*Bliss, A. J. *The Metre of Beowulf.* 2nd ed. Oxford: Basil Blackwell, 1962.

Pope, John Collins. *The Rhythm of Beowulf: An Interpretation of the Normal and Hypermetric Verse-Forms in Old English Poetry.* Rev. ed. New Haven: Yale University Press, 1966.

Translations into Modern English Prose

Chickering, Howell D. *Beowulf: A Dual-Language Edition.* Garden City, NY: Anchor Books, 1976.

*Donaldson, E. Talbot. *Beowulf: A New Prose Translation.* New York: W. W. Norton, 1966.

Garmonsway, G. N., and Jacqueline Simpson. *Beowulf and Its Analogues.* London and New York: Dent and Dutton, 1968.

Bibliographies

Hasenfratz, Robert J. *Beowulf Scholarship: An Annotated Bibliography, 1979–1990.* New York and London: Garland, 1993.

Short, Douglas D. *Beowulf Scholarship: An Annotated Bibliography.* New York and London: Garland, 1989.

Other Important Works

The Anglo-Saxon Poetic Records: A Collective Edition. Edited by George Philip Krapp and Elliott Van Kirk Dobbie. 6 vols. New York: Columbia University Press, 1931–1953.

Bjork, Robert E., and John D. Niles, eds. *A Beowulf Handbook.* Lincoln: University of Nebraska Press, 1997.

Bonjour, Adrien. *The Digressions in Beowulf.* Oxford: Blackwell, 1950.

Brodeur, Arthur Gilchrist. *The Art of Beowulf.* Berkeley: University of California Press, 1959.

*Chambers, R. W. *Beowulf: An Introduction to the Study of the Poem.* 3rd ed., with a supplement by C. L. Wrenn. Cambridge: Cambridge University Press, 1959.

Clark, George. *Beowulf.* Boston: Twayne Publishers, 1990.

Earl, James W. *Thinking about Beowulf.* Stanford: Stanford University Press, 1994.

Hill, John M. *The Cultural World of Beowulf.* Toronto: University of Toronto Press, 1995.

Irving, Edward B., Jr. *A Reading of Beowulf.* New Haven: Yale University Press, 1968.

———. *Rereading Beowulf.* Philadelphia: University of Pennsylvania Press, 1989.

*Niles, John D. *Beowulf: The Poem and Its Tradition.* Cambridge, MA: Harvard University Press, 1983.

*Orchard, Andy. *A Critical Companion to Beowulf.* Cambridge: D. S. Brewer, 2003.

Sisam, Kenneth. *The Structure of Beowulf.* Oxford: Clarendon Press, 1965.

Stanley, E. G. *In the Foreground: Beowulf.* Cambridge: D. S. Brewer, 1994.

*Tolkien, J. R. R. *Beowulf: The Monsters and the Critics.* Sir Israel Gollancz Memorial Lecture, British Academy, 1936. *Proceedings of the British Academy,* XXII (1936), 243–95.

Whitelock, Dorothy. *The Audience of Beowulf.* Oxford: Clarendon Press, 1951.